THE RIDD

FOXWOOD GRANGE

THE RIDDLE OF
FOXWOOD GRANGE

A SHERLOCK HOLMES MYSTERY

DENIS O SMITH

Paperback ISBN 978-1-78705-038-9
ePub ISBN 978-1-78705-039-6
PDF ISBN 978-1-78705-040-2

Published in the UK by MX Publishing
335 Princess Park Manor, Royal Drive,
London, N11 3GX

Cover illustration by Ann Cordery & Stuart Dorman

For Phyllis, with love, for

all her help and encouragement

CONTENTS

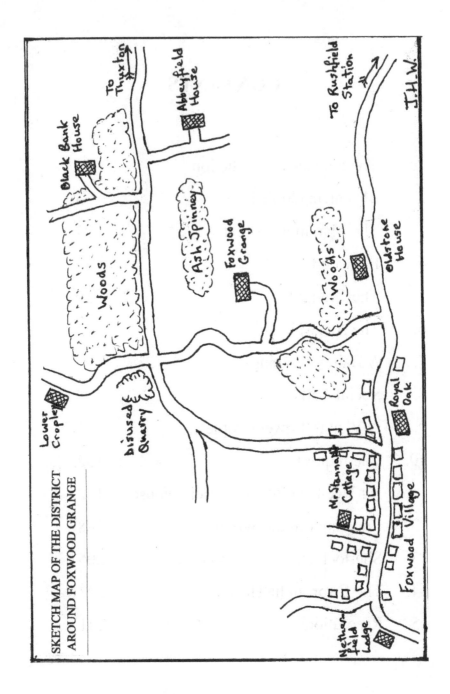

SKETCH MAP OF THE DISTRICT
AROUND FOXWOOD GRANGE

To Thuxton

Abbeyfield House

Black Bank House

Woods

Ash Spinney

Foxwood Grange

Woods

Oldstone House

To Rushfield Station

J.H.W.

Lower Copley

Disused Quarry

Royal Oak

Mr Stannard's Cottage

Foxwood Village

Netherfield Lodge

1: THE SCIENCE OF DEDUCTION

SHERLOCK HOLMES stood up from the breakfast-table and selected his long-stemmed cherrywood pipe from the rack on the mantelpiece, as he was wont to do when in a discursive rather than a reflective mood. It was a pleasant morning in the summer, and although my friend had been continuously busy for several weeks with a succession of interesting cases, he had no immediate calls upon his time that morning, and we had been discussing his theories with regard to the detection of crime. I had ventured the opinion that although he frequently referred to his theories as forming the basis of a science, the fact that no-one but Holmes himself seemed able to apply his theories in practice suggested that it might more accurately be termed an art.

"I could not disagree with you more," said he, as he seated himself beside the hearth and put a match to his pipe. "The fact that no-one else yet applies my methods in a regular sort of way indicates only that no-one else has yet been taught to do so. It is, in essence, simply a matter of education."

"Of course, I am aware that you have written numerous monographs upon the subject," I remarked, "but there is as yet no standard general text-book that students could consult."

"You are quite correct, Watson. That is a deficiency which I shall remedy as soon as I get the opportunity. It is my intention that *The Science of Criminal Detection* will be the magnum opus of my later years, perhaps preceded by *A Scientific Approach to Observation and Deduction.*"

"You raise another matter there which has often puzzled me," I responded after a moment. "You frequently speak of observation and deduction as if they were separate; but, surely, the one implies the other. How would you distinguish between them?"

My companion nodded his head. "There is indeed a single continuum of mental processes on which both these activities lie, and the one passes imperceptibly into the other, so that it can sometimes be difficult to draw a dividing line between the two of them. Nevertheless, there are instances which one would unhesitatingly place in one category or the other. To take an elementary example: one evening, a week ago, I was working at my chemical bench when you pushed the door open and entered the room, having been out for a time. I glanced up and thought 'Watson has returned'. That was clearly an instance of observation."

I burst out laughing. "If I may say so," I said when I had recovered myself, "that strikes me as a ridiculous example, Holmes, scarcely even deserving the name of observation. Why, it is simply a matter of instant recognition. No-one could possibly suppose otherwise!"

"Perhaps not," returned my companion in a serious tone, "and yet the matter is not so straightforward as you seem to suppose. For all that I knew, the man who entered the room might not have been you, Watson, but someone who closely resembled you – after all, there are those who claim that each of us has an exact double, somewhere in the world – and the fact that he entered without knocking may simply have been because he was ill-mannered or absent-minded."

"But that is absurdly unlikely!"

"Perhaps so, but it is still possible. You should never confuse the two. All our ideas are either possible or impossible, and whether something is regarded as likely or unlikely does not affect that. Indeed, to say that something is unlikely implies by its very definition that it is possible. However, in that instant when I glanced up from my test-tubes, I observed that the newcomer was wearing exactly the same clothes as you had been wearing when you went out an hour previously, and I recalled also that you had said before you left that you would be absent for about an hour. With these supporting facts, I concluded in an instant that the newcomer was indeed you, and returned to the contemplation of my chemicals. In the most elementary of observations, you see, we rely on innumerable items of memory to assist us in reaching a conclusion. But the facts we rely on are themselves elementary and directly related to that which we are observing. They occur to us in an instant, and require no conscious process of thought to link them with the present circumstances.

"Now," he continued, "to give a simple example of deduction: two days ago, if you recall, I was the one returning to these chambers, when I found you sitting in a chair with a teapot and a cup beside you. I remarked that I was sorry that you had missed your friend Stamford at the Criterion Bar, and expressed the hope that he was not ill. You replied that he was perfectly well, so far as you were aware, but you had learned from someone else that he had left London for a few days to visit

3

relatives. You then asked me how I knew that you had failed to find him."

"Yes, I recall the the conversation very well. We were then interrupted by the door-bell. Inspector Lestrade had called with some information for you, the two of you left together soon afterwards, and our conversation was never concluded. I never did learn how you knew I had missed Stamford."

Holmes nodded. "I shall explain it to you now, then," said he. "It is a very elementary matter, but it does at least illustrate the difference between deduction and the simple observation of the previous example.

"In the first place," he continued, ticking off the points on his fingers with the stem of his pipe, "we had left the house together, at which time you had remarked to me that you hoped to run across Stamford at the Criterion. You had made no specific arrangement with him, you said, but you knew that it was his habit to have a drink with friends at the Criterion on Wednesday lunchtime. When I returned, I touched the teapot, thinking that I might join you in a cup of tea. I found, however, that it was almost cold, and also noted that there was very little tea left in it. I then drew on my knowledge that when Mrs Hudson makes a pot of tea, there is always enough in it for three or four cups, and it was clear to me that you had been back some time. A rough calculation for how long it would take for you to call for a pot of tea, how long it would take for the kettle to boil and how long it would take for you to consume, say, three cups, suggested that you had been back home for at least an hour and a quarter. If that were so, then, subtracting the time it must have taken you to reach the Criterion and get back home again, you had clearly spent little more than five minutes there.

"Furthermore, this implied that you had not only failed to run across Stamford, but you had not bothered to wait fifteen or twenty minutes to see if he turned up. Evidently, you had been given some information as soon as you reached the bar which made it certain that he would not be coming. I then expressed the hope that Stamford was not ill, and you replied that, on the contrary, he was taking a short holiday.

"Why this counts as a series of deductions and my other example did not is because in reaching my conclusion I did not draw simply on recollections from earlier in the day, but also on other general truths – of Mrs Hudson's usual speed in making a pot of tea, of the rate at which you usually consume it, of how long you would generally wait to see if someone turned up at the bar and so on. Only by consciously – if very swiftly – bringing these facts together could I arrive at my conclusion. That is therefore a deduction."

"I understand," said I, although I could not help thinking that, knowing my habits as well as he did, it was all rather a simple matter for him.

"Of course, it is a very elementary example," he remarked, responding to my thoughts rather than my words, as was his wont. "I should not have mentioned it at all, but for your request that I attempt to define the distinction between observation and deduction."

As he was speaking, there came a ring at the door-bell. A brief conversation at the front door ensued, and a moment later Mrs Hudson appeared in the doorway of our room.

5

"There is a man downstairs with a message for you, Mr Holmes," said she. "I told him I would bring it up, but he says he would rather hand it to you himself."

"By all means," returned Holmes. "Pray show him up, Mrs Hudson."

The man who entered our chamber a moment later was about forty years old, of medium height, clean shaven save for a neat dark moustache, and clad in a black overcoat and cap. For a moment he looked from one to the other of us.

"I believe you have a message for me," said Holmes, holding out his hand. "Is it from one of your colleagues at Paddington?"

"No, sir," the other replied, as he unfastened his coat: "a stranger to me, a very respectable-looking gentleman in a tweed suit – respectable, but mighty nervous."

"What made you think he was nervous?" Holmes queried.

"Why, sir, he kept looking over his shoulder as we were speaking. He showed me this envelope and asked me if I knew of anyone coming this way who might deliver it for him. When I saw what the address was, I said I could go this way, and would do it myself."

"I see. You were presumably just coming off night duty at the time."

"That is correct, sir."

"At the goods depot on the far side of Paddington station, where you are employed as a checker."

"Yes, sir."

"You have not been there all your career, though," Holmes continued. "I imagine that your employment with the Great Western Railway commenced in Bristol – no doubt at the goods depot there – and that your move to London was occasioned by the offer of promotion to checker – or perhaps from checker to senior checker."

"The latter, sir. I have been here just two years."

"I trust that you are not always on night duty?"

"No, sir; just one week in three."

"I am glad to hear it, especially now that the fishing season has begun, for I know you take a keen interest in angling."

"I do indeed, sir," replied the man with a chuckle. "I am a member of both the Paddington Angling Club and the one at Brentford."

"Thank you," said Holmes, taking the envelope which the man held out to him. He took a coin from his pocket and offered it to his visitor, but the latter shook his head and declined it.

"The other gentleman has already paid me adequately for the job," said he.

"It is always a pleasure to meet a man of integrity," remarked Holmes with a smile. He held out his hand which the other man took and shook vigorously. "Might I know who it is I am addressing? You already know my name."

"Yes, Mr Holmes," the visitor replied. "My name is Coleford, John Coleford. I wonder, sir," he added after a moment, "if you would not mind doing me a small favour?"

"Certainly," said Holmes. "What is it?"

"I should be obliged if you would explain to me how you know all those things about me, when we have never met before."

Holmes nodded. "Just before you arrived, Mr Coleford, my esteemed friend and colleague, Dr Watson, and I had been discussing the subject of observation and deduction – that is, the reading of facts about a person from details of his appearance – and your arrival provided an opportunity for a practical demonstration. You do not mind that I used you as a laboratory specimen?"

"Not at all, sir. I am honoured."

"Very well," said Holmes, laughing. "I will explain. When you entered the room, I, of course, knew nothing whatever about you. Your coat, however, appeared to be of railway issue, a conjecture which was supported by your cap, which appeared to be from the same source, and the monogram 'GWR' on the buttons of your coat. You were therefore employed by the Great Western Railway, probably at Paddington. No doubt you observed these points, Watson?"

"I thought Mr Coleford's coat might be that of a railway man," I replied. "I did not notice the monogram on the buttons."

"So far we are in the realm of simple observation. But then I asked myself why our visitor should be wearing such a heavy-looking coat on such a balmy morning. The obvious answer is that he had been working through the night, for although the days may be fair at present, the nights can be very chilly,"

"They can indeed, sir," interjected Coleford, "especially when you are working in a large shed which is open to the sky at one end!"

"But if Mr Coleford had been on night-shift at Paddington, he was almost certainly employed in the goods depot rather than the passenger station. There are generally no passenger trains in the night time, but the goods side of the business, I imagine, continues without remission throughout the twenty-four hours."

"It certainly does, sir," said Coleford. "Oftentimes the night is busier than the day."

"Now, the fact that Mr Coleford is wearing an official uniform suggests he is not simply engaged in clerical duties in an office. But his bearing, which speaks of authority and experience, suggests that neither is he simply a porter. Then, as he unfastened his overcoat to take out the envelope, the answer was given to me by that horizontal line on his regulation waistcoat."

I looked and saw that there was a faint but definite line across the middle of his waistcoat, as if the material had been constantly rubbed by something.

"It comes from continually leaning upon the little portable desk on legs that the checkers carry about with them and use to lean their papers on. It was clear, then, that Mr Coleford was a checker, one of the most important and responsible positions in the goods depot. But his accent, although not strong, is not quite a London accent, and I thought I detected a mild west-country intonation in it, such as one hears in Bristol. He has clearly not lived in London long enough to lose this accent, and I conjectured that his change of residence might have come upon the occasion of his promotion. As to the interest in matters piscatorial, there is a rolled-up newspaper protruding from his right-hand coat pocket which looks to me like the *Angling Chronicle*."

"It is indeed, sir," said our visitor, glancing down at his pocket in surprise.

"I was a little puzzled at first," Holmes continued, "as to why a man of Mr Coleford's obvious seniority should have offered to bring the message himself, rather than directing the gentleman to some more orthodox messenger service. We had heard from Mrs Hudson that he had declined her offer to bring the message upstairs, from which I had rather assumed that in delivering the message himself, he had perhaps hoped to receive payment from me. His refusal of what I offered, however, disabused me of that notion and made matters clearer. I believe, Mr Coleford, that you have seen my name in the paper in connection with some investigation or other, and thought it might be interesting to see this great detective enterprise for yourself, from the inside, as it were. Am I correct?"

"You are indeed, sir," replied our visitor, looking a little discomfited. "You have divined my motive exactly. I hope you do not mind my intruding," he added in an embarrassed tone.

"Not at all," cried Holmes, breaking into a smile. "This, I'm afraid, is all there is to it," he continued, waving his arm about the room. "No super-modern equipment for the detection of crime, no rows of desks at which clerks are busily recording facts and figures, nothing, in short, but me, my colleague, Dr Watson, and a couple of shelves of books. The solution of crimes is not done at desks but up here," he added, tapping the side of his head.

"I can't wait to tell the wife," said Coleford, looking about him. "She will be mightily interested, I know."

"I hope so," said Holmes with a laugh, as Coleford nodded his head to us and wished us good day. "Now," said he, as we heard Coleford's heavy step descending the stair, "let us see what this is all about."

He tore open the envelope and extracted the letter, which he studied in silence for a few moments. Then he passed it to me and I read the following:

My Dear Mr Holmes,

I flatter myself that I am generally quite adept at negotiating myself through the vicissitudes of life, but something has occurred recently which has left me quite at a loss. It is both inexplicable and sinister, and I really do not know what to make of it.

I wish to consult you with some urgency, but for reasons I shall explain to you later I would very much prefer not to call at your chambers. I wonder, therefore, if you would be so good as to take lunch with me at one o'clock on Friday, at the Great Western Hotel in Praed Street.

Yours sincerely, Farringdon Blake

"Not much to go on," said Holmes as I finished reading. "The name seems vaguely familiar. I think he may be a journalist."

"Of course!" I cried. "I remember now. I have read several of his articles in different newspapers and magazines. I think his speciality is to explain the most abstruse of scientific concepts in simple, everyday language – or, at least, to try to. They are the sort of articles that make you feel extremely clever while you are reading them, as you seem to understand the subject perfectly. An hour later, however, you find you cannot recall it all with sufficient clarity to reconstruct the matter for yourself. Will you accept his invitation?"

"I may as well. I have nothing else on at the moment, and will at least get lunch out of it. My brain could certainly do with a little fresh stimulation. Will you come?"

"I haven't been asked."

"Oh, I shouldn't worry about that," said my companion in a dismissive tone. "I can't imagine that Farringdon Blake will object to your presence, and if you hear his account first hand, it will save my having to repeat it all to you when I get back. Of course, one must always be prepared for disappointment. Journalists have a knack of making things sound more interesting than they really are. Despite the terms in which Mr Blake describes the matter, it may amount to nothing of significance and be simply a waste of our time."

In this pessimistic conjecture, however, my friend was completely mistaken.

2: MR FARRINGDON BLAKE

THE DINING-ROOM at the Great Western Hotel was crowded, the clatter of knives and forks and the buzz of conversation almost deafening, but upon our giving Farringdon Blake's name to the waiter, we were at once shown to a table at the far end of the room where a man in a tweed suit was sitting alone. He stood up as we approached, Holmes introduced us and we all shook hands.

"I am so glad you were able to come," said he as we took our seats. He was a tall, slim man of perhaps five and thirty, with black hair and a neatly trimmed beard and moustache. In his eyes as he addressed us was a thoughtful, intelligent look. "I have been debating with myself for a couple of weeks whether to consult you or not," he added.

"Even in the last twenty-four hours you were still undecided," remarked Holmes.

"That is true. How do you know?"

"You evidently wrote your letter earlier in the week, as you state the day of our meeting as 'Friday' rather than 'today' or 'tomorrow', yet you did not submit it to the postal authorities in the usual way. I can only assume that having written it you were unsure whether to send it, and made a decision on the spur of the moment to hand it to a chance acquaintance this morning."

"You are quite correct. I should perhaps explain that I don't reside in London any more. I come up just once a week, usually on a Friday. I had brought the letter with me in my satchel, but remained undecided about it until the train reached Paddington, when I saw something that made my mind up for me."

"What was that?"

"A man. A particular man. At least, I think I saw him. I'm not entirely certain about it."

"Hum!" said Holmes. "Let us be clear. Is your indecision as to whether to consult me because you think that your problem may, after all, be but a trifling business, which will likely sort itself out in due course and is thus not worth looking into further, or is it because you believe you may have misunderstood the matter altogether and there may actually be nothing to look into? Or is it something else?"

Mr Blake hesitated. "I'm not sure I can even answer that question with any confidence, Mr Holmes. It's an odd thing: I spend my time trying to explain difficult scientific questions to the general public, and here is something bearing directly upon my own life that I cannot even explain to myself!"

"I imagine," said Holmes after a moment, "that sometimes when you are trying to explain a scientific point to your readers and you are not sure where to begin, you find it helpful to return in thought to the period before that particular theory was propounded. That is, you describe what it was that led Galileo or Newton, say, to find previous views inadequate, and led them to propound their own new theories. Sometimes, a chronological approach rather than an analytical one can clarify the issues involved. The chronological approach can also be clarifying in the case of personal mystification, Mr Blake, and that is the approach I suggest you adopt."

"You are quite right," said Blake, "and you express the matter eloquently. As a matter of fact, your powers of expression are one of the two things that led me to consider consulting you. I have read one or two of your articles in journals," he added, as Holmes raised his eyebrows in surprise. "I was impressed both by your analysis and by the way you presented it."

"Thank you. That is gratifying," said Holmes with evident pleasure. "From the response I got at the time, I rather feared that my humble essays had passed, unmourned and forgotten, into oblivion. What was the other reason you decided to consult me?"

"An account Dr Watson wrote of one of your cases, entitled 'A Mysterious Murder'. I think it was in *Tit-Bits* that I saw it. It concerned the murder of two American men who had been staying in London by – as it turned out – a fellow-countryman of theirs. It was rather brief, and thus somewhat condensed, and I should like to have known more details of the matter, especially the antecedents of the case, but it made it clear that it was entirely due to your powers of observation, Mr Holmes, that the culprit was apprehended."

I laughed. "I readily concede it was too brief and too dense," I remarked, "but that was because I was allowed less than a thousand words to describe the whole business. I had no sooner described the strange circumstances in which the first murdered man was found than I had to detail Holmes's analysis of the matter, the conclusions it led to and the surprising capture of the murderer. The antecedents of the matter were in fact unusually interesting, and it is my hope to one day bring out a fuller account of the case. The banal title was not my choice, by the way. I had wanted to call it 'A Tangled Skein', but the editor rejected that on the grounds that many of his readers would not know how to pronounce 'skein'. I did not trouble to argue the point very forcefully: I had had to abbreviate my account so much that it no longer seemed quite so 'tangled' anyway!"

"I have had similar experiences," said Blake with a chuckle. "On one occasion, because an editor wanted to fill up a page in a hurry, I was allowed precisely three hundred words to try to say something interesting and enlightening about volcanoes!"

"Having now established that we are all distinguished men of letters," said Holmes in a tone of amusement, "let us now move on to the business that has brought us together today. Pray begin your chronological account, Mr Blake!"

"Certainly," said the other. "As you appear to know, I contribute articles to all manner of newspapers and periodicals, generally on scientific or medical matters."

"I have read several," I interjected. "I have often been struck by the very broad range of your knowledge."

"Ah! There, I regret, you make an understandable error, Dr Watson. In fact, my scientific knowledge is considerably slighter than you suppose. I should be obliged if you did not mention it to anyone else, but I will confess to you that I myself don't always fully understand the subjects that I attempt to explain to others. I subscribe to numerous learned journals to keep up with the latest research, leave aside all the things I myself don't understand and select from the rest anything which I think might be of interest to the average reader. Like a schoolboy before an examination, I cram myself full of all the relevant facts I can find, so that my article will be both accurate and interesting, but if you were to question me on the subject two weeks later, I might not be able to give you any sensible answers, as my brain will have moved on to fresh material, and the new knowledge will have pushed out the old. Sometimes this makes me feel something of a fraud, but I console myself with the thought that I am at least serving a useful purpose: entertaining and educating the general public on matters about which they probably know little, and giving publicity to the latest theories of really clever scientific and medical men which might otherwise remain unknown outside the pages of obscure learned journals.

"However," Blake continued after a moment, "to return to my chronological account: I began my career as a journalist with the *Standard*, moved after some years, to the *St James's Gazette* and later the *Telegraph*. At the same time I used to contribute occasional anonymous short pieces to other papers and magazines – 'sketches of London life' and that sort of thing. But I was often struck by the very large number of letters we used to receive which demonstrated profound ignorance of some very basic scientific and mathematical truths, or which freely admitted the writer's lack of knowledge and asked for enlightenment. Gradually, my own independent articles began to have a scientific slant to them, if only to describe how certain scientific and mathematical notions underlie our everyday life, especially in a modern city such as London, and my name began to appear frequently above them. Soon, I was earning more from these articles than I did from my regular journalistic work. People were always writing to me, asking me to explain something or other, or suggesting subjects that I might write about, and I always did my best to satisfy their curiosity. Eventually, I was so busy that I could hardly cope with the amount of work I had. A decision had to be made: either I give up most of my independent work and concentrate all my energies on my work at the *Telegraph*, or I throw up that job, cast myself adrift upon the uncertain seas of independence and trust to fortune that I didn't end up on the rocks. I much preferred the idea of independence, but it was a path bestrewn with pitfalls and uncertainties, promising little in the way of security and much in the way of anxiety and endeavour.

"By chance, at precisely the same time as I was considering this momentous decision, I received a letter from my late father's cousin, George Stannard, an elderly man from whom I had heard nothing for several years. He lived in an ancient house known as Foxwood Grange, in the wooded country of north Oxfordshire, close to the border with Warwickshire. He invited me to pay him a visit whenever I could get away, when he would, he said, put a proposal to me. Of course, I had no idea what was in his mind, but two weeks later I went down there to see him.

"He appeared much older than the last time I had seen him, but although physically frail he was still mentally alert. Save for an elderly couple, the Caxtons, who were his only servants, he lived all alone in that rambling old house, which stands by itself in its own extensive grounds. It is a very handsome old place, late Tudor in origin, built on the side of a gentle hill, so that the gardens drop away below it in a series of terraces, down to a little brook in the wooded valley below. At one time, I understand, there was a considerable amount of farmland attached to the Grange, but most of it had been sold off over the years, until just two fields now remained, which Mr Stannard let out to local farmers for grazing. When I had visited there with my father, as a boy, the house had seemed to me to be miles from anywhere, but in truth it is little more than half a mile from the village of Foxwood, and only a mile and a half from the railway station at Rushfield.

"Mr Stannard greeted me very cordially, I must say, and we soon slipped into easy and amiable conversation. Much of it was about the past, when he and my father had been good friends, but he was also very interested in what I was doing now, and questioned me closely about my work. That evening, as we sat after supper with a glass of port, he put his proposal to me. So far as he was aware, he said, I was his closest living relative, and would one day inherit Foxwood Grange. This came as a surprise – a shock, almost – to me. It was not something I had ever given a moment's thought to. There were some other relatives on the other side of his family, he said, some people called Betteridge, who lived near Nottingham. He was not certain which of us was, legally speaking, his closest relative, but it did not matter, he said, as he intended to leave me the house in his will.

"I was so taken aback by this that I scarcely knew what to say. I thanked him profusely, but he waved aside my thanks.

"'I come now,' said he, 'to the proposal I mentioned in my letter. Although I am very fond of this old place, I am becoming a little old to enjoy it properly, and would dearly love to move to somewhere smaller. I have friends in Foxwood village and have my eye on a cottage there which will shortly fall vacant. I am willing to sell you Foxwood Grange now, for a fairly nominal sum – just enough to enable me to purchase the cottage in the village. What do you say?'

"I hesitated. 'The prospect is a very enticing one,' I replied, 'but I am not very flush of funds at the moment.'

"'I can sympathize with that,' said my host with a chuckle. 'I have a little money invested in consols which provides me with sufficient income to just about tick along, but no more than that. But surely you can raise a small loan against the value of this estate? You will not lose by it: when I die the cottage will be yours, too, and you can sell it and pay off the loan there and then.'

"As I sat there, considering the matter, uncertain what to say, Mr Stannard spoke again. 'If you give up your job at the *Telegraph*, and devote yourself to your scientific articles – as I certainly think you should, my boy – you could live comfortably here - far more cheaply than in London - and just send off your articles in the post.'

"'It is not always so simple as that,' I said, laughing at his enthusiastic tone. 'Editors sometimes need a little personal persuasion. Things they receive in the post tend to be put on one side to be looked at later, and "later" may mean not for several weeks' time.'

"'I understand,' said Mr Stannard, nodding his head. 'In that case, you could do all your work here in peace and quiet, and perhaps just travel up to town one day a month. My library has plenty of scientific volumes in it – although I can't claim I have the latest editions of anything.'

"'Very well,' said I, laughing again at his pleading manner. 'You have persuaded me, Mr Stannard! I accept your proposal with grateful pleasure and shall set about raising some money as soon as I get back to London!'

"That was about three years ago, near enough. Within three months I had raised sufficient money for Mr Stannard to move into his cottage, had resigned my position at the *Telegraph* and had moved myself and my possessions to Foxwood Grange. I have gone into some detail on the matter so you will understand how I came to be living in such an odd, out-of-the-way spot.

"When I moved into the Grange, incidentally, I not only took over the house and its library, together with most of the old furniture and pictures, but I also took over the Caxtons, Mr Stannard's only domestic staff, as I mentioned before. When Mr Stannard moved into his cottage, he judged that he could get by with the daily help of a woman from the village, and asked me if I would keep the Caxtons on here. I was only too pleased to do so. Mr and Mrs Caxton have been at the Grange as long as I can remember, and know the place and its requirements inside out. I knew, too, that Mr Stannard had always found them to be completely reliable and trustworthy. Since then, the three of us have rubbed along very harmoniously for the last three years.

"About six months ago, however, I could see that Mrs Caxton's work was becoming a little too much for her, so I took in a young local girl, Ann Wallingford, to help her. This has proved most successful, as Ann is a good worker, with a lively and pleasant disposition, and her cheery presence has definitely brightened the old place up a bit. Then, about three months ago, I had a letter from the secretary of St Matthew's College, Oxford, with which I have had considerable contact over the last three years in the course of my work, to ask if I would consider taking on one of their graduate students, Alexander Whitemoor, as a secretary or assistant for a term or two. I readily agreed to this request, as my papers had got into a very disordered state, and I had been too busy to sort them out myself. Whitemoor's intention had been to read for a doctorate, his interest being in the history and development of scientific thought, but his studies had been interrupted by his widowed mother's falling seriously ill, which had obliged him to return home at frequent intervals. It was felt, under the circumstances, that it might be best to postpone the resumption of his formal studies until next year, and in the meantime he could assist me and perhaps learn something as he did so of the way in which scientific theories are built upon what has preceded them. His presence, too, has been a success, and, young though he is, it has been stimulating to me, I must say, to have someone else of an intellectual bent about the house. Staying at Foxwood, incidentally, also means that Whitemoor is much closer to where his mother lives, at Towcester in Northamptonshire, and he returns home to visit her most week-ends. I think that brings the household of the Grange up to date. I can give you any further details later, should you require them."

Farringdon Blake paused and poured himself a glass of water from a carafe. "Now," said he, as he took a sip, "to tell you what has happened recently. I must first emphasize what a peaceful and delightful part of the country it is in which I live, with woods on the hills, meadows in the valleys, and pretty little villages nestling between them. As I have got to know my neighbours, I have found them on the whole charming and friendly. I have never once regretted moving there and am sure I could not be happier living anywhere else in England.

"The first inkling I got that my contentment with life might be misplaced, and that something strange was afoot, something mysterious about which I know nothing even though I seem to be the focus of it, was just two weeks ago today. I had come up to town on an early train as usual, arriving about half past ten. As I was leaving the station here I chanced to observe a man in a light overcoat standing by the main entrance. For a second our eyes met, then he looked away, as can happen at any time with a total stranger. There was nothing especially notable about him, and I dare say I should normally have soon forgotten I had ever seen him, were it not for what happened later that day. I had gone down to see the editor of *Redfearn's Magazine* which has offices just off the Strand. As I was leaving their building, I saw the man I had seen here at Paddington standing on the other side of the street. As I glanced across at him, he turned away, whether deliberately or simply by chance I could not tell. In any case, his turn was not quick enough to prevent my seeing his face, and I was certain it was the same man. At the time, I simply thought it was an odd coincidence, and gave it no more thought. On the train home that afternoon, however, the mental picture I had of his turning away when I looked at him came back to me, and I could not help feeling that there was something furtive in his manner."

"It was no-one you had ever seen before?" Holmes interrupted.

"No, never."

"Do you have any keen rivals in your line of work?" Holmes queried. "Is there anyone, that is, who might feel he could gain some kind of advantage over you by learning which editors you had been to see?"

Blake shook his head. "Not really. I don't think anyone else is producing the same sort of articles as I am. Besides, there is nothing secret or confidential about anything I do. My name is attached to almost everything I write, so anyone wishing to know who it is I am working for can find out by simply reading the various papers and magazines. Following me about town in a furtive manner would add absolutely nothing to that knowledge."

"So I imagined," said Holmes, "but one must consider all possibilities. Pray continue with your account."

"One afternoon, a few days later, during that fine weather towards the end of June, I had been working hard in my study for several hours when I decided that I had had quite enough for the day of poring over books and journals, and took myself out for a walk. During my three years' residence at Foxwood I have wandered all over the surrounding countryside in all the seasons of the year, but there are so many oddly-shaped little fields and woods in the area that there are still lots of places I am not very familiar with. On that day, I left the garden by a side-gate and followed a track up the hilly field beyond, into a narrow belt of trees which stands on the very crest of the hill and is known locally as the ash spinney. It separates one farmer's land from that of another, and I had never been sure to which of the two the wood actually belonged. I have been that way many times before, but have usually passed straight through the trees and into another field on the other side of the hill. On this day, however, for no particular reason, I decided to turn to the right and follow the wood along the crest of the hill. I had wandered along a little way beneath the huge ash trees, when all at once I came across something odd and surprising. Into the trunk of one of the trees had been hammered several large iron staples, each one eighteen inches or so above the one beneath it and thus forming the rungs of a ladder up the side of the tree, rather like something out of a fairy story.

"The staples didn't look particularly new, although they were in good condition and not rusty. I had never seen anything quite like it, and stood there for some time, regarding it with amazement. I supposed that at some time in the past, whoever owned the wood had fixed these steps in the tree for his children to play on, and I looked up to see where they might lead to. There seemed to be some kind of wooden platform there, up among the leafy branches, and, on the spur of the moment I decided to climb up and have a look at it. It did not take me long to reach it. It was, I suppose, about twenty feet from the ground, although it seemed much higher than that as I was climbing up."

Farringdon Blake paused, and took another sip of water. "I like to think I am a fairly level-headed man, Mr Holmes. I take most things in my stride. But when I reached that wooden platform, I found something there that knocked all the sense out of my head, so that I thought I was losing my mind. The shock sent me reeling and dizzy, so that I had to grip the branches about me to prevent myself tumbling off the platform. I doubt you could ever imagine what it was I found there, what it was that made me feel I was losing my wits."

3: THE MAN IN THE STREET

"WELL?" SAID HOLMES in an affable tone, as Farringdon Blake paused. "If we could never imagine what you found, you will have to tell us."

Blake took a long draught of water. The hum of conversation in the dining-room seemed to have subsided a little as we waited to hear what he would say. "You may think it foolish," he began at length as he put down his glass, "that such a thing could disconcert me quite so much; but please hear my whole account before forming your opinion." He leaned forward and lowered his voice. "Upon the platform, high in that ash tree, was a telescope, standing on a tripod. It was a large, modern and expensive-looking piece of equipment. I was very surprised to see it there, and, just out of curiosity, leaned down to look through it. Imagine my shock when I found that it was pointed at my own house, Foxwood Grange, which was clearly visible from that vantage-point up the tree. Not only that, but it was pointed at, and precisely focused on, my study window. The telescope was a very powerful one. Through it I could see right into the room and clearly see my large desk, spread with books and papers, where I had been sitting, just half an hour previously."

"That is where you sit to work?" asked Holmes.

"Yes, with my back to the window. It is the lightest place in the house."

"Could the telescope have simply slipped into that position?"

"Absolutely not. The nuts and screws on it were all tightened, to hold it exactly in the position in which I found it. When you consider my circumstances, you will perhaps appreciate why this discovery came as such a very great shock to me. There was I, happy and content, writing my scientific essays in a lovely old house in beautiful countryside, pleased that everything seemed to be going so well, when suddenly – quite by chance – I had discovered that someone had been secretly and furtively spying on me. My equanimity and confidence have been utterly destroyed, Mr Holmes, and I have found it a terrific struggle these last two weeks just to keep my mind on my work."

"It is certainly an interesting and curious state of affairs," remarked Holmes after a moment. "It is always possible, though, that the explanation for the telescope is a simple and innocent one. Perhaps someone was up on the viewing platform, observing the countryside or the local bird-life, and at the end, purely on a whim, turned the telescope in the direction of your house, without any malice in his heart. Perhaps something had just caught his eye: your opening or closing the study window, for instance, might have caused a momentary flash of light as the window caught the rays of the sun."

"That was the sort of thing I kept telling myself, Mr Holmes, but against that was the fact that the screws were all fastened to hold the telescope in that precise position. Then, as I tried to consider the matter calmly, I recalled the man I had seen in the street in London, and I could not help wondering if the two things were related, and I was being spied upon by the same agency, both at home at Foxwood and here in London."

Sherlock Holmes nodded his head, and considered the matter for a moment. "I take it you have not discovered to whom the telescope belongs," said he at length.

Blake shook his head. "I wanted someone else to bear witness as soon as possible to what I had discovered. The following day, therefore, when my secretary returned from a visit to his mother, I took him up to the tree with rungs. To my great disappointment, however, the telescope had vanished from the wooden platform, and there was no sign that it had ever been there. Later that same day, I called on two of the local farmers to try to establish who owns the land on which the ash spinney stands, and learnt that it belongs to the farm on the other side of the hill, Lower Cropley, owned by a man called Thomas Pearson. He has farmed there for about twenty years, but he informed me that, so far as he could remember, he had in all that time set foot in that little wood only once or twice, and had never noticed the rungs on the tree. He suggested that his predecessor, a man called Davis, who had had a large family, had fixed the staples to the tree so that his children could have a tree-house to play in – much as I myself had initially surmised."

"You are not aware of anyone in the district who possesses a telescope such as you saw?"

"No, although my enquiries have not been exhaustive."

"Very well. Has anything further occurred?"

"Yes. Last Friday, a few days after I had discovered the telescope, I came up to town as usual. I looked out for the man in the light overcoat as I was leaving the station, but, to my relief, I did not see him anywhere. Later that day, however, when I was visiting the offices of the *Pall Mall Gazette*, I was in an upstairs room and happened to glance out of the window. Across the street, standing in a doorway, was the very same man. It was then I decided that I must consult you, Mr Holmes."

"And yet you were still not certain."

Blake's features expressed doubt and indecision. "Despite the relative shallowness of my scientific credentials, as I confessed to you earlier, I am of a naturally logical and scientific turn of mind, and am always ready to see and admit alternative explanations for anything. In this case, it was still possible, I thought, that I was mistaken, and that these things were, after all, simply coincidence. I wrote you a letter, but, as you know, I did not post it. Then, this morning, as I arrived here at Paddington, I thought I saw the same man again. There was a large crowd of people by the station entrance, though, and when I looked for him again, he seemed to have disappeared. Had I really seen him? I don't know. My nerves are shot, and I am beginning to start at shadows. Who is this man? What does he want with me? It is horribly unpleasant to think that, wherever you go, some unknown person is secretly watching you. I cannot go on like this, Mr Holmes."

Again Holmes nodded his head. "It was, I take it, because of this man that you did not wish to come to my chambers."

"Exactly. I thought he might just follow me there and make enquiries as to your business. Then he would know who it was I was consulting and perhaps be able to guess the reason, which would put him on his guard. I wished my consultation with you to be private, so that whoever it is that is watching me has no knowledge of it."

"Can you describe the man to us?"

"Yes, but not very helpfully, I'm afraid. He appears to be middle-aged and somewhat taller than average, with a broad chest. He has a greying moustache, and wears a light brown overcoat and a bowler hat."

Holmes sat in silent thought for a few moments. "Tell me," he said at last, "where did you go this morning?"

"An office in Fleet Street."

"You did not see the man there?"

"No. He may have been there, but I did not see him. The street was very crowded."

"And your plans for this afternoon?"

"I have another appointment in Fleet Street. Ordinarily, I should have found somewhere down there to take lunch. I only suggested that you and I meet here as I thought that Paddington would be more convenient for you."

"That was very considerate of you. What I suggest now is that when we have finished our meal, I will leave first, while you and Dr Watson sit here talking for a few minutes. Unless the man following you is in this dining-room now, which I very much doubt, he will not know that we have dined together and that there is any connection between you and me, so I should be able to pass out of the hotel unremarked. Then, when you leave, do not take a cab straight away, but walk off together, at least as far as Marble Arch. I will be loitering further along Praed Street

31

and will follow you at a distance. I should be able to see if there is anyone else following you. Do you understand?"

"Certainly. Might I know what else you intend to do?"

"Would you be able to put us up at Foxwood Grange for a night or two?"

"With pleasure."

"Then if you would give Dr Watson directions as to how to get there, what I propose is that we run down to Foxwood tomorrow, equipped with a good map and Dr Watson's excellent field-glasses. I should very much like to have a look about there for myself. Is that agreeable to you, Watson?"

"Very definitely. I am absolutely fascinated by Mr Blake's problem."

"It is certainly a *recherché* little mystery! Indeed, it is quite the most *outré* little problem I have come across in some time! Now, Mr Blake, there are a number of questions I wish to ask you, but they can wait until I see you again. The first thing I hope to do is to identify this man who appears to be dogging your footsteps in London, as that is the more immediate question."

The street was very crowded when Farringdon Blake and I left the hotel. Holmes had instructed him that he was on no account to look about him in a searching manner, but that if he did happen to catch sight of the man in the light overcoat, he was to raise his hat with his right hand and scratch his head with his left. As we looked to right and left before crossing the street, however, Blake's hat was never raised. Along Praed Street we walked in a leisurely manner, and so down the Edgware Road towards Marble Arch. There, Blake and I said goodbye, he hailed a passing cab and I strolled into Hyde Park and sat on a bench for some time, smoking my pipe.

I had no idea whether we had been followed or not, but my thinking was that if we had, and if our pursuer had decided to turn his attentions to me, then I would try to exhaust his patience by sitting there for half an hour or more. When I eventually rose to my feet, after about forty minutes, I saw no-one there who had been there when I sat down. In an unhurried fashion, I made my way back to our lodgings in Baker Street.

Sherlock Holmes had not returned, and it was almost five o'clock before he did so. He seemed in good spirits, and I asked him if he had had any success in identifying the man who had been following his client.

"More than that," returned my friend. "I now know all there is to know about him. I soon picked him out, standing in a doorway across the street from the hotel. Then, when *he* set off to follow you, I set off to follow *him*. There was something about him that struck me as vaguely familiar, and, as I followed you all down to Marble Arch, I tried to remember where I had seen him before.

"When Blake took a cab and you strolled in your ostentatiously leisurely fashion into the Park, your shadow stood a moment and appeared undecided whether to follow Blake or follow you. In the end, after watching you fill your pipe, he did neither, but hailed a passing four-wheeler. There was quite a crowd on the pavement at the time, and I was able to get close enough to hear him call out 'Long Acre' to the driver. A minute later, I managed to secure an empty hansom, and set off for the same destination. As we clattered along, it became evident that my brain had been chugging away quietly by itself, like a little steam engine set in motion, for into my mind, for no apparent reason, came the name 'Wilson Baines', and I recognized at once that that was the man I was following. He is by way of being a private enquiry agent, Watson, with a somewhat dubious reputation. As I recollected his name, I also remembered that he had at one time been among the ranks of the detective force at Scotland Yard, although no-one there ever mentions him now.

"When I reached Long Acre, Baines had just paid off his cab and was entering a large, drab-looking building. I told my cabbie to carry on a little further, then, when I was sure that Baines was out of the way, I walked back to see where it was he had gone to ground. It is one of those fairly modern but depressingly gloomy buildings that are let out to dozens of different businesses. Just inside the main entrance is an array of small brass plates, and there, among those of the second-floor occupants, was one declaring 'John Wilson Baines. Private and discreet enquiries undertaken'. Satisfied that I had confirmed my suspicions as to who it was I had been following, I then made my way down to Scotland Yard. My idea was that if one of the policemen I know well was about, I might be able to learn a little more about Wilson Baines.

"I was in luck, as Inspector Lestrade was in his office, working on some papers. He was reluctant to speak of Baines at first, but when I assured him that any information he was able to give me was for my own personal interest and would not be passed on to others, he nodded his head.

"'Very well,' said he. 'You have done me one or two favours, Mr Holmes, I can't deny that, so I'll tell you what you want to know. But,' he added, sinking his voice to a whisper, 'you must swear not to pass it on to anyone – except for your colleague, Dr Watson, of course – I'll make an exception in his case.'

"I gave him my assurances once more, and this, in brief, is what he told me. Wilson Baines had been some years on the force when several of his colleagues began to have serious doubts about his honesty. He seemed to some to be just a little bit too close to the villains they were supposed to be keeping an eye on, and there was more than one instance when someone who was about to be arrested appeared to have got wind of the fact and had disappeared just before the arresting party arrived. In every such instance, Baines had been involved in the case.

"Matters came to a head one evening when Baines was seen by one of his colleagues apparently accepting a bribe from a suspected criminal. Of course, he tried to talk his way out of it, but no-one believed him. The difficulty though, was that although they knew Baines was guilty, there was not really sufficient evidence to guarantee a conviction in court. In the end, Baines was offered a choice. He could stay on the force, but he would be reduced in rank – and, in any case, none of his colleagues would work with him any more – or he could voluntarily resign his position, in which case no further action would be taken, and the charges against him would be struck from the record. Understandably, he chose the latter option."

"He sounds a bad lot," I remarked.

"Undoubtedly," said Holmes. "From what Lestrade tells me, they were very glad to be rid of him. Now he makes a living by small-scale enquiry work. A lot of it, I understand, is people simply wanting to know the whereabouts of those who owe them money, or wives and husbands spying on each other – sordid work, Watson. And now, it seems, someone has engaged Baines to spy on Farringdon Blake."

"I can't imagine why," I said, shaking my head.

"Nor I, at the moment. But perhaps when we learn more details of his circumstances tomorrow we shall be able to form some sort of hypothesis."

The following day dawned bright and sunny. Sherlock Holmes was in the very best of spirits, no doubt pleased at the prospect of an interesting and challenging case. I had observed many times before that whereas inaction had an almost morbidly soporific effect on my friend, an intellectual challenge of any kind acted like a stimulating tonic upon him, invigorating his whole being. For myself, I confess that I could not imagine how he would set about the matter. Something was afoot – that much seemed certain – but what? All we knew – or thought we knew - was that someone had employed this man Wilson Baines to spy on Holmes's client on his weekly visit to London, and that someone in north Oxfordshire had spied upon him through a telescope. It seemed very little to go on, and I found myself wondering if the whole business might not earn a place in Holmes's records only as a failure, a completely impenetrable mystery.

From my own point of view, although I would naturally be disappointed if my friend failed to make any progress in the matter, the outcome of the investigation was not my immediate concern. I had had sufficient experience of Holmes's profound inner resources to know that if anyone could get to the bottom of a problem and solve the apparently unsolvable, it was Sherlock Holmes. I could therefore leave all the anxiety about the case to him. For myself, I was simply delighted at the prospect of getting away from London for a few days. The weather had been good, and it was certainly more enjoyable to have sunshine rather than fog or rain, but the streets of London had become somewhat stifling in recent days, as they nearly always did in the summer, and I thought it likely that the air in the wooded hills of north Oxfordshire might perhaps be a little fresher.

Holmes had sent a telegram to say that we would catch a train at Paddington in the early afternoon and arrive at Rushfield station at about half past five. Our plans were, however, destined to be altered. Some time after breakfast, when we had unhurriedly packed our travelling bags and were sitting reading the morning papers, there came a ring at the bell. A moment later, the maid showed a middle-aged man into the room, and I was surprised to see that it was Mr Coleford, our railway friend of the previous day, who appeared extremely agitated about something.

"What can we do for you today?" asked Holmes, as he showed the visitor to a chair.

"Something very strange has happened, Mr Holmes," Coleford began. "As I was leaving the station this morning, I was approached by a tall, middle-aged man – "

" – wearing a light overcoat and bowler hat, and with a grey moustache?"

"That's exactly right," said Coleford in surprise. "He said to me 'You took a letter from a gentleman yesterday morning.'

"'What if I did?' I asked.

"'You must tell me the address you took it to,' said he. 'It is most important.'

"'Who are you to tell people what to do?' I demanded, as there was something in his manner I didn't care for.

"'I'm a plain-clothes police-officer,' he said. He pulled some sort of card from his pocket and held it in front of my nose, but so quickly that I had no chance to read it. That's not the way of an honest man, so I decided I wouldn't tell him anything.

"'I didn't notice the address,' I said. 'I just put it in a post-box for him.'

"'You're lying,' he said. 'He could have put it in a post-box himself. You delivered it by hand.'

"'He didn't have a stamp,' I said. 'He gave me some money to pay for one.'

"'You listen to me, my man,' he said, fair shouting now. 'You'll find yourself in serious trouble, withholding information from an appointed officer of the law!'

"I didn't believe he really was a policeman, so I just walked off and left him, but I thought you ought to know about it. I didn't come earlier because I thought he might be following me."

"You have done well," said Holmes. "I think I know who that fellow is, and he's no more a policeman than you are. You did right not to tell him what he has no business asking about, and I am very grateful for your letting us know about it."

When Coleford had left us, Holmes sat for some time with his brows knitted in thought. "I am wondering," said he at length, "if we can turn this incident to our advantage. I've a mind to go and see Wilson Baines now. Of course, he won't tell me anything, but I might be able to put the wind up him a little. It is, after all, a criminal offence to impersonate a police officer. If I can shake him a little over this matter, then he might just let something slip. I really think I should take advantage of this chance to learn something about what is otherwise a somewhat opaque case, and postpone our visit to Oxfordshire until tomorrow. If you would be so good as to wire Farringdon Blake to that effect, I should be obliged."

Holmes was back in little more than an hour, but there was no expression of satisfaction on his face. "Baines is out somewhere," said he. "There is a cardboard notice pinned to his office door, stating that he will be back at seven o'clock, and will then be there until nine. What I therefore suggest, Watson, as Mrs Hudson is already under the impression that we shall not be here for supper this evening, is that the two of us stroll over to Long Acre later and find somewhere to eat. We can then call on Baines between half past seven and eight."

We did as Holmes suggested and found a pleasant little restaurant in St Martin's Lane. Unfortunately, they were very busy and there was some delay in preparing the food, with the result that we did not get to the office building in Long Acre until nearly half past eight. By then, the sun had been set for some time, night was closing in, and the street lamps were lit.

The interior of the building presented an even gloomier appearance than the outside had suggested. A single lamp was lit in the hallway, the dim light of which illuminated just a few feet on either side of it and left the further reaches of the hall in deep shadow. The floor was covered with some hard, unyielding material, as were the stairs, and as we mounted the latter our footsteps rang out and echoed round the tiled stairwell. At the second floor, Holmes led the way along a narrow, shadowed corridor, but we had gone only a few yards when he abruptly stopped and put his finger to his lips.

"What is it?" I asked in a low voice.

"Footsteps," he responded in a sibilant whisper. "Downstairs. Light and furtive, as if on tip-toe."

For a few moments we remained perfectly still, listening, but, as far as I could tell, the building was in complete silence. At length, my companion shook his head, and we resumed our progress along the corridor, passing several offices which I could see through their frosted glass panels were in darkness. Near the furthest end of the corridor, however, a dim light showed through one of these glass panels, and Holmes stopped at a door which bore the name "J Wilson Baines: Enquiry Agent".

"The card notice has been removed and a lamp is lit," remarked Holmes in a low tone, "so he must have returned."

He rapped with his knuckles on the frosted glass panel of the door, but no answering sound came from within. Twice more he knocked, without drawing any response. After waiting a further moment, he put his hand on the door-knob, turned it and pushed open the door. Within was a sort of ante-room, in complete darkness. The light we had seen came from an inner office, the door of which stood slightly ajar. Holmes knocked on this and pushed it open.

I do not think that either of us could have been prepared for what we saw in that inner office. The lamp on the wall was turned down very low, but its dim illumination was sufficient to reveal a dreadful scene. A large desk took up half the space of the small room, and in the chair behind this desk a grey-haired man was sitting, his head slumped forward onto the desk-top. The hair on the back of his head was matted with blood, and it was evident he had been struck a terrible blow there. All about his head, on the papers which littered the surface of the desk, was a thick dark pool of blood, and upon these papers lay a heavy-looking marble book-end, smeared with blood and evidently the murder weapon. For a moment, I was rooted to the spot with horror, as Holmes stepped forward and felt the man's neck for a pulse. Then he turned the man's head slightly, so I could see his face.

"Is it Baines?" I asked.

Holmes nodded. "He'll not let anything slip now," said he. "He's dead."

4: FOXWOOD

IT WAS LATE and the streets were deserted by the time we reached our lodgings again that night. After a brief examination of the horrific scene in Wilson Baines's office, Holmes had suggested that I find a policeman while he remained on guard there. The constable I brought communicated with one of his colleagues, and the local station sent two more men and also notified Scotland Yard, from where a detective officer, Inspector Fellowes, arrived twenty minutes later. I was glad to see Fellowes, for he and Holmes were well acquainted and he was prepared to accept our account of how we had discovered the murdered man's body, which the constables had been reluctant to do, eyeing us with the utmost suspicion.

I let my companion do all the explaining, simply nodding my head in agreement with what he said. I could tell, from the answers he gave to the policemen's questions, that he was keen to keep Farringdon Blake's name out of the matter and, even more so, that of our railway friend, Mr Coleford. "Every detail may have to come out at the inquest," said Holmes to me as we made our way back to Baker Street, "but for the moment I would rather neither of them was pestered by the police when we can be certain that neither of them has anything to do with this terrible crime."

Back at our lodgings, Holmes used the Bunsen burner on his chemical bench to heat up a little water and make two cups of cocoa, with a generous dash of whisky in each, then we lit

42

our pipes and, sitting either side of the hearth, discussed the evening's surprising and dreadful events.

"I take it that when I went to find a policeman you took the opportunity to have a good look round in Baines's office," I remarked. "I have been wondering ever since if you managed to turn anything up there."

"Very little, in truth," responded my companion with a shake of the head. "I looked through as many of Baines's records as I dared in the little time available to me, shortening the task somewhat by ignoring anything that was more than a year old. The end result of this search, however, was that I found nothing whatever in his records that I could possibly connect with my client. In the fireplace, though, there was a small heap of blackened ashes, and it was apparent that someone had very recently burnt a number of papers there. Whoever it was had clearly been determined that no-one should see what was on those papers, for he had not only burnt them, but had then scattered the ashes with a poker. I sifted through this charred heap as carefully as I could, but it was practically impossible to make anything out. Then, just as I heard your footsteps on the stair outside, as you returned with the constable, and I was about to give it up, I found one tiny edge of paper which was not quite so burnt as the rest, on which I could make out part of a single word. That fragment of writing, Watson, was '-oxwood'."

"'Foxwood'!" I cried. "Your client's address!"

Holmes nodded. "Perhaps; but there is another possibility. It is not just my client's house that bears the name 'Foxwood', but the whole parish in which his house lies. The fragment I saw could thus just as well have been part of someone else's address, the address of whoever it is that hired Wilson Baines to follow my client about London."

"Yes, I see you are right."

"In either case, whether the scrap of paper I saw refers to Farringdon Blake's address or the address of whoever has been spying on him, the fact that the papers had clearly been burnt this evening must surely mean that this mysterious spy and the murderer of Wilson Baines are one and the same person."

"I agree. It must be so. But why on earth should Baines's own client have attacked him so viciously?"

"There is no way of telling. Perhaps Baines had demanded more money for what he was doing; perhaps, in the course of his enquiries, he had discovered something about his client that his client did not wish him to know, and, on the strength of that, was attempting to extort money from him."

"That certainly sounds possible, from what we have heard of Baines. But where does that leave us?"

"It means that the trail in London has gone cold, at least for the moment, and we must now seek for answers at Foxwood. I think that I shall turn in now, Watson, and I advise you to do the same. It is best that we are as fresh as possible tomorrow, for I fancy that our task in north Oxfordshire will not be an easy one."

The following day being Sunday, the trains were few and far between, and although we made an early start, we were obliged to change twice, with a long wait each time, and did not reach Rushfield station until late in the afternoon. Farringdon Blake met us with a pony and trap, and we set off at a slow trot along a dusty country road. As we jogged along, Holmes described to his client the events of the last two days, from our parting at the Marble Arch on Friday to the discovery of Baines's body the previous evening. At this latter news, a look of disbelief and horror came over Blake's features, and for several minutes he did not speak.

"That is terrible – dreadful," he said at length. "Whatever this man Baines has done, I would not wish such a fate upon him. From what you have told me of his line of work, I imagine he must have made many bitter enemies – angry husbands, for instance, whose wives had hired Baines to spy on them – but such extreme violence seems incomprehensible, the act of a madman. I suppose, from my own point of view, there is one thing from which I can take solace," he added after a moment: "at least this dreadful business can have nothing to do with my own little mystery."

"I am very much afraid it may have," returned Holmes with a shake of the head. He described to his client the charred papers he had discovered in the hearth of Baines's office. "Someone had clearly gone to great lengths to cover his tracks; but the one tiny clue he overlooked points directly and unequivocally to this district."

Again, an expression of horror mingled with astonishment passed over Blake's face. "The matter seems to have passed from bad to worse," he said at last with a shake of the head.

"Do not be despondent," returned Holmes in a brisk tone. "Things may look dark and incomprehensible at present,

Mr Blake, but there is a stage in almost all investigations when that is so. There is no point in dwelling on things we cannot affect. I am confident of making some progress in the matter when I get a little more data. To begin with, I shall need the details of all your neighbours in and around Foxwood," he continued, taking his note-book from his pocket, "especially those who are educated and moderately well off. Perhaps, if it is not too much trouble, you could give me such details now."

"My neighbours?" queried Blake. "But these are people with whom I am on terms of affable friendship. I cannot believe that any of them would stoop to spying on me! The very thought seems absurd!"

"Nevertheless, all possibilities must be considered. You don't know why you are being spied upon. Would you not agree?"

"Absolutely. I have no idea."

"It follows, then, that you cannot know who it is that is doing the spying, or what his purposes may be, and, thus, no-one can be ruled out. Now, there are, I think, two assumptions we are justified in making to begin with. If our investigation of the matter proves either of these assumptions to be false, then we can discard them. The assumptions are these: first, that only someone moderately well off could afford the sort of telescope you discovered up the tree in the ash spinney. Second, that with the possible exception of the farmer who owns the land on which the ash spinney stands – who, you mentioned to us, has denied all knowledge of the rungs in the tree – whoever has climbed those rungs to spy on you can only have discovered them by chance, and only then recognised the opportunity they presented. If so, then the person spying on you is most likely to be someone who lives in the district and takes walks in the fields and woods as you do."

"Very well," responded Blake after a moment's consideration. "I can see the point of your argument, even if I find the conclusion unpalatable. I don't really have many neighbours, and fewer still who fall into the categories you mention. For what it's worth, I can soon give you a list of them. First of all there is Thomas Pearson, the farmer on whose land the ash spinney stands. He could, I think – like many farmers – be described as 'a man of few words'. He has, as I believe I mentioned to you, farmed the land there for about twenty years, and generally seems to have no interests apart from that work."

"His household?" queried Holmes as Blake paused.

"He has a wife and two sons, James and Anthony, who are both in their early twenties, a couple of years apart. These two young men both have a reputation as madcaps, but in a fairly conventional way, and their interests, so far as I have been able to discover, are as narrowly circumscribed as those of their father. He keeps a couple of servants, local girls, one of whom, so rumour has it, may marry the older son in the not-too-distant future. That is, I think, the extent of my knowledge. I have taken tea with them a few times and found their company pleasant enough but their conversation somewhat limited.

"The other farmer who is a neighbour is Oliver Ashton, whose land immediately adjoins my own gardens. He is of a completely different character. His wife, sadly, died about five years ago, and his two children, a boy, Giles, and a girl, Fiona, aged about seventeen and fifteen, are away at school most of the year, so, apart from a married couple who are his only domestic servants, he has the house to himself. As a result of this, I suppose, he is a very great reader. This certainly makes his conversation more interesting than that of Thomas Pearson, but he is one of those people whose conversation tends to be dominated by whatever book he is currently reading. Thus, on one occasion when I passed an evening with him, almost the entire conversation was taken up with a discussion of King Alfred the Great, a biography of whom Ashton had just finished reading. As I knew little more about Alfred than that he had united some previously warring factions against the Danish invaders, and had absent-mindedly burnt some cakes, you will imagine that Ashton did most of the talking. On another occasion, he had been reading a book about Captain Cook's voyages of exploration, and the evening's conversation was dominated by the subject of Australia and New Zealand, about which I knew almost as little as I knew about Alfred the Great. I have always found Ashton agreeable enough, but as both he and his children are regarded as conducting themselves with a rather manifest air of superiority, they are not very popular in the district. We'll drive past his farmhouse, Oldstone House, a little further on. I'll point it out to you as we pass.

"Then," Blake continued after a moment's thought, "there is Mr Matthias Needham of Abbeyfield House. He would certainly fit into your categories of 'educated' and 'well off', although he keeps himself to himself most of the time and I can't think of the slightest reason he could have for spying on me. I know nothing whatever about his antecedents, so I can only describe him as I find him now. He is unmarried and lives alone at Abbeyfield House, which is even more isolated than my own house, where he spends his time in studying, so far as I can gather. Quite what subjects he studies, I cannot say, as he is, as I say, a very private man and speaks of himself only rarely. We have dined together, either at his house or mine, on a number of occasions, and the conversation has always been very lively, ranging over almost every abstract topic you could imagine, from politics, science, history and law to the possible existence of intelligent life on other planets.

"He is congenial enough when he is in the mood, although his manner is never an open one. I cannot quite put my finger on it, but there seems something about him, even in his most expansive moments, that is opaque and calculating. And now that – in order to answer your questions – I reflect on our acquaintance in this way, I do recall a couple of odd things about him. I remember that he once asked me if I ever thought that I was being spied upon. I said not, and enquired as to what had made him ask the question, to which he answered that he had occasionally heard someone in his garden at twilight, and had once thought he had caught a glimpse of a face at the window. I suggested that it might have been some local boys looking to find some apples in his orchard, and we did not pursue the matter further."

"When was that?" Holmes asked.

"Not recently – some time last autumn, I think. He has not mentioned the matter since. The other odd thing occurred one evening when Mr Needham was dining with me at the Grange. It was, I suppose, about two years ago. The conversation had drifted from one topic to another until it had alighted upon the subject of Foxwood Grange itself and its history. During the course of this, he mentioned that he had dined with my cousin, Mr Stannard, on numerous occasions in the past, but the latter had never showed him round the house. He said this in an odd tone, as if trying to imply that Mr Stannard had had some reason of his own for not doing so, which I felt sure was not true. There and then, I offered to remedy the deficiency and we set off for a tour of the old place. It was quite dark by then, however, so the tour was conducted by lamplight, and I'm not sure how satisfactory Mr Needham found it. I told him that if he ever wished to see any of it again in daylight, he had only to ask. It is, after all, a very historic place, and I can certainly understand anyone having an interest in it."

"Did he ever make such a request?"

"Only once. About six months later, he asked if he might have another look in the library at the Grange, for, he said, it had been so dark on the previous occasion that he had been unable to make out the titles of many of the books there. I readily agreed, and we spent an enjoyable afternoon poring over the old volumes together, for there were, as you will imagine, many that I myself had never opened since I had lived there."

"Did Mr Needham appear interested in any book in particular?"

"Not really. He was certainly more interested in the philosophical works than the others, as I recall – Bacon's essays, an early edition of Locke, an eighteenth-century translation of Descartes and so on – but not in any one of them especially. He mentioned that he had many of them himself, in more modern editions. I did get the impression from some remark he made that he had hoped to find some esoterica there – books of hidden secrets, magic incantations and so on – but if so he must have been disappointed, for we didn't come across anything like that."

"Very well. Pray continue."

All the time that Blake had been speaking, the pony had been proceeding at a slow trot along that quiet rural road. Now, with a pull on the reins, he drew the trap to a halt, and indicated the view to the left ahead of us, where a valley wound its way towards a series of gentle wooded hills in the distance.

"I always think that the view from this spot must be one of the most beautiful in England," said he. "Those hills you see are part of the Cotswold chain. When you look across from here, you see the hills and the woods, and very little else, so it is a little like looking back in time to some prehistoric age, before even ancient man had made any impression upon the landscape."

"It is certainly a lovely view," I agreed.

"While you sit here a moment and admire it," said Holmes, "perhaps you could continue your survey of your neighbours."

"I think there is really only one more household to mention," returned Blake, "but it is a decidedly odd one. Some distance on the far side of the ridge on which the ash spinney stands is another isolated house, Black Bank House. It was unoccupied when I first came to the district, but about eighteen months ago a singular group of people moved in there. I often saw them out walking when they were first here, but although I generally gave them a cheery 'hello' when our paths crossed, I received only a silent nod of the head in return. There are three of them, a man and a woman of middle age, and another man who appears somewhat older. I had seen them out walking several times before I had any idea who they were, and had formed the impression that the older man was the head of the household. He is a very learned-looking man and I had often seen him talking as they walked along, sometimes gesticulating as he did so, as if to emphasise some point or other. As the other man generally walked beside him or just behind, occasionally making some remark and often jotting things down in a note-book he carried, I had conjectured that he was perhaps the older man's secretary or assistant. As to the woman, I could not say, but she seemed to act in an easy, familiar sort of way towards the older man, and I thought she might be his wife.

"On one occasion, when I saw them in the distance, they had paused in their walk and the two men seemed to be having a heated discussion about something. Indeed, so heated did they appear that I thought they might almost come to blows over the issue, whatever it was, but the woman seemed to come between them, make some point to each of them in turn and eventually calm them down, whereupon they resumed their walk and discussion in the usual peaceful way.

"Some time later, I heard – from Mrs Caxton, my cook, of all people, although I imagine the ultimate source of the information was probably someone at the village post office – that the head of the household at Black Bank House was one Professor Crook. That probably meant nothing to most people in the parish, but it was a name I was familiar with, and I knew that Professor Crook had formerly held the chair of astronomical physics at Cambridge. When Mrs Caxton supplied me with the name, I at once recalled reading somewhere, a year or two earlier, that Professor Crook was about to retire from the post he had held with great distinction for so long. Although giving up his teaching duties, the report had said, he would continue his own work, and hoped to publish a comprehensive account of his theories in a few years' time. This clarified the mystery of Black Bank House considerably, as far as I was concerned. Evidently, Professor Crook is one of those people who find it helpful to walk about when meditating on abstract problems, and the other man, who is undoubtedly his amanuensis and is probably highly qualified himself, keeps notes of all the professor's thoughts.

"Once I had discovered who it was I had as a neighbour, I made a point of calling round at Black Bank House at the earliest opportunity, thinking what a thrill it would be for a toiler in the foothills of science such as myself to meet so eminent a scientific scholar. When I did so, however, I was informed by his secretary, who introduced himself as Dr Taylor, and who seemed a very pleasant gentleman, that Professor Crook was resting and could not be disturbed. I asked if there might be any more suitable time for me to call, but he shook his head. 'Pray do not be offended,' said he. 'Professor Crook is not as strong as he used to be, and tires very quickly. I am always concerned lest he over-tax himself, so we have made it a general rule not to entertain any visitors. If we meet when we are out on one of our walks, however, you may be sure I will introduce you.'

"I found this most disappointing, I must say. I have since seen them in the distance several times when I have been out walking, but our paths have never crossed, so I have never had the pleasure of shaking the great scholar's hand. There," added Blake in a tone of finality. "On that somewhat disappointing note, this survey of my neighbours is concluded!"

"And is your cousin, Mr Stannard, still flourishing?" asked Holmes.

"Very much so," returned Blake. "He is very pleased with his little cottage, and pleased to be living in the centre of the village. I see him fairly frequently. Not so long ago, he was visited by his distant cousin, old Mr Betteridge from Nottingham, and as Mr Stannard's cottage is rather small, I entertained them both at the Grange. Mr Betteridge had himself recently relinquished his very large house in favour of his son, and he and Mr Stannard spent much of the evening disparaging old, rambling houses and singing the praises of smaller properties, but they were very amusing about it, which made it an entertaining evening."

"Very well," said Holmes, shutting up his note-book. "Let us now proceed!"

Blake flicked the reins and the pony set off at a gentle trot. After about half a mile, we passed an old, stone-built farmhouse on our right, which Blake informed us was Mr Ashton's house. A little further on, a side-road went off to the right, and as we turned that way, Blake pointed along the main road.

"The village is that way," said he. "The thatched roof you can see in the distance, above that hedge, is that of the village pub, the Royal Oak, where old Caxton goes every Friday evening, to play skittles and the like. He is a very sociable old fellow, and seems to know everyone there is to know in the parish. Speaking of the people of the parish, by the way," he added after a moment, "I have let it be thought that you are personal friends of mine, fellow scribblers for the weekly periodicals, taking a few days' holiday from London. I would rather that people did not know your real reason for being here."

"That is probably sensible," returned Holmes. "It is best that our presence does not arouse too much curiosity. And as Dr Watson has been speaking for some time of getting away from London for a few days, I am sure he will have little difficulty in playing the part of a holiday-maker!"

Our way took us, now rising a little, now falling a little, between high hedges and tall trees that met in a green arch above our heads. Presently the trap slowed again, and we turned to the right, in between two brick gateposts and onto a narrow, curving drive. We passed two or three large, spreading trees and a series of well-trimmed bushes, and came round a hedge to the front of what I thought the loveliest Elizabethan building I had ever seen, its dark red brickwork bathed in the late afternoon sunshine. It was not a large building, at least as to height, but it seemed to ramble off, to left and right, in an attractively haphazard fashion. Its sections of brickwork, some of it laid in that characteristically diagonal Tudor fashion, were separated at regular intervals by black wooden beams and broad lattice-paned windows, so typical of the Tudor period. The roof was covered with dark red, lichen-blotched tiles, above which rose several tall and highly ornate brick chimneys.

55

As Blake reined in the pony before the house, the front door was opened and an elderly man emerged in the garb of a manservant. "Shall I put Henrietta away, sir?" he asked as we climbed down from the trap.

"Yes," replied Blake, "We shall not need her again this evening."

We were entering the front doorway, when Blake paused and looked after his servant, who was leading the pony and trap round the left-hand corner of the building. "There's something wrong with old Caxton," he remarked to us, a frown on his face. "He is not usually so morose and gloomy-looking as this."

As he spoke, a young man appeared in the doorway. "Ah, Whitemoor," said Blake. "This is Mr Holmes and Dr Watson, the friends and fellow-scribblers I mentioned to you earlier. Would you mind showing them in and entertaining them for a minute? Do excuse me, gentlemen," he continued, turning to us. "I just want to have a quick word with Caxton and see what the matter is." With that he hurried off after the elderly servant, and we followed the young man into the house.

We were sitting in an oak-panelled drawing-room, having a cup of tea and discussing our journalistic activities, when Blake returned. The expression on his face was a sombre one.

"What is it?" asked Holmes.

"A local tragedy," returned Blake. "An old fellow, Jacob Brookfield, who is a crony of Caxton's from the Royal Oak, has not been seen for about two weeks. Everyone just assumed he had gone to visit his sister in Banbury, which he had been talking of doing for a while. Earlier today, however, his body was found by some village boys at the bottom of a disused quarry. Apparently, it looks as if the body has been there for some time, perhaps as long as two weeks."

"Where is this quarry?" asked Holmes.

"Not far from here, as a matter of fact. Brookfield lived with his married daughter, whose house is out this way, on the road to Thuxton. He would have passed the old quarry, which is not very well fenced off, every night he walked home from the pub. The quarry comes very close to the road-edge at one point. It seems that he was quite intoxicated on the last evening that anyone saw him, so it is thought he must have wandered off the road and slipped over the edge of the quarry before he knew what was happening."

"Did his daughter not wonder what had become of him?" I asked.

"Apparently they had had a bit of a quarrel earlier in the day, and he'd declared that he would go to his sister's if he wasn't wanted here, so that's where the daughter thought he had gone. He was well known for being a bit of an eccentric, coming and going unpredictably, without ever letting anyone know what he was doing."

"What an unfortunate business," I remarked, shaking my head. I glanced at Holmes, who was sitting in silence. The expression on his face was an impassive one, revealing nothing of his inner thoughts, but I, who knew him well, could see from a thoughtful look in his eyes that he was weighing this new information carefully along with everything else we had been told by Farringdon Blake. Quite what my friend would make of it, I could not imagine. It did not, on the face of it, appear to bear any relation to the business that had brought us to Foxwood, and seemed, as Blake had described it, simply a local tragedy. Whether Holmes could see any greater significance in it, I could not tell. For myself, I can only confess that all the recent shocking events had left me in a state of utter mystification.

5: THE GRANGE

THERE WAS, UNDERSTANDABLY, a somewhat subdued air in the drawing-room, and for some time we sat drinking tea and smoking our pipes in silence. A young and pretty dark-haired girl in a maid's uniform came in to ask if we required anything else, but Blake said not. Eventually, Whitemoor got to his feet and said that, if no-one minded, he would return to his room to carry on with the work he had been doing earlier.

"I suppose we all ought to carry on," Blake remarked in a flat tone when Whitemoor had left us. "It's just that I've felt a little knocked back by all this grim news – first that man in London, and now old Brookfield." He shook his head. "Still," he continued, rising to his feet, "I'll give you a little tour of the house as I intended, before the daylight goes."

We followed our host from the drawing-room into the very broad entrance hall, where the dark oak panelling gleamed in the low rays of the late afternoon sun and a stately staircase ascended to the upper floors, then along a short corridor at the side of the staircase until we came to a door on the right. "This is my study," said he, pushing open the door.

It was a medium-sized room, its walls oak panelled like those of the drawing-room, save where tall bookshelves lined the walls. At the far end was a large bay with windows on all sides, and in this bay was a wide desk. Holmes squeezed past the side of the desk and gazed out of the window. "This is what was visible from up in the tree, presumably," he said, to which

Blake nodded his head. "It doesn't appear that there would be much for the spy to see," Holmes continued. "He could certainly see whether you were at your desk or not, and perhaps whether you were working from books or simply had papers on your desk, but I doubt if he could have made out in any detail what any of them were. Hum! We shall have to take a look from the other end – from the viewing-platform – tomorrow. At present, I confess, this spying seems fairly pointless to me – as pointless, in fact, as the spying on you in London!"

"Pointless or not, it certainly occurred," remarked Blake.

"Indeed," returned Holmes. "That is the enigma."

"I suppose if it appears pointless, then there is nothing we can learn from it," observed Blake after a moment.

"Not necessarily. On the contrary, it is often what seem the most pointless features of a case that are in the end the most instructive."

"Does anything suggest itself to you in the present case?"

"Yes, several things; but some of them are mutually contradictory, so there is no point in listing them at present."

As we left the study, Blake gestured to the right. "The kitchen is that way," he said. "There is also a corridor across the back of the house which is jocularly known as 'the long gallery', in imitation of such rooms in far grander houses. In truth, it is not very long, and is not really much of a gallery, either, although it does have a row of windows which overlook the back yard!"

Our guide then took us on to the other rooms of the ground floor, each oak-panelled in the same dark way as the study, and I confess I began to find it a little oppressive. It was certainly all interesting, historically speaking, and very handsome in its own way. But as we passed from one room to the next, a vision of the light and airy sitting-room in our own lodgings in London arose unbidden in my mind, and I found myself reflecting on the differences, and concluding that, personally speaking, I was happy in Baker Street, and should not really care to live at Foxwood Grange.

Presently, our circular tour of the ground floor of the Grange came to the final room, the library, which occupied the front west corner of the building, directly across the hall from the drawing-room in which we had been sitting earlier. As Blake opened the door, I was for a moment almost dazzled by the sudden burst of golden sunlight, for the low sun was shining straight in through the diamond-paned windows, and onto a highly polished reading table in the middle of the room. It was a large room, and save for the broad windows and an immense stone fireplace on our right, all the walls were lined with bookshelves.

"This is a very fine room," I said.

"It is indeed," agreed Holmes. "Ah!" he cried, and, following his gaze, I saw that he was looking up at the deep lintel over the doorway through which we had just entered. Three lines of lettering had been carved with great precision into the wood there, which read as follows:

TRUTH ITSELF IS ALWAYS
THE HIGHEST AND BEST GOAL
OF HUMAN EFFORT

"It is Francis Bacon," cried Holmes in a voice suffused with delight. "What a splendid observation to have above one's head in a library!"

"I am glad it pleases you," responded Blake in an appreciative tone. "Bacon stayed here in 1620, and the carving was done then, in his honour. I think you are the first visitor I have had who has recognized the source of the quotation."

"Well, well," said Holmes, "it is an inspiring maxim not just for those in the scientific and scholarly disciplines, but for everyone who reflects on life, and perhaps above all for anyone in my own humble profession. Perhaps I should have it carved above my own doorway! This is certainly a splendid room, Mr Blake! Some of these books look very old. Are any of them from Elizabeth's reign?"

"Yes, quite a number, although several were rebound in the first half of the seventeenth century to match some of the books acquired then. There are some wonderful books here – enough to keep one fully occupied for a year or two, I should think!"

"No doubt. And what is this? Yet more worthy maxims?"

I turned from the book I was examining, to see what Holmes was looking at. Over the fireplace, hanging in a gilded wooden frame on the chimney-breast, was a large document of some sort, written in black ink, in a flowing, old-fashioned hand, the initial letters of each line decorated with loops and twirls done in red ink.

"It looks like a charter of some kind," I remarked. "Or is it a poem?"

"Of a sort," said Holmes, examining it closely. "Or perhaps one should deem it more a moral tract."

I joined him by the fireplace and read the following:

> If error be in the heart
> Nor all thy diligence nor all thy talent
> Nor all that learning can bestow
> Shall bring forth fruit.
> Like seed scatter'd unto rocks
> Or bulbs thrust into mud
> All that might have been
> Is but a vain and empty vision

"What is the source of this passage?" asked Holmes. "It has an eighteenth century flavour to it, but I don't recognize it."

"Nor me," I said.

"That is not surprising, gentlemen," replied Blake. "It was composed by a former owner of this house, a man not previously noted for putting pen to paper very often except to write out gambling slips and sign his name to the debts he owed to all and sundry."

"An ancestor of Mr Stannard?" queried Holmes.

"No, not at all," returned Blake. "Foxwood Grange was only in the Stannard family for three generations, Mr Stannard's grandfather having bought it in 1795. Before that, the house had had a very chequered history, and had passed through many hands." Blake indicated the chairs set round the table. "Take a seat." he said, "and I'll give you a brief history of the house and of that document. I'm sure you'll find it interesting, for there is something of a mystery surrounding it.

"First of all," he continued after a moment, "the house was built for Sir William Stamford in 1592. His estates were the largest in the district at the time, and this house was of some importance. It remained in his family for about forty years, but in the 1630s there was no direct heir, and it passed by marriage to some people called Hollings. They seemed to have managed to keep out of the political upheavals that engulfed most of the country in the middle of that century, and the house remained in their family until the 1680s, when it was sold to a man called Podmore. He didn't live here for very long, however, and there were then three more short-lived owners, until it came, in 1746, into the hands of one Samuel Harley, the author of that document you were looking at over the fireplace. This was undoubtedly the most notorious period in the history of this old place. You have perhaps heard of the 'Hell-Fire Club'."

"What, Sir Francis Dashwood and his disreputable circle?" I asked.

"Exactly. If you know anything about Dashwood, then you will have a good idea what Samuel Harley was like, for he was cut from the same cloth. In short, he was a rake and a libertine, notorious for his behaviour even in an age which had no shortage of such figures. If I mention that his cronies included George Augustus Selwyn, Bubb Doddington, George 'Swine' Darcy and all those people, you will understand the sort of thing I mean. To call them a dissolute, debauched gambling set scarcely does their behaviour justice. They scandalised mid-eighteenth-century society, and one of their chief haunts was this house, Foxwood Grange. Harley had, by a series of chances, inherited enormous wealth when still a young man, and proceeded to work his way through it with the speed of a forest fire. Among his possessions were a large house in Mayfair, in London, another near Derby and this one, Foxwood Grange, which seems to have been the one he regarded as his home, probably because he had spent a large part of his childhood here.

"At the height of his notoriety, the pattern of Harley's debauchery was well established. He would go up to London for a few weeks, spend money there in colossal amounts, waste even more and gamble away yet more, then return to Foxwood with his cronies and other guests, both male and female, and repeat the performance here. When he was at length tired of having the house full of drunken revellers, he would pack them all off to London and spend a few weeks recovering from his excesses until boredom overcame him and he set off once more for London, to begin the whole sordid round once again.

"Even such great wealth as Harley possessed cannot last forever in the hands of a committed wastrel, and so it was in this case. Bit by bit, Harley's fortune dribbled away until there was very little of it remaining. He sold all his houses but this one, and sold all the land he owned save for a few small fields. All his other valuables – gold, silver and so on – had by this time long gone. Then, one fateful night here at Foxwood, when Harley was even more inebriated than usual, he made a disastrous mistake. He had been gambling all day and all evening, and had lost heavily. In the end, in a desperate attempt to recoup his losses, he staked Foxwood Grange itself against all his debts. Some accounts say it was staked on a roll of the dice, others say it was on a hand of cards. Whichever was the case, it scarcely matters, as he lost. In a matter of moments, Foxwood Grange and what was left of its estate no longer belonged to Harley, but were the property of George 'Swine' Darcy. This concluded a month or more of such bad decisions and ill-fortune, and Samuel Harley was now a ruined man. He was given three months to get his affairs in order and leave the house. It was during this period that he composed that document you were looking at, and left it here for those who came after him to read."

"I suppose he was overcome with remorse," I observed, "and wanted to leave a warning to others to avoid his wretched fate."

"Presumably. He was by all accounts not a stupid man, and without the influences he had fallen under at an early age might well have made a worthy citizen, in which case his life might have been completely different."

"What became of him?" asked Holmes.

"No-one knows for certain, but it seems he went out to Italy, to stay with some old crony of his. How long he lasted there, though, I have no idea, as he dropped completely out of sight and nothing was ever heard of him again. The general belief is that he drank himself to death."

"What a wretched tale," I remarked with a shake of the head.

"Indeed," said Blake, "but that wasn't quite the end of it. Rumours began to circulate, two or three years later, that he had not been quite so destitute as it had first appeared, and that before his final, miserable decline he had used some of his wealth to purchase items of value – rubies and other precious stones were suggested – which he had secreted away somewhere."

"That seems a little unlikely from your account," said Holmes. "If he possessed such assets, why then did he not sell them to raise the money to save himself from destitution?"

"I agree," returned Blake. "I believe the rumour only arose because of a letter he had written from Italy to his heir – a distant cousin – in which he stated that he had left something for him at Foxwood which he might find of value. But I think he was probably just referring to the moral lesson in that document over there. There is certainly no record of anything else ever having been found here, and Darcy, who owned the house at the time, declared that the rumours were utterly untrue."

"Perhaps Darcy himself had found whatever it was, and pocketed it for his own use." I suggested.

Holmes shook his head. "That is of course possible," he said. "But if it seems unlikely that Harley really possessed the objects of value that were rumoured, it is surely even more unlikely that he would simply have left such things here, for he would have known that they would be more likely to be found by Darcy than by anyone else."

"My conclusion precisely," said Blake, "which is why I think he was simply referring to the moral tract he had left here. Anyway, gentlemen, that is the sorry story of Samuel Harley, and of the most notorious period in the history of this old place."

"What became of the house afterwards?" I asked.

"I don't think Darcy ever spent much time here," Blake replied, "although Harley's moral composition evidently amused him in some way, for it was he that had it framed and hung where you see it now. Anyway, he sold the house about five years later, to someone called Mayhew. It then passed through several other hands until Mr Stannard's grandfather bought it in 1795, as I mentioned before."

As he was speaking, the library door opened and the elderly servant put his head in.

"What is it, Caxton?" asked Blake.

"I do beg your pardon, sir, but the news of old Mr Brookfield knocked me quite out of my stride, and I forgot to inform you that Mrs Booth called this afternoon, while you were absent."

"Oh? Did she want anything in particular?"

"No, sir. She specifically asked me to convey that fact to you. She was in her little trap with the boy, and said she was simply out for a Sunday drive round the district."

"She did not leave any other message?"

"No, sir."

"Who, if I may ask," said Holmes when the servant had left us, "is Mrs Booth?"

"Just a neighbour of mine."

"But you did not mention her in the list of neighbours you gave me earlier."

"I had to draw the line somewhere, Mr Holmes. I can hardly imagine Mrs Booth climbing up a tree to spy on me!"

"Nevertheless, as she is evidently someone who feels able to call on you without notice, she is a part of the tapestry of this parish which I am trying to get clear in my mind. Is she an elderly woman?"

"No, not at all. She is not yet thirty."

"A widow, perhaps?"

"No. I suppose I shall have to tell you, even though she can have nothing to do with my little mystery. She is simply someone with whom I have become friendly over the last year. She is separated from her husband and lives with her three-year-old boy, Henry, in a house on the other side of the village. We happened to meet and strike up a conversation at the village fete last summer, and hit it off rather well. On the strength of that, she invited me to call round at her house for a cup of tea any time I was over in that direction."

"And have you?"

"Yes, many times. And she has come here many times."

"I am sorry if my questions seem unnecessarily intrusive, Mr Blake," said Holmes, taking his note-book from his pocket, "but I must get all the facts straight in my mind if I am to make progress in the case."

"I understand."

"What is Mrs Booth's first name?"

"Penelope," replied Blake, appearing a little discomfited.

"And that is, perhaps, how you customarily address her?" queried Holmes, eyeing his client keenly.

"Yes, I suppose it is."

"Do you know anything about her husband, or why the two of them are separated?"

"Not really. I have never raised the subject. It would seem to me impolite – indeed, grossly impertinent – to do so.

But from occasional remarks she has made, I have gained the impression that her husband treated her very badly. Eventually, she felt she had little choice but to leave the marital home. She has a little money of her own and just about manages to get by on that, but she is not very well off."

"Do you know where her husband is living now?" asked Holmes.

"Somewhere near Birmingham, I believe. It might be Solihull, but I am not certain."

"Very well," said Holmes, shutting up his note-book. "That will do for the moment."

"I might say," Blake added in a somewhat hesitant voice, "lest you get the wrong impression, that I am not the only one in Foxwood who pays visits to Mrs Booth. I know for a fact, for instance, that my neighbour, Ashton, has called upon her on several occasions, although I like to think that she finds my conversation somewhat more interesting than his."

"I seem to detect a note of rivalry in your tone," remarked Holmes with a little smile. "Would I be correct in inferring that Mrs Booth is a woman of some attractions?"

"You could say that," returned Blake with an embarrassed chuckle. "I think so, anyway."

At dinner that evening, we discussed our host's work, and, largely because he himself had an unpretentious, self-depreciating view of it, the conversation was a very light-hearted and amusing one. This came as something of a relief, I must confess, after the gloomy and disturbing matters with which we had been concerned over the last couple of days. I asked Blake if he had ever found himself repeating things he had already written about before, at which suggestion he nodded his head vigorously.

"Many times," he replied. "For instance, I think I must have explained the general principles of the telephone at least five times in different publications."

"Seven, actually," corrected Whitemoor. "I found two more this afternoon."

Blake laughed. "That is one of the most important tasks that Whitemoor is doing for me," he remarked. "He is going through all my past articles and cross-indexing them all, something I have never had the time to do. Then, in future, if I am asked to write about the telephone, say, or the rainbow – I've explained that three or four times, too – I shall only need to consult the index to see what I have written before on the subject. This will make my work a lot easier. In some cases, indeed, I shall probably be able to completely re-use an old article, with just a few words changed here and there to freshen it up a little!"

Thus the conversation proceeded in a gay, light-hearted manner, brightening up that dark and somewhat severe dining-room in which we were taking our meal. And yet, despite the gaiety of the gathering, my mind kept wandering, in each brief moment of silence, back to the room next door, the library, in which Blake had recounted to us the melancholy tale of Samuel Harley, and back, also, to the dark office in London where, less than twenty-four hours earlier, we had encountered such a scene of horror. When I retired to my bed that night, my thoughts were an incoherent jumble of all that we had seen and heard since that fateful moment on Friday morning when Mr Coleford of the

71

Great Western Railway had arrived with a letter for Sherlock Holmes. As I drifted off to sleep, I wondered what, if anything, my friend was making of the case, or if he was, in truth, as mystified by it all as I was myself. Knowing his keen intellect as I did, I looked forward to hearing a word from him which might bring a little light into the darkness.

6: THE ASH SPINNEY

AFTER BREAKFAST the following day, Blake took us up to the ash spinney. It was a fine, bright morning, and I was glad to be out of doors in such weather and to hear the birds singing gaily as they flitted from tree to tree. As we passed through the side-gate from the garden into the sunlit, hilly field beyond, all speckled over with the bright colours of wild flowers, I confess it was hard for me to remember what our real purpose was, that we were seeking answers to Farringdon Blake's odd mystery. Sherlock Holmes, however, was silent, and I could see from the intent look upon his features that he was quite oblivious to the beauties of nature, and had thoughts only for the problem to be solved.

"Is this field one of Mr Ashton's?" I asked our guide.

"Yes," returned Blake. "As you see, it is lying fallow this year. Last year he just had a few sheep in it. Next year, I believe he is going to grow a crop in it. What crop, exactly, I don't know, but I know that he intends to plough it this autumn. He seems to follow a system of crop rotation which is different from that of anyone else."

"Perhaps he is following a system recommended in one of those books he is always reading," I suggested with a chuckle.

"Perhaps he is," agreed Blake. "That wouldn't surprise me. Not all his reading is on obscure or 'far-away' topics. As a matter of fact, when I was first here he showed me a slim volume written by a local historian about fifty years ago which detailed the history of Foxwood parish and of the Grange in particular. It was from that book that I learnt some of the details of what I was telling you yesterday about Samuel Harley."

"Do you not have a copy of that book in your own library?" asked Holmes.

Blake shook his head. "Surprisingly not," he replied. "You would think that Mr Stannard's father or grandfather or whoever was here at the time would have bought a copy, but if there is one there somewhere, I have never been able to find it. I borrowed Ashton's copy for a couple of weeks, and after I'd returned it to him I asked a bookseller in Banbury to try to get me a copy. I've never heard from him since, though, so I presume he couldn't find one."

It took us only a few minutes to reach the ash spinney, at the top end of the field. It appeared, as far as I could see, to be the highest point for some distance around. I had brought my field-glasses with me, and I turned and surveyed the countryside below us, back the way we had come, towards a row of low, undulating hills far in the distance. Down in the valley I could see chimneys and part of a roof peeping out from a small clump of trees, which Blake informed me was Ashton's farmhouse, Oldstone House.

Holmes, meanwhile, had passed through the narrow belt of trees and was gazing across the landscape to the north. The field immediately beyond the ash spinney sloped gently down until it met a narrow road, which Blake informed us was the road to Thuxton. Beyond the road lay a dense-looking wood.

"Where does the quarry lie in which the body of the old man, Brookfield, was found?" Holmes asked Blake.

"Over to the left there," replied Blake, indicating a spot to the left of the wood. "The narrow lane which passes the Grange, up which we drove yesterday, continues on until it meets that road at a crossroads. The quarry is just to the west of that."

"And Pearson's house – Lower Cropley, I think you called it – where is that?"

"A short distance on the other side of the crossroads. You can't see it from here, as it's just over the brow of the next hill. Somewhere else you can't see is Black Bank House, where Professor Crook lives. That lies to the right, on the other side of that wood. The track to the house goes off the road you can see, and passes through the wood, but it's difficult to make out from here."

"Very well," said Holmes. "Now we have got our bearings, let us have a look at the viewing-platform up the tree."

We turned to the side and followed the path along the ridge through the ash spinney. Presently, Blake stopped at the foot of a huge ash tree.

"This is the one," said he, slapping the broad trunk of the tree with the flat of his hand. "As you can see, there is no sign of anything out of the ordinary on this side of the tree, so you will appreciate how one could pass along this path many times without knowing that there was anything unusual about it."

He led us round to the other side of the tree, which faced towards the sloping field down which we had just been gazing, and there were the stout iron rungs which he had described to us in London.

Holmes looked up at the wooden platform, high above our heads. "How much space is there on the platform?" he asked.

"I'm not sure it would take the three of us," returned Blake, "so if you and Dr Watson would care to climb up, I'll wait down here."

I handed Holmes my field-glasses and he led the way up that strange steep stairway. The climb was surprisingly hard work, and, when we reached the top, the ground seemed a very long way beneath us. On the platform, although it was not at all a windy day, I was very conscious of the gusts blowing this way and that, and held on to an overhead branch for support.

"Some of these small branches have been broken off and some removed with a pair of clippers," said Holmes as he examined the foliage around the viewing-platform. "Let us see what that permits us to observe. I can see the desk and chair in Mr Blake's study clearly enough," he said after a moment, as he peered through the field-glasses, "but I can't really see any further into the room than that. I can't see into the drawing-room at all, as there's a bush in the way. If I swing the glasses round to the right, however," he continued after a moment, "I can see a large open area behind the house, which appears to be cobbled. To the right of that is another building, facing the back of the house. It appears to have been built against the hill which rises behind the house, and looks somewhat more architecturally distinguished than the usual row of outhouses. What is that, I wonder? Here, Watson, take a look," he added, handing the glasses to me.

I peered through the glasses, and confirmed all that he had said. A few moments later we descended to where Blake was awaiting us, at the foot of the tree, and Holmes looked about him once more.

"If we continued along this path through the wood, where would we come to?" he asked Blake.

"The path meanders along the ridge for some distance," replied Blake. "At the end of the spinney, it crosses the top of a field and comes to a narrow lane – little more than a farm-track, really – which leads to Abbeyfield House, Mr Needham's place."

"Does he ever come this way?"

"I don't know. He might, I suppose, if he were on foot, but when he has visited me, he has always driven himself over, *via* the Thuxton road."

As we made our way back to the house, down the hilly field, Holmes described to his client the broken and clipped branches he had observed on one side of the wooden platform.

"It makes it certain that you and your household are the focus of the spy's interest," said he.

"I never doubted it," returned Blake.

"Perhaps not, but it was always possible that the Grange was just one among a number of things that he wished to spy on. The fact that no branches on the other side have been removed rules out that possibility, as the foliage makes it impossible to see in any direction other than that of the Grange."

"I see what you mean. I am impressed by your scientific thoroughness in testing for other possibilities," remarked Blake.

"Thoroughness is one of the most important aspects of detective-work," said Holmes. "If you are not thorough you will miss some little detail or other, and the little detail you miss will invariably turn out to be the key to the whole problem. Incidentally, I observed that branches had been removed to enable a clear view not only of your study, but also of a large open area at the back of the house where there is another building, small but architecturally elaborate, which has been constructed against the hill behind the house."

"That," replied Blake with a chuckle, "is what has always been known, somewhat optimistically, as 'the orangery'. It was built in the first half of the eighteenth century, about a hundred and fifty years ago. I very much doubt that any oranges have ever been grown there, but as you perhaps observed, it does at least face in the right direction to catch the sun all day. It's just a glorified greenhouse, really. We use it to raise a few bedding plants and so on for the garden. At least, old Caxton does. I've been too busy to give much thought to that sort of thing, but as Caxton seems to like pottering about in there, I give him free rein to grow whatever he thinks best. I'll extend your 'guided tour' to the orangery when we get back to the house. It's not without interest in itself, as there is another little mystery in there, something else connected with Samuel Harley."

When we reached the garden of the Grange we followed our guide round the side of the house, past the French windows of the drawing-room and the bay window of the study, into the large cobbled yard behind. On our right was the "orangery", an elaborate single-storey structure, the front wall of which was topped with numerous ornamental gables and pinnacles above a row of large windows. Blake opened the door and we followed him in. It was a large chamber, perhaps twenty feet wide and fifteen feet deep, devoid of all furniture save a few old wooden tables and benches, so that our voices rang and echoed around the bare walls. What immediately seized my attention, however, was the rear wall of this chamber. Unlike the other sides, which were bare red brick below the large windows, the rear wall had been plastered and decorated along its whole length with an elaborate fresco. Depicted in this were vines and fruit-laden branches, and in between this twining, luxuriant foliage were numerous female figures in a classical style, each holding a cornucopia overflowing with fruits, flowers and other natural produce. Incongruously, in the very centre of this fresco was a large square panel, about six feet high and six feet wide, composed of a great number of square tiles, each bearing a single capital letter. These appeared to be placed in a perfectly random order, forming no recognizable words. As I examined the tiles more closely, I realised that they were in fact wooden blocks, each incised very neatly with a letter of the alphabet in the centre and a small number in the bottom right-hand corner.

"What is the meaning of this curious panel?" asked Holmes, frowning as he studied it.

"It is, apparently, more of Samuel Harley's work," replied Blake. "There is no record of its having been here before he owned the house. George Darcy made some disparaging remarks in a letter about what he termed 'another of Harley's idiotic follies', which is probably a reference to this, and all the subsequent owners of the house referred to it without ever being able to understand it, or suggest what the purpose of it might be. It has generally been regarded as some kind of puzzle devised by Harley, but if it is, no-one has ever been able to solve it, or work out what it might mean."

E	C	T	O	A	S	T	F	U	L	O	N	R
T	S	B	R	U	O	L	E	A	B	T	L	S
A	L	H	V	I	T	R	L	I	T	R	M	E
L	U	N	A	T	E	T	D	N	R	A	L	O
S	R	D	K	L	R	L	E	F	N	I	E	B
T	N	B	H	I	N	R	A	B	L	O	D	T
H	D	E	I	N	L	T	W	H	S	H	A	L
G	T	N	N	T	A	O	E	A	C	L	H	R
A	H	A	T	Y	P	S	M	U	T	A	G	T
I	C	E	G	V	G	L	E	I	H	U	R	S
O	S	I	O	H	I	O	N	Y	T	A	I	N
N	M	O	I	D	U	A	N	T	K	V	A	I
Y	C	B	E	N	E	T	R	T	S	E	N	L

"I'm surprised he ever had the time to make up puzzles," I remarked with a chuckle. "By all we have heard of him, he seems to have been either drunk or otherwise occupied most of the time."

"I think he made up such things when he'd got rid of all his rowdy visitors and was all alone here. There are several accounts that mention that Harley's puzzles and riddles were an important and perhaps unique part of the riotous gatherings that took place here. According to one source, he would hide something somewhere in the house and present a clue to its whereabouts in the form of a riddle. Then, for each room they entered without finding anything, each of the participants would have to pay a forfeit."

"He sounds an ingenious sort of person," I said. "It is a pity his talents were not put to better use."

"Precisely, Dr Watson. That is what I have often thought. He was, as I believe I mentioned before, a highly intelligent man. Perhaps that is why his fall was so catastrophic. Perhaps only someone truly brilliant could contrive such a disaster for himself. Most of his acquaintances were distinctly mediocre, both in character and in intellect, and, as mediocre people tend to, they all had a strong instinct for what you might call self-preservation, whereas Samuel Harley seems to have had none at all. The mediocre life had no appeal for him: for Harley, life would bring either dazzling success or abject failure. With Harley it was all or nothing; for a time it seemed he had all that life could offer; in the end he had nothing."

"Are there any instructions anywhere in the house relating to this puzzle, or any indication as to what its purpose might be?" asked Holmes, who had been studying the panel intently.

Blake shook his head. "No, nothing at all. It is therefore not simply a single puzzle, but, in a sense, a double puzzle, for it may well be that it is impossible to solve it until one has worked out quite what the point of it is, and what one is supposed to do with it. That has not stopped many people – including me, I confess – trying to make some kind of sense of it. Interestingly, it is not mentioned in the memoirs or correspondence of anyone who visited the house during Harley's time here. The general belief, therefore, is that he created it during that three-month period of grace that Darcy allowed him before he had to leave the house for the last time, as a sort of final farewell challenge. Of course, those who thought that Harley had hidden some 'treasure' somewhere in the house believed that this puzzle held the secret to its whereabouts. That may be so, but, as I mentioned yesterday, I was always somewhat sceptical about the 'hidden treasure' theory. Still, it has provided an added motive for those who have tried to solve the puzzle, but, despite that, no-one has yet been successful. Anyway, I can tell you one thing about it which may not be instantly obvious: the blocks of wood can all be moved."

He picked up a small gardening fork which lay on one of the wooden benches and pushed the tips of it in between two of the wooden blocks. Then, using the fork as a lever, he prised out one of the blocks. Behind where the block had been, in the black-painted wooden back wall, were five small holes, arranged symmetrically, like the spots on a dice.

"It is the same behind each of the blocks," said Blake: "five holes, as in this case. But some of the holes are dummies, and have no depth." He took a pencil from his pocket and inserted it into each of the little holes in turn. In the first three it went in to a depth of two inches or so, but in the last two it went in only about a quarter of an inch. It was clear those holes were blocked, but it was difficult to see, as all was painted black. "On the back of all the blocks are protruding wooden dowels, like prongs, which fit into the holes in the back wall," he continued, turning over the block in his hand. "This one, as you see, has two such prongs, but the number varies from block to block. Some have five prongs, some four, some three and some, like this one, have just two."

"So that some of the blocks will probably fit in most positions," said Holmes, "but some will not, depending on which of the holes in the back wall are blocked and which are not."

"Exactly, Mr Holmes. And as this array is thirteen by thirteen, giving a total of one hundred and sixty-nine blocks, the different possibilities of arrangement are absolutely astronomical. There may well be some correct positioning of the blocks, but, if so, it would, practically speaking, be virtually impossible for anyone to discover it simply by trial and error. The possibilities are simply too great."

"Yes, I can see that," said Holmes in a thoughtful tone. "And yet, as the letters are movable, then it must be by moving them that one solves the riddle. I wonder," he continued, "what the purpose may be of the little numbers in the corner of each square."

"I can see that this puzzle has caught your imagination, Mr Holmes," remarked Blake with a chuckle.

"Well, well," returned Holmes. "It is certainly a challenge, and I enjoy a challenge. But you need have no fears that I shall neglect your case, Mr Blake. I can assure you that it has my undivided attention. But just as someone wrestling with a difficult mathematical problem may open a book of verse in the evening, to give himself a few minutes' diversion before sleep, so I may free my mind for a few moments from the riddle of the murderous stranger who has been spying on you by considering this much older riddle. Sometimes such a diversion is beneficial: one returns to the main problem with one's mental energy refreshed and renewed."

Over lunch we discussed our morning's expedition further. Young Whitemoor asked Holmes if we had made any more discoveries in the ash spinney to rival "the stairway up the tree", as he put it.

"Not really," replied Holmes, shaking his head. "We did discover that a few small branches had been cut away near the viewing platform to give an uninterrupted view of this house, but that was much as one might expect."

"No more indications, then, as to what it might all mean?"

"I'm afraid not," said Holmes with a chuckle.

"Mr Blake also showed us the letter-puzzle in the orangery," I remarked, "although I don't think any of us could make anything of it."

"I thought you had a theory about that, Mr Blake," said Whitemoor. "I seem to remember that when I was first here and you were showing it to me, you said you had covered dozens of sheets of paper with your ideas on it."

Blake laughed. "You're quite right," he said. "I certainly covered plenty of paper, trying out different possibilities, but none of them got me anywhere at all, and in the end I gave it up as impossible."

"Do you still have those sheets?" I asked. "After all, two heads are better than one, as they say – or four heads in this case. It may be that although you felt you had come to a dead

84

end with your workings, they might suggest to one of us something that you hadn't thought of."

"That's a fair point, generally speaking," returned Blake, "but unfortunately, in this instance, my workings really were all useless, believe me. In any case, I don't have them any more. I think they were used to light the kitchen fire one day, which is all they were really any good for!"

Holmes had been silent throughout this exchange, and when I glanced his way, I saw a thoughtful expression on his face. What he was thinking, I did not know, but I knew that he would not care overmuch that Blake's papers had been destroyed. He was never what one might term a co-operative person; rather, he preferred to act alone, and reason things out for himself. When he spoke, it confirmed my reading of his thoughts.

"No offence, Blake," he said, "but it is probably a good thing that your papers are destroyed. If I were to see them, it might prejudice my mind irrevocably and thus hamper my own consideration of the matter."

"You intend to tackle the mysterious puzzle, Mr Holmes?" asked Whitemoor in a tone of surprise.

"In a purely amateur sort of way," returned Holmes. "I might as well see if I can get anywhere with it. Perhaps my efforts will end in failure, and will only provide more kindling for the kitchen fire. We shall see!"

After lunch, Holmes announced, to my very great surprise, that he intended to take a walk over the local countryside, to experience the *genius loci*, as he put it. Although he generally kept himself fit, I knew he had no taste for taking exercise purely for its own sake, and I suspected that he had some specific goal in his mind. When I put the point to him, however, he was unforthcoming, and when I asked him if he would care to have a companion with him he declined the suggestion, so I remained in ignorance as to what the purpose of his expedition might be. Shortly after he had gone out, it occurred to me that he had not asked to borrow the field-glasses, from which I deduced that he was not intending to survey the countryside from a distance but to examine something closely, although what that might be, I could not imagine.

A little later, Blake and Whitemoor were discussing some reference the latter had turned up in a volume of mathematical history. "I do apologise, Watson," said Blake, turning to me, "but you will have to excuse me for a couple of hours. I've been commissioned to write an article on the ramifications of Pythagoras's theorem for the *Ludgate Magazine*, and I've got to get it done this week."

"That is perfectly all right," I returned. "I wouldn't want my presence to hinder your work. Incidentally, although I'm of course familiar with Pythagoras's theorem – we had to learn how to prove it at school – I didn't know it had any 'ramifications', as you put it."

"You'd be surprised," responded Blake. "I'll show you the article when I've finished it. Anyway, I've got to hand it in this Friday at the latest, and I haven't even started it yet, so I'll have to get on with it! I'm afraid I shall have to leave you to your own devices this afternoon."

Blake and his young assistant thereupon disappeared into the study, discussing Pythagoras as they went, and I was left wondering what I should do with myself. It was a lovely summer's day, and I strolled for a time round the pleasant gardens, and then sat a while in a sheltered corner, smoking my pipe. Eventually, though, this idleness bored me and I decided to go off on an expedition of my own. My chief concern was to avoid running across Holmes. I did not wish him to think that I was following him or getting in his way. As I made my way out of the side-gate from the garden into the field, I decided that I would not loiter in the ash spinney but pass straight through it and into the field on the other side.

When I reached the crest of the ridge, I stood a moment, surveying the prospect ahead of me. The field before me was a large one, which sloped gently down to what Blake had described as the road to Thuxton village. As I let my gaze wander all round this pleasant rural prospect, I observed a small group of people walking along the bottom edge of the field, where it was separated from the road by a hedge and a row of trees. As I watched them, I saw that there were three of them, two men and a woman. The taller of the two men seemed to be striding out ahead, with his two companions following behind. I could not doubt that this was Professor Crook, his wife and secretary.

Abruptly, the leading figure stopped and turned back to face the others. They were obviously discussing some point or other, the two men close together, the woman standing a little to the side. Then, as I watched, I had the impression that the discussion was becoming more heated. The two men moved even closer together, and both seemed to be raising their arms in gesticulation. All at once, the shorter man, whom I took to be the secretary, seemed to push the taller man violently in the chest. He staggered backwards and might have fallen, but the other two stepped forward and caught hold of him. A moment later, after a few more words had passed between them, they resumed their walk at a steady, even pace, as if nothing had happened.

I did not know what to make of this. To see two grown men, presumably both highly educated, quarrelling in this violent fashion was both strange and shocking. But what was stranger still was the way the altercation had seemed to be instantly forgotten and the walk resumed as if it had never been interrupted. As I watched, this strange group of people reached a gate in the hedge, passed through it onto the road, and so vanished from my sight behind the hedge. On the other side of the road was a dense wood, where, Blake had said, the house of these singular people was situated. There and then, I resolved that I would walk over that way, and, if it were possible, see the house for myself.

I sat on an old log at the edge of the ash spinney for five minutes, watching the fleecy clouds drifting slowly across the broad blue sky. I wanted to give Professor Crook and his companions time to reach home, so that I did not encounter them in the woods. It was a very peaceful spot, and as I sat there I found myself wondering where Holmes was, and what he was doing.

At length I got to my feet, made my way down the margin of the field and passed through the gate at the bottom. There I turned right, towards the village of Thuxton, and strolled on until I came to a track on the left which disappeared into the woods. I stood there a moment, listening, but heard nothing but bird-song, then set off up the track. It was very narrow, scarcely wide enough for a farm-cart to pass, and deeply rutted. It must have been very muddy and difficult of passage in the winter, I reflected, but now the ruts were dry and hard, and walking was easy.

After a few minutes, I came to a fork in the track. The main route, to judge from the deep ruts, continued straight on through the woods, but I decided to take what appeared to be a less-used branch to the right. A short distance along this way the track curved to the left, and as I rounded the bend I caught sight of chimneys and the roof of a house over a tall hedge to my right. I was just wondering if this might be Black Bank House, when a medium-sized, dark-bearded man emerged suddenly and in great haste through a gap in the hedge.

I was somewhat startled by his abrupt appearance, but I doffed my hat and bade him "good afternoon". He returned my greeting in a perfunctory sort of way and was hurrying past me when he abruptly stopped.

"Excuse me for bothering you," said he, "but have you seen an elderly man with a grey beard anywhere about?"

I shook my head. "Would that be Professor Crook?" I asked.

He shot me a suspicious look. "Yes." said he. "How do you know?"

I explained that I was a visitor to the district and was staying at the Grange, where my host, Mr Blake, had mentioned that the eminent Professor Crook had a house over this way. "Have I the pleasure of addressing Dr Taylor?" I asked.

"Yes," he replied in an abstracted tone, as if his mind was absorbed by something else. "The fact is," he added abruptly, "that Professor Crook and I had a slight disagreement about something earlier on, and he has gone off in a huff. I wanted to find him and apologise for what I said."

"Well, if I should see him, I'll tell him that you're looking for him," I said.

"Good," said Dr Taylor in a preoccupied tone as he turned away. "Thank you," he added over his shoulder. "I hope you enjoy your little holiday."

As he was making his way further up the track, away from me, and as I didn't want to appear to be following him, I decided I would go back the way I had come, and return to the road. There was no sign there of Professor Crook, nor of anyone else. Not just the road, but the whole of the countryside appeared deserted and peaceful. For one accustomed to the constant tumult of the London streets, it felt strange and almost disconcerting to be all alone in those wide open spaces. For a moment I could not think what to do next. At length I decided I would return along the road towards Foxwood village, and see if I could find the quarry into which the elderly Mr Brookfield had apparently fallen to his death. It was not that I had any morbid desire to see the spot where he had lost his life, but I recalled that when we had first heard of the matter from Blake, the previous evening, Sherlock Holmes had seemed particularly struck by it, and if something was of interest to Holmes, then I thought that it might be worth my while to learn a little more about it.

As I walked along, I pondered the household at Black Bank House. It was certainly a singular one, as Blake had described it to us, and I admit it puzzled me greatly. There was undoubtedly something strange about it, but what lay behind the strangeness I could not imagine. Dr Taylor, for instance, had been perfectly polite to me, but in a way that was so absent-minded as to make me feel that although he had spoken to me, he had in reality scarcely registered my presence there at all. I shook my head in puzzlement.

Presently, I came to a cross-roads. If I had my bearings correct, the road to the left was the one that went past the Grange, the one to the right was the way to Pearson's farm, Lower Cropley, and the one straight ahead was the more direct way to the village of Foxwood. It was along this last road that old Brookfield had come on the night of his death, on his way home from the Royal Oak at Foxwood, and that was the road I followed. On the right, a short distance past the crossroads, was a thick hedge. I walked on a little way, until I came to a narrow gap in this hedge. I pushed my way through it and found myself on a flat area of short, springy turf. Ahead of me lay a large quarry, its edge just a few yards from the hedge. At the farther end, the surrounding land was much lower. That was evidently the way the workmen and their vehicles had entered the quarry. But at the near end, where I stood, the ground was much higher, and it was a fearsome drop to the floor of the quarry. Lying on the grass at my feet was a small and faded wooden sign which had clearly fallen over some time ago. On it was painted in red the single word "DANGER". Cautiously, I made my way to the edge of the quarry, crouched down and peered over. A sheer drop of about forty feet met my gaze. Anyone falling over that would undoubtedly be killed.

Were it not for the recent tragic death there, it was a pleasant spot to sit on such a sunny day. I moved slightly forward, put my legs over the edge of the quarry and, sitting there, I took out my pipe, filled it and lit it. I am not one much given to foolhardy escapades, but it felt safe enough, as I sat there in the sunshine, smoking. It did occur to me, though, that if someone were to suddenly come up behind me and give me a good push, I would be quite unable to stop myself falling to my death. This thought had scarcely crossed my mind when the silence was broken by a rapid footstep behind me and the sound of someone pushing his way through the hedge. I turned in alarm as a figure loomed up behind me.

7: A BALMY EVENING

"THAT DOES NOT LOOK the safest of spots in which to take a rest," came a familiar, somewhat strident voice.

"Holmes!" I cried. "You startled me!"

"Perhaps so," said he, "but I doubt you would have felt quite so startled had you not been sitting on the edge of the quarry in the first place."

"You may be right," I conceded, rising to my feet. "Where have you appeared from so abruptly?"

"I was up in the ash spinney, from where I had a very good view of the road and your progress along it. I saw you turn in here, and as my own investigations were concluded for the moment, I thought I would join you."

"And have your investigations – whatever they are – turned anything up?" I asked as I sat down beside him, next to the hedge.

"A few details," he replied as he filled his pipe and put a match to it. "I'd rather not say more at the moment, Watson. The details may not be significant, and may not lead anywhere. What about you, old fellow, have you learned anything of interest? I saw you enter the wood beyond the Thuxton road earlier."

"I ran across Professor Crook's secretary, Dr Taylor, there," I replied. "He struck me as pleasant enough, although the household as a whole is certainly an odd one." I told him then all that I had seen, and my surprising encounter with Dr Taylor.

"My impression," I said, "is that Professor Crook is one of those people whose brilliant intellect makes him impatient with those not so quick-witted as himself, but whose great gifts do not extend to being polite to anyone."

Holmes chuckled. "They are certainly a singular group of people," said he. "Still, if you look closely enough, no doubt every household in the country is 'odd' in its own particular way."

"That may be true," I remarked, "and, in a way, that is the trouble. We are not really learning anything – so it seems to me, anyway. I have encountered an odd household, you have observed what you term 'details' in the wood, which you say, however, may be of no significance. In other words, we have between us come across nothing so far that sheds even the faintest of lights upon your client's mystery, and I fear that that will be the case however long we stay here. I can't see how we will ever learn anything of importance."

My companion shook his head. "I fear you are slipping into your old pessimistic ways, Watson. It is not true that we have learned nothing this afternoon. There is at least one interesting fact that we have both learned independently."

"Oh? What is that, pray?"

"This hedge through which we have both pushed our way: it is very thick."

"What of it?"

"Do you not see? Much of it is hawthorn. It is therefore not only thick, but prickly, too. Furthermore, there is no gap in it for thirty feet save only the one that we both found, which is by no means easy to penetrate. It is therefore extremely unlikely that the old man, Brookfield, could have stumbled through the hedge by accident. Nor is it very likely that Brookfield – an elderly man who had made the journey home from the village inn an uncountable number of times – would on this occasion have chosen to push his way through a prickly hedge in the dark to this narrow strip of turf by the quarry-edge. It is possible, of course, but highly unlikely."

"What, then?"

"I believe he was murdered, Watson, murdered in cold blood on the road, and his lifeless body dragged through the hedge and cast into the quarry."

"But that is an appalling thought!" I cried. "Why should anyone murder a harmless old man?"

"Perhaps because he was not so harmless as you suppose, Watson. Perhaps, by chance, he had witnessed something on the road that night which made him a danger to someone."

"Do you have any reason for advancing such a theory?"

My friend hesitated for a moment. "I shall tell you one of the things that came to light when I was examining the path through the ash spinney," he said at length, "but you must keep it to yourself. Around the base of the tree with rungs the ground is so scuffed up that it is difficult to make anything out. In general, however, the path is little used, and further along it I was able to pick out some individual footprints, although I can't, of course, tell when they were made. At the far end of the path, where it meets the track which connects the Thuxton road to Abbeyfield House, one particular set of prints turned left, down to the road. This track meets the road just a short distance beyond that on the other side of the road which leads to Black Bank House, up which you ventured earlier and on which you met Dr Taylor. It is possible, then, that whoever removed the telescope went that way and emerged onto the road just as old Brookfield was walking past on his way home. If so, it was an unfortunate and tragic chance for him. I cannot say for certain that that was what occurred, but it is a distinct possibility. However, Watson, I should be obliged if you would say nothing of this view to Blake. I would not wish to cause him any further anxiety. He has had enough surprises and alarms recently, without our adding to the list. Would you not agree?"

"Absolutely. I shall keep your theory to myself, and not say a word to anyone about it. Do you think that Blake himself may be in danger?"

"It is difficult to say. It is possible. Part of our duty must therefore be to keep a watchful eye on our client. But, come," he continued, as he consulted his watch, "the afternoon has almost passed. Let us return to the house and see if they can provide us with a little refreshment!"

On our return to the Grange we were greeted by Farringdon Blake, who told us he had "had enough of Pythagoras for the day", and rang for a pot of tea. He also informed us that in our absence a telegram had arrived, addressed to Holmes. My friend ripped it open and scanned the contents for a moment.

"It is as I thought," said he to Blake. "It is from our landlady, Mrs Hudson. I had instructed her to open my post and let me know at once if there was any news of the inquest on

Wilson Baines. She informs me it is to be on Wednesday morning, and we have received a summons to appear."

"We shall have to return to London, then," I said.

"I shall, at least. As the inquest will probably begin fairly promptly on Wednesday morning, I shall have to travel tomorrow, to ensure I'm there in time. But I don't think it's necessary for you to attend, Watson. After all, your evidence would be identical to mine, and I would rather you stayed here for the moment."

I hesitated. "I shouldn't want to get into trouble with the authorities," I said.

"I shall take full responsibility," said Holmes. "I shall tell them that you are out of town, visiting someone in the country, and that your testimony would be the same as mine. Perhaps if you would sign a paper to that effect, giving me full authority to speak on your behalf, it would be a good idea. All they will be interested in at this stage are the immediate cause of death, the weapon employed, the approximate time of death, the names of those who discovered the death and the report of the first policeman on the scene. In any case, the police will probably request an adjournment, to give them more time to look into the matter, so I don't think your absence from this first hearing will be crucial."

Blake brought writing materials to the drawing-room, where I wrote and signed a brief note as Holmes had suggested. I had just finished it when the maid brought in the tea. As he poured it out, Blake asked us if we had made any further discoveries that afternoon, but Holmes shook his head.

"I spent most of my time in the ash spinney, looking at footprints," said he, "but it was largely a hopeless task. There are so many different footprints around the bottom of the tree with the rungs that it could scarcely be any more difficult if a herd of buffalo had passed that way on their annual migration. I think that Dr Watson had a somewhat more interesting afternoon than I did!"

I told Blake then what I had seen of Professor Crook's household. Whitemoor came in to take tea with us as I was speaking, and was fascinated by my account.

"I have never actually spoken to any of them," said he, "but I have often seen them in the distance, and they always seem to be the same: Professor Crook striding out in front, gesticulating to emphasise the points he is making, the other man just behind him, taking notes, and the wife, apparently silent, bringing up the rear. She never seems to be paying much attention to what they are saying, and I have sometimes wondered what, if anything, she gets out of their discussion."

"She gets fresh air and exercise, anyway," suggested Blake with a chuckle. "It may be that the technical discussion is of no interest to her, but she probably enjoys getting out of the house for a while, rather than staying indoors all day."

Thus the conversation meandered about for a while, from the local countryside and its curious inhabitants, *via* a detour into Pythagoras's Theorem, to a consideration of the balmy weather. At the back of my mind all the time throughout this enjoyable discourse was a vague sensation of strangeness, which I could not quite put into words, even to myself. It was, perhaps, the contrast between our conversation, which was that of leisured holiday-makers, and the air of hidden mystery and menace which surrounded our presence in that remote, rural corner of the country. Holmes had been silent throughout most of this conversation, but at length, when the tea-pot was empty, he rose to his feet and said he would like to make a copy on paper of the array of tiles in the orangery.

"It will give me something different to think about on the train-journey to London," said he, "should the scenery from the carriage-window begin to pall."

I offered to help him, and Blake went to bring more writing-materials from the study.

In the orangery, Holmes seated himself at one of the tables, and, with the aid of a ruler, began to draw a large network of squares on one of the sheets of paper.

"Let me see," said he, murmuring to himself. "There are thirteen rows and thirteen columns in the array, which means that there are one hundred and sixty-nine squares altogether. If you will call out the letter on each block, Watson, followed by the little number in the corner, it will save me having to look up and down repeatedly from the paper to the wall and losing my place each time I do so."

I laughed. "Certainly," I said. "Just let me know when you are ready."

I began with the top left-hand tile and in a few minutes my friend had filled in the whole of the array.

"Now," said he, "I think I shall also make a copy of that intriguing little poem in the library."

"Do you think the two could be related in some way?" I asked as I followed him into the house.

"It is possible," he returned. "After all, according to the information we have, Samuel Harley composed both of them at the same time, in that brief interval between losing the house in a game of chance and being obliged to leave it for the very last time. But, of course, even if there really is some connection between the puzzle in the orangery and the poem in the library, we can have no idea at present what that connection might be. It might be a very close and direct one, or a subtle, indirect one. It may be that the tract is simply what it appears to be – a moral reflection on life, inspired by the writer's own sorry experiences – or it may in reality be something quite different, a puzzle which must be solved just as much as the puzzle in the orangery."

We had reached the library as my companion had been speaking. Now I stood and gazed at Samuel Harley's last testament, where it hung on the chimney-breast.

"I can't really see anything cryptic about it," I remarked after a moment. "It appears perfectly straightforward."

"So it does," returned my friend, as he seated himself at the table and began to copy the poem onto one of his sheets of foolscap, "but we can take nothing for granted, Watson. We have heard that Samuel Harley had a great taste for puzzles and riddles of all sorts. We must therefore bear that in mind when examining anything that is the product of his evidently unusual brain."

I turned as the library door was pushed open and Blake entered.

"Ah, there you are!" said he. "I had been wondering where you had got to! More reading material for your train-journey?" he queried with a chuckle, leaning over to see what Holmes was writing.

"Holmes believes there may be some connection between this odd little composition and the puzzle-square in the orangery," I said.

My friend laughed. "I only said it was possible," said he, as he finished his writing. "We were discussing the question just a moment ago," he said to Blake.

"I don't mean to sound discouraging," responded Blake, "but I should perhaps inform you that you are not the first to consider that possibility, Mr Holmes. Mr Stannard's grandfather, for one, tried to solve the puzzle by linking it in some way to this moral exhortation. He put all his thoughts on the matter in a small note-book which is in this library somewhere – although I've looked for it several times without managing to find it."

"I take it he didn't reach any conclusions."

"No. His idea, according to Mr Stannard, was to re-arrange the letters in the puzzle-square so that they spelt out this poem. That sounds straightforward enough, although it is difficult to see how that could tell one anything, or identify the location of any hidden treasure. But there is in any case one major stumbling-block to any such theory, which is that the number of letters in the puzzle-square and the number of letters in this document are not the same, this being appreciably longer."

"I am aware of that fact," said Holmes. "It was one of the first points I noted."

"I should have known you would be thorough," said Blake, sounding a little abashed, "but I thought I had better mention it, all the same. I can't really see how this poem could shed any light on anything, anyway – other than Harley's view of life – unless the references to rocks and mud have some hidden significance, which I can't really believe."

"Well, well. We shall see," said Holmes, as he gathered his papers together.

It had been the most pleasant of summer days, and, even after the sun had declined in a blaze of golden glory and slipped below the horizon, the air remained warm. Outside the French window of the drawing-room was a small paved terrace on which an old table and several chairs were set out. When our meal was finished, Blake suggested we repair to this terrace and enjoy the soft evening air. He brought out a jug of wine, glasses and an oil-lamp from the drawing-room, and there we sat, drinking wine, smoking our pipes and making light-hearted conversation beneath the stars. All about us, the silence and stillness of the countryside was broken only by the soft hum of insects and the occasional distant bleat of a sleepy sheep.

"This must seem very different from your previous life in London," I remarked to our host, and asked him if he had always lived in London before moving to Foxwood.

He shook his head. "I was born and raised in London, near Bow," he said. "My father had a clerical position with the Royal Navy, and spent all his time in an odd little office just a stone's throw from the Tower of London. But when I was about eight years old, he was promoted to a more senior position, which brought him a little more income, and he and my mother decided to move. Bow had, I believe, been a quiet and pleasant place when they had first set up house there, but was becoming dirtier and smokier with every year that passed. At length, they decided to move out of London altogether, and we decamped to Brentwood, in Essex. It meant that my father had a fairly long railway journey every morning and evening, but he didn't seem to mind that, and Brentwood was certainly a much healthier place to live than Bow. It was still fairly rural in those days, and I spent much of my boyhood there rambling about the nearby woods and fields. Later, my mother and father revealed a previously unseen taste for sport and became founder members of the Brentwood Lawn Tennis Club."

"And now," I said, "after a period back in London, you are again out in the country, in an even more rural spot, and having to travel up to London regularly, as your father did."

"That is true, but I foresee the day when even places like this are connected by telephone to London and other cities. It may not come in my lifetime, but if it did I should not need to travel up to town so much. Sometimes, of course, a personal visit is necessary, but at other times I could just telephone the newspaper offices and read out my latest article to them, and someone at the other end of the line could take it all down in shorthand."

I laughed. "That sounds a somewhat fanciful notion," I said. "One might even call it fantastic. Just think of all the equipment that would be required – the exchanges, switchboards, cables and so on – not to mention all the people who would have to be employed to work it all – to make a telephone connection between London and a little place like Foxwood! Surely, it could never be worth anyone's while to do it."

"So you might think, but that is what many people said about the railways when they were first proposed, that we should never need more than about half a dozen lines in the whole country. The idea that the railways might reach small country towns was regarded by some as ridiculous. But now one can travel from almost anywhere in Britain to almost anywhere else with just a couple of changes, and without once leaving railway premises."

"I doubt whether the telephone will ever reach Towcester," interjected Whitemoor. "Even the main railway line ignored Towcester, and passed us by, just a few miles away. Our only connection to the rest of the railways now is by a local company which always seems to be standing on the brink of bankruptcy. My father invested a fair amount of money in the local line when it was promoted, but I don't think he ever saw much of a return on his investment."

"If it's any consolation to you, Whitemoor," Blake remarked, "your father was not alone in his misfortune. My cousin, Mr Stannard also sank money in that particular railway which he has never seen since."

"Some railway schemes were certainly built on decidedly shaky ground," I said, "especially some of these little local lines. Have you always lived in Towcester?"

"Yes," replied Whitemoor. "Both my mother and father were born there."

"And you, Dr Watson," said Blake: "where were you raised? I usually consider myself quite good on the nuances of accents, but I can't quite place yours."

I had opened my mouth to reply when Holmes, who had been silent throughout this discussion, as was his wont, abruptly raised his hand.

"What was that?" he said in a sharp tone.

"I heard nothing." I replied.

"It sounded like a pebble falling from somewhere," said Whitemoor.

"Perhaps a bit of mortar from the roof which some bird dislodged earlier," suggested Blake. "Some of the mortar under the tiles is very old and is beginning to disintegrate."

"There is another one!" said Holmes, and this time I heard it, too.

"It seemed to strike the wall of the house before falling to the ground," I said.

"I agree," said Holmes, turning in his chair and looking behind him, at the tall hedge which separated the garden from the field beyond: "almost as if someone—"

Even as he spoke I had the impression of some flash of movement in the air above us. I saw Holmes duck his head instinctively, as I myself turned quickly away. At almost the same instant there came an ear-splitting crash, as some heavy object struck the top of the table with tremendous force, smashing the lamp, the wine-jug and the glasses and sending the broken glass flying in all directions.

"What the devil – !" shouted Blake, his voice hoarse with shock, as Whitemoor let out a cry of pain. Holmes was already on his feet and racing towards the hedge. I followed him as quickly as I could and we ran down beside the hedge in the darkness, until we came to the gate into the field. Holmes pulled it open and I followed him into the field. For a moment we stood perfectly still, listening for any sound that might reveal the whereabouts of whoever it was that had thrown something at us. My eyes had rapidly adjusted to the darkness and I could see some considerable distance across the field, but no sign of movement was visible.

"Can you see anyone?" asked Blake in a breathless voice, as he and Whitemoor joined us.

"No," replied Holmes. "We can't tell if he has got away or is in hiding nearby. And if he's fled, we don't know if he's gone up the field or down."

"It's a great pity we don't keep a dog here," said Blake with feeling. "A dog would soon get on his trail!"

"We'll have to do the best we can," said Holmes. "Watson: you and Whitemoor go up the field. Keep to the edge, but watch for any movement further out in the field. Blake, you come with me. We'll go down the field. Come on!"

Whitemoor and I walked at a brisk pace to the very top of the field, near the ash spinney, but caught neither sight nor sound of anyone. We returned to the gate just as Holmes and Blake reached it. They had had no more luck than we had.

"Let's get back and see at least what was flung at us," said Holmes in a tone of disappointment.

When we reached the terrace, Blake brought out another lamp from the drawing-room, lit it and placed it on the table amid the litter of broken glass.

"Would you mind having a look at my head, Doctor?" said Whitemoor to me. "I think I may have a cut."

I held the lamp up to his face. Above his left eye was a nasty gash, red with blood.

"Thank goodness for eyebrows!" I said. "You must have been struck by a chunk of flying glass, but your eye has been saved from harm by the brow above it. Come inside and I'll clean you up a little."

"Mrs Caxton should still be in the kitchen," said Blake. "She can show you where the medical box is."

We returned a few minutes later. Holmes was holding a large, rough-edged stone in his hand.

"This was the missile," said he. "We were fortunate it didn't strike any of us, or we might have needed more assistance than Mr Blake's medical box could provide. Evidently the two smaller stones the attacker threw just before were to give him his range."

"What a brutal, vicious act!" I cried. "What can be the meaning of it?"

"There was a little note attached to this stone with twine," returned Holmes. "It appears to be a warning or threat, presumably to our client, although that is not certain."

Blake handed me the slip of paper he had been examining. I held it next to the lamp and read the following, written in capital letters: "KEEP AWAY FROM PEOPLE AND PLACES THAT DON'T CONCERN YOU".

8: SOCIAL CALLS

AS THE WARNING MESSAGE had, in its dramatic fashion, been delivered, and as the messenger had apparently departed, it seemed unlikely that we would be assailed again that evening by flying stones. Still, we reasoned, there was no point in taking unnecessary risks, so we moved into the drawing-room and closed the French window. Both old Caxton and the maid appeared, to ask if they should attempt to clear up the broken glass and other debris from the terrace, but Blake told them to leave it until the morning when it would be easier to see what they were doing.

"Now," said Holmes, "we must, I think, assume that the warning message was meant for Mr Blake. Dr Watson and I have been here scarcely twenty-four hours, during which time I have met no-one other than the members of this household. Dr Watson did run across Professor Crook's secretary, Dr Taylor, this afternoon, in the wood near Black Bank House, but it is difficult to see why that encounter should occasion such a warning, especially as Mr Blake has himself conversed with Dr Taylor in the past without anything of the sort ensuing. Mr Whitemoor, I imagine, is not very familiar with the people of the parish."

"That is true," said Whitemoor. "I have met a lot of the locals, but know most of them only well enough to bid them 'good morning' as we pass."

"Quite so. Therefore, as I say, the message must be assumed to be intended for Mr Blake, although why it should be sent on this particular evening, we don't know."

"I suppose you must be right," agreed Blake, "although I cannot imagine for a moment who might have sent it, or why."

"The mode of delivery being unusually violent," remarked Holmes, "during which any one of us might have been seriously injured, it is surely not too extravagant a speculation to suggest that the motivations of the author of the message arise from a deep well of rage."

"That seems clear enough," responded Blake, "but I'm sure I know no-one in the district to whom that could apply."

"It may not be anyone you know," said Holmes. "Indeed, it may not be anyone who lives in the district."

"What are you suggesting?" asked Blake.

"You have struck up a friendship with a woman who is estranged from her husband. He, it seems to me, would be the most likely candidate for our nocturnal stone-thrower. There is in my experience nothing which is so reliable in stirring up rage and violence as relations between the sexes."

"But my relations with Mrs Booth have always been perfectly honourable," returned Blake in a defensive tone.

"I do not doubt that that is how it seems from your point of view, Mr Blake, but your point of view is in this case perfectly irrelevant. It does not matter in the least how you view the matter. All that matters is how Mr Booth sees it. It may be that, from his point of view, you have come between him and his wife."

"That is absurd!"

"You may think so, but he may judge the matter otherwise."

"How could Booth know anything about me, anyway?" retorted Blake after a moment in a heated tone.

"He may have made enquiries, or Mrs Booth herself may have mentioned your name in some connection."

Blake sat in silence a moment. "What should I do, then?" he said at length.

"It is important that we attempt to confirm or refute the hypothesis. As a scientific writer you will understand that. The first thing you should do, therefore, is pay a visit to Mrs Booth and ask her if she has seen anything of her husband recently."

"I understand. I shall call upon her tomorrow morning. It would certainly explain a lot if it is Booth who has been behind all these recent events. I take it you believe it was he who was spying on me through the telescope?"

"It is possible. We can say no more than that at present."

Blake put his head in his hands and sighed. "Life is unpredictable," said he. "I have certainly never meant to cause any trouble between Mrs Booth and her husband. There seemed enough trouble there already."

"Life may be unpredictable," returned Holmes, "but one thing you may depend on is that all our actions have consequences."

When I sat down at the breakfast-table with Blake and Whitemoor the following morning, there was no sign of Holmes. I was surprised at this, as it was unlike him to be a late riser, at least when he had a case to occupy his mind. The matter

110

was explained soon enough, however, as he came in while we were eating, wearing his outdoor clothes and bringing the fresh air of the countryside with him.

"I have been up for a couple of hours already," said he as he sat down at the table, "and have, I must say, worked up something of an appetite! I have been examining the footprints in Ashton's field," he continued in answer to our queries, as he helped himself to rashers and eggs. "Whoever it was that flung that rock at us last night came down the field from the top end, by the ash spinney, and returned the same way. Of course, some of his footprints were covered by Watson's and Whitemoor's, but they were still clear enough. As you saw no sign of him," he continued, turning to me, "he had evidently run off like a hare after his attack upon us. Indeed, many of his prints ascending the hill show only the toe-end of the sole, indicating that he was running at great speed."

"Were you able to follow the prints any further than the ash spinney?" I asked.

My friend nodded his head. "It appeared he stopped there briefly, at the top of the hill, probably to catch his breath, and then made his way down the margin of the field on the other side, towards the Thuxton road. At the road, I lost him, I'm afraid. I spent some time endeavouring to pick up his trail again, but the surface of the road is hard and dry, and I could find no trace of him."

"That is a pity," said Blake.

"It doesn't matter too much," returned Holmes. "I was almost bound to lose the trail somewhere on the road. I am satisfied with my findings. I made a sketch of his footprint, complete with measurements."

"You sound amazingly thorough!" exclaimed Whitemoor in surprise.

"Footprints are a peculiar interest of mine," said Holmes with a chuckle. "I have written a brief monograph on the subject – although I doubt you will run across it in any of the college libraries in Oxford!"

"It is unfortunate that the footprints around the tree with the rungs in it were all so scuffed up," remarked Blake after a moment. "If they had been clearer, you might have been able to establish whether our assailant from last night was the same person who had carried the telescope up the tree – although I feel certain it must have been."

Holmes nodded. "Well, well," said he in a philosophical tone. "I am sure we shall get it all sorted out in the end."

"I sincerely hope so," said Blake.

After breakfast, Blake said he would tell Caxton to get the pony and trap ready, to take Holmes to the railway station, but Holmes declined the offer.

"I have been looking at the map," said he, "and I don't think it will take me much more than half an hour to walk there, so that is what I should like to do. The exercise will do me good!"

"I had the impression you had already had an adequate amount of exercise this morning!" I remarked.

Holmes shook his head. "Hardly," said he. "When I was out earlier, I spent much of the time bent over, studying the ground at my feet. A brisk walk to the railway station is quite a different prospect and, fortunately, I shall have no luggage to encumber me. I shall just collect my razor and toothbrush, and the papers on which I copied Samuel Harley's puzzle, and then I shall be off!"

"I understand Mr Holmes is obliged to attend an inquest," said Whitemoor as we watched my friend run rapidly up the stairs.

I nodded. "It is a not uncommon occurrence in his line of work," I returned. "As I understand it, he believes it will probably be a fairly routine matter, and he does not think he will be away for very long."

"We shall have to see that you don't get bored in the meantime, then," said Blake in a humorous tone. "I wonder, Dr Watson," he continued after a moment's thought, "if you would care to accompany me on my visit to Mrs Booth this morning?"

I hesitated. "I should not wish to be in the way," I responded. "You might find my presence somewhat irksome if it caused Mrs Booth to act differently towards you, or prevented her from speaking her mind."

"On the contrary," said he with a shake of the head, "I would deem it a very great favour if you would come. I intend to ask her about her husband, and I should much prefer it if someone else were there when I put my questions. In any case, I am sure that you will enjoy meeting her, and she will enjoy meeting you."

"Very well, then," I said, "if you are sure, I should be delighted to come."

The rapid clatter of footsteps on the stair announced Holmes's return. With a glance at his watch, he declared he would leave at once, saying he would keep us informed by telegram if there was anything interesting to report. I walked with him a little way down the drive, where we stood a moment. He was interested when I told him of Blake's wish that I accompany him to Mrs Booth's house.

"I think that an excellent idea," said he. "I had been rather hoping that one of us might be able to go along with him. I cannot, if I am to get to the railway station on time, so you will have to be my eyes and ears, Watson. What is it, old man?" he added. "You look a little apprehensive. Surely you are not daunted at the prospect."

"It is simply that I am not as observant as you are, Holmes," I returned. "I fear that any report I make to you will only disappoint you."

"Nonsense!" cried my friend. "Do not look on this commission as an unbearable burden, Watson, for it is nothing of the sort! I simply want your impressions – of Mrs Booth in particular, but also of anyone else you chance to run across, either in the company of Blake or by yourself. Make a few notes in your pocket-book, if that will aid your memory, and I shall very much look forward to hearing your report when I return!"

"When might that be?"

"I cannot say for certain. I shall return as soon as I can, but there are one or two matters I wish to look into first. Until then, keep your eyes and ears open at all times, and, in particular, keep a watchful eye on our client."

With that, my friend set off on his solitary walk to the railway station. As I watched him striding briskly down the drive, I confess I felt all at once a great weight of responsibility resting upon my shoulders. Whenever Sherlock Holmes was about, I always had someone with whose opinion I could compare my own observations, someone whose judgement I could trust when I was puzzled. Now that I found myself alone amongst strangers, I had an odd sensation of solitude, much, I imagine, as an explorer in a distant land might feel when surrounded only by the native inhabitants whose language he does not speak. If this sounds an exaggerated or absurd comparison for someone in the attractive and gentle Oxfordshire countryside, I can only say that it is the closest I can come to describing the effect my friend's departure had upon me. Strange things had happened, and were continuing to happen, in that apparently idyllic spot, and although life no doubt carried on in its customary uneventful way for most people in the parish, there was something else afoot beneath the peaceful surface, and I did not really know whom I could trust and whom I could not. Sincerely, I hoped that Holmes's absence would not be too prolonged.

As I walked slowly back to the house, another thought struck me. As I have remarked already, my friend had no interest whatever in taking exercise for its own sake, and I could not help wondering if he had some other reason for turning down the offer of a ride in the trap. Try as I might, however, I could think of no reason that made any sense, so with a sigh and a shake of the head, I reluctantly put the matter out of my mind. I knew from experience that if he were acting on some train of thought of which I was unaware, he would enlighten me as to its nature when he judged the time was right.

When I returned to the house, Blake and I discussed our proposed visit to Mrs Booth. He had, he said, intended to take the pony and trap round there, but as it was not far and the day was such a fine one, he suggested that we follow Holmes's example and make our way there on foot. With this I was in complete agreement. The prospect of a walk through the village on such a bright, balmy day was an attractive one. Half an hour after Holmes had left, therefore, we ourselves set off.

It was very sunny as we made our way down the lane to the village, and it seemed the perfect morning for a walk. Had our purpose not been such a serious one, I should have rejoiced at the wild roses and honeysuckle twining in the hedgerows, and the heady scents of summer that surrounded us in the still, warm air. As it was, such appreciation as I felt for the bounties of nature was tempered somewhat by a feeling of apprehension at the prospect of meeting and questioning Mrs Booth. This was not simply the natural nervousness one might feel before meeting someone of the opposite sex whom one had never met before, and who, one knew, might not welcome one's presence. After all, if Holmes was right in his supposition that it was Booth who had flung stones at us, then Mrs Booth's husband was a violent and dangerous man. Moreover, if he was behind all the other recent occurrences that had troubled Holmes's client so much – which seemed to me very likely – then he was almost certainly the murderer of Wilson Baines in London. I also knew, of course, which Blake did not, that Holmes strongly suspected that the local man, Brookfield, had also been brutally murdered. If that were so, as Holmes believed, then, presumably, Booth was responsible for that death, too. All in all,

I had rather more disturbing matters on my mind that morning than the beauties of nature.

My friend Sherlock Holmes had often struck me as a man perfectly devoid of all natural human emotions. This meant that, sometimes at least, his company was not so congenial as it might otherwise have been, but I had always supposed that this was in some way a necessary component of his unusually logical and analytic brain, without which his achievements would not have been so striking. One consequence of this singular trait in his character was that he never – or hardly ever – had any emotional reaction to the cases he was investigating, however dreadful or tragic they might have seemed to someone else. His detached manner in this regard inevitably rubbed off a little on me, so that while ever he was about, I, too, was able to maintain a relatively detached view of the matter in hand. Now that he was no longer with us, however, I found that as I walked with Farringdon Blake down that leafy country lane and my thoughts turned once more to the details of the strange business in which we were embroiled, I was struck afresh by the sinister and horrific nature of it all. Men's lives had been ended in brutal fashion in this strange chain of events which had begun for Blake with his discovery of the rungs up the tree to the old wooden platform on which he had found a telescope. The whole business struck me all at once as so confused and chaotic as to seem like a meaningless but disturbing dream, or the senseless ravings of a madman.

"I think you will like the village of Foxwood, Watson," remarked my companion, breaking in upon my thoughts. "It is a charming little place in its own way, and some of the cottages are very old."

"That reminds me," I said, extricating myself with some difficulty from my own gloomy reflections: "I have been meaning to ask you if there are many foxes in the woods around Foxwood."

Blake chuckled. "As a matter of fact there are," he replied, "although that's not where the name comes from. The parish is recorded in the early middle ages as 'Fulke's Wood', that is, woodland belonging to someone called 'Fulke' – whoever he may have been. 'Foxwood' is simply a later corruption of that, as the centuries passed and Fulke's name was forgotten. But there are certainly plenty of foxes about in the district, and I don't doubt there always have been. You can hear them sometimes at night, barking to each other in the woods, in that distinctive high-pitched, dry-throated sort of way. I don't think I'd ever heard it before I moved out here, but I quickly became so used to it that I could do a reasonable impression of it myself."

He stopped, tilted his head back and let out a series of sharp, high-pitched barks.

"That's very good," I said. "You ought to be on the stage."

"Thank you," said my companion with a chuckle, and for a moment a little smile flickered across his face. Next moment, as we resumed our walk, the smile had gone and a serious expression had returned to his features. "If only all our problems could be solved by making little jokes about them and acting the clown," he said with a sigh and a shake of the head.

We turned into the main road, passed a number of scattered cottages, and came at length, on our left, to the Royal Oak. Almost immediately opposite it, a narrow road went off to the right, along which I could see more cottages. This, I surmised, was the direct road up to the old quarry, along which old Brookfield had walked on the night of his death. The village high street beyond the inn was very quiet and almost deserted. On either side were picturesque little cottages and a few larger houses, some set back behind neat gardens, and some standing at the very edge of the road. In one row of the latter were a number of small shops. Further along the street, we passed the village school and a large playing-field on our left, and, up a slight rise on the right, an ancient-looking church within a large and neatly-kept churchyard. Beyond that lay an orchard, after which another narrow road went off to the right. A little further on we rounded a bend in the road and came, on our right, to a small but handsome house with large square windows, which stood alone behind a small garden. A painted sign on the gate identified this as Netherfield Lodge.

"This is where Mrs Booth lives," said Blake as he pushed open the gate.

The maid who answered our knock at the door conducted us to a room at the rear of the house, overlooking the long back garden. There, sitting at a table, a sewing-machine before her, was a very handsome, fair-haired young woman in a grey dress, frowning slightly as she pinned two pieces of patterned material together. Kneeling on the carpet by her feet was a small boy, who was playing with a box of toy soldiers and horses. As the maid announced us, the woman put down the material she was holding and rose to her feet, a look of surprise on her face.

"How very pleasant, to see you on such a sunny morning, Mr Blake!" she said with a smile of delight.

"This is my friend, Dr Watson, a fellow-toiler with pen and ink," returned Blake, as the woman's eyes turned towards me. "Dr Watson, Mrs Booth."

"I'm very pleased to meet you, Dr Watson," said she, holding out her hand which I took and shook gently. "Would you care for some refreshment?" she asked. "Yes, I'm sure you would! You are in luck, actually, as Susan has just been making some fresh lemonade." She turned and nodded to the maid, who had been loitering by the door, no doubt in anticipation of such an instruction. "Let us go out into the garden and enjoy the sunshine," Mrs Booth continued. "You can bring your soldiers outside, Henry," she said to the little boy, "and make them a camp beneath the tree."

I helped the boy gather his soldiers into the box, then followed Blake and Mrs Booth out to the back garden, where a table and chairs were set out in the shade of a large apple tree. As we sat down, she turned to me once more.

"Do you also write scientific essays, like Mr Blake?" she asked me.

I shook my head. "I do not have that sort of knowledge," I replied. "In any case, I am a mere beginner. I have written a couple of pieces on criminological matters, that is all."

Mrs Booth's features expressed doubt. "I am sure that that must be interesting in its own way," she remarked in a thoughtful tone, "but is it not also a little lowering, to be dwelling so much on the bad things people have done? Oh, forgive me," she added quickly; "I didn't mean to be rude. It was simply the first thought that came into my head. I am sorry if I have offended you."

"Not at all," I said with a smile. "You are quite right. Crime and criminals could certainly be lowering – and more than a little, too – if one were to spend one's time dwelling on them. But I tend to gloss over the bad things people have done, as you put it, and concentrate on the way the crime was solved. A friend of mine, Sherlock Holmes, is particularly skilled at solving mysteries – criminal and otherwise – and as he has no real interest in recording his own exploits, I thought I should do it for him."

"I see. That does sound interesting."

"It is. It is the mystery that attracts Holmes, you see, rather than the crime in itself. If we lived in a perfect world, in which there were no crime, he would no doubt devote himself to other mysteries. I imagine he would probably be an experimental chemist, discovering new elements."

"It is a pity this Mr Sherlock Holmes is not also staying with you," said Mrs Booth to Blake with a smile. "He could apply his skills to that mysterious letter-puzzle you have in your greenhouse!"

Blake laughed. "As a matter of fact he *is* staying with us – and already bending his mind to that puzzle – but he has had to return to London today on professional business."

The maid reappeared then with a jug of lemonade and some glasses on a tray, which she set out on the table. As the lemonade was being poured out, Blake asked Mrs Booth what it was she had been making when we arrived.

She laughed, a light, musical laugh. "You would never guess," said she. "It is a miniature Tudor dress – something like one of Queen Elizabeth's, but for a girl of nine! She is going to take part in the village summer pageant in a few weeks' time."

"I was not aware that you did such needlework," said Blake in a tone of surprise.

"I used not to – I was hopeless at it when I was younger – but I got the sewing-machine two years ago, and that has revolutionized my existence. You can do the routine sewing so much more quickly, you see, so that you can spend more time on the tricky bits that you have to do by hand. To begin with, I made a few outfits for myself and for Henry – they weren't very good – and then, last summer, I offered to make something for the child of a neighbour who was an even worse seamstress than I used to be. She was very pleased with it, and told everyone else, and I soon started to receive commissions from all and sundry. It's not just children's clothes, either; I make things for their parents, too!"

"Well, I never!" exclaimed Blake. "Good for you!"

Mrs Booth laughed again. "I do my best," she said. "People generally seem pleased with what I do for them, and it brings me in a few shillings fairly regularly which is very useful. I don't know how I could get by if it weren't for the needlework. It keeps Mr Stubbs at the draper's shop very happy, too, as I'm always ordering odd bits of fabric from him!"

For a few minutes we discussed the intricacies of Mrs Booth's needlework and other matters, then, as the conversation lapsed, Blake leaned forward.

"Penelope," said he, "I must be honest with you. This visit is not simply a social call. There is something I must ask you."

The lady's eyebrows went up in surprise. "You sound very serious," she remarked.

"I am," said he. He then described to her the events of the previous evening, and Holmes's suggestion that her husband might be our mystery assailant, and asked her if she had seen him recently.

Mrs Booth shook her head. "No, I haven't," she replied, "but it is an odd coincidence that you should ask, for I have recently received several letters from him, after not hearing anything from him for a long time." She paused then, as if collecting her thoughts on the matter.

"I am sorry to be asking you about such personal matters," said Blake.

"That is all right," she returned. "You already know, I think, how things stand between my husband and me, and, after the events of last night and the discussion you must have had, I imagine Dr Watson, too, is privy to the matter. The fact is that Richard – my husband – wrote to say he wished to pay me a visit. I wrote back and said I did not wish to see him. He then wrote again, saying that he wished to discuss our situation with me, with a view to my returning to the marital home. I wrote back to say that I was not interested in this proposal, at least for the moment. He then wrote a third letter, making vague threats of legal action."

"Legal action?" Blake queried. "Of what sort?"

In answer she nodded her head slightly in the direction of the little boy, who was playing with his soldiers in a nearby flower-bed.

"You must be very anxious," said Blake in a voice full of concern.

"I will cross each bridge when I come to it," returned Mrs Booth. "There is no point in worrying too much about things that may never happen. Anyway," she added after a moment, "the last letter I received was about two weeks ago. I have heard nothing since, and, so far as I know, he has dropped the idea of coming here."

"Has he ever visited you since you moved to Foxwood?" asked Blake.

"Yes, just once, about eighteen months ago, but the visit ended in our having a violent quarrel, and I vowed to myself that I would not have him here again. He has a very short temper, and although he is a small man, he is certainly capable of great violence, as I know from personal experience. But, although I might be mistaken, I cannot think that he would come all this way without trying to see me. And as for throwing a stone at you, I can't see why he should. He can know no more about you than he knows about anyone else in the parish. I have never mentioned anything about my friends and neighbours here in any correspondence I have had with him, so I think you may have to look elsewhere to find your stone-thrower."

"I see," said Blake with a frown. "It is all very puzzling, I must say. Incidentally," he continued after a moment in a lighter tone, "speaking of neighbours, have you seen anyone else lately – Mr Ashton, for instance?"

Mrs Booth hesitated a moment, and looked, I thought, slightly embarrassed at the question. "No," she responded at length. "I haven't seen Mr Ashton for some time. But your question reminds me: I ran across your cousin, Mr Stannard, in the street the other day and he asked me if I had seen anything of you. I got the impression that he thought you had neglected him a little recently."

"It's true. I haven't seen him for several weeks," said Blake. "Perhaps we should pay him a visit now. Would you mind, Watson?"

"Not at all" I replied.

Shortly afterwards, therefore, when we had finished our lemonade, we bade farewell to Mrs Booth and her little boy, and retraced our steps along the village high street.

"She is a charming woman," I remarked. "I can well understand why you enjoy visiting her."

"I'm glad you think so," returned Blake. "However," he continued as we walked along, "I don't really know what to think about what she told us. Mr Holmes's suggestion that it was Booth who attacked us certainly seemed to make sense. And, if Booth did think I was seeing too much of his wife, he must surely be the likeliest person to have spied on me through the telescope."

I nodded my head in agreement. "He might also have had a motive for hiring that enquiry agent to follow you about

London," I observed. "He might have thought, for instance, that you might be going to consult a lawyer there on Mrs Booth's behalf."

"About the possibility of a divorce, do you mean?"

"Yes, something on those lines. Look, I know it's none of my business, Blake, but don't take offence. I'm simply suggesting to you what Booth might have thought."

"I understand. You may be right, Watson, although, if so, it would still be a complete mystery as to why Booth should have murdered his hired spy."

"Perhaps he simply lost his temper for a moment and struck out at the other man, not intending to do him serious harm, far less kill him. Mrs Booth describes him as having a very short temper."

Blake nodded, but there was an expression of puzzlement on his features. "It must be so," he said, "and yet Penny – Mrs Booth – seems sure that her husband has not been here in the last eighteen months or so. If that is the case, how could he possibly know anything about me? It is not yet a year since I spoke to Mrs Booth for the first time in my life."

"It is certainly a puzzle," I agreed.

We had been passing the churchyard as we spoke, and now came to a narrow lane on our left. "Mr Stannard's cottage is just up here," said my companion. We turned into the lane, which I could see led up to a side-entrance of the churchyard. On either side were neat little cottages, several of which had window-boxes overflowing with bright summer flowers.

"This is a very attractive little nook," I remarked.

"I think Mr Stannard would agree with you," returned Blake. "I know he is very content, living here. He makes his own contribution to the summer gaiety, incidentally, as you will see. His is the house with a climbing rose in the tub by the door," he continued, indicating a white-washed cottage a little way ahead.

Our knock at the door was answered by a ruddy-cheeked, middle-aged woman with a duster in her hand. She smiled as she recognized my companion, and ushered us into the house. "Mr Stannard is in the garden, catching up with his newspaper-reading," said she, leading the way towards the back of the house.

In the narrow garden behind the house, an elderly, white-haired man was sitting at a small green-painted table, a newspaper spread out before him. My first impression of him was that he was bent and frail-looking, but he surprised me by springing to his feet when he saw us.

"My dear boy!" he cried in an enthusiastic tone, addressing Blake. "It is good to see you! I had thought you had quite forgotten me!"

"Not at all," returned Blake, laughing, "but I have been rather busy lately." He introduced me and the old man shook my hand vigorously.

"A doctor, eh? Are you a medical man, sir? A doctor of divinity? Or perhaps a doctor of philosophy?"

"Medical," I said. "I am a retired Army surgeon."

"'Retired'?" he queried. "You look a bit young to be retired!"

"Well, not so much retired as invalided out of the service," I explained. "I was badly wounded in Afghanistan."

"I'm sorry to hear that. It often seems to be the fate of medical men in the Army. You join up to treat others and end up needing treatment yourself! Exactly that happened to a friend of mine. He told me he was known as the most frequently injured man in his regiment. Mind you, even he admitted he was somewhat injury-prone: when he first went to India, he slipped and broke his leg just getting off the boat. Anyway, enough of these reminiscences! Come and sit down and we can share our news! Have you heard the latest folly that our idiotic Government are considering?"

We sat round Mr Stannard's little table and had an enjoyable discussion about every subject imaginable, from the latest news from overseas to the most recent happenings in Foxwood. Mr Stannard delivered his opinions in a very forceful manner, but always with a tinge of humour, which made his conversation highly entertaining. He was interested when Blake mentioned that Sherlock Holmes was staying at the Grange for a few days.

"I believe I know that name," said Mr Stannard. "I think he was mentioned in a newspaper report concerning the theft of the Temperley Emeralds some months ago."

"That is possible," said Blake. "He is a man who is rather good at solving puzzles and unravelling mysteries."

"You must get him to look at Samuel Harley's puzzle while he is with you, then," said Mr Stannard.

Blake laughed. "He is already working on it," he said. "I didn't need to ask him. He seemed naturally drawn to it."

This appeared to trigger some train of reflection in Mr Stannard's mind, for after a moment he abruptly asked if Blake had seen anything of Mr Needham lately.

Blake shook his head. "Why do you ask?"

"He was always interested in Samuel Harley and his puzzles." replied Mr Stannard. "In fact, 'interested' scarcely does his state of mind justice; 'obsessed' would be a more accurate description of it. He stole two books from me as a result of it."

"You never mentioned this to me before," said Blake in a tone of astonishment. "Are you sure about it?"

"I'm morally certain of it," said Stannard, "although of course I can't prove it. He borrowed a book of local history from me once, some years ago – there was a lot in there about Samuel Harley – and returned it a few weeks later. When I happened to look for it in the library some months afterwards, however, I couldn't find it anywhere. Then I remembered that Needham had called round to see me one day when I happened to be out, and had waited for me in the library for half an hour. I think he must have taken the opportunity to slip the book inside his coat. It was only a slim volume. I could think of no other explanation for its disappearance. No other visitor had ever been in the library when I wasn't there. I later discovered that my grandfather's note-book, in which he wrote down all his thoughts about Harley and his puzzle, had also disappeared, and I could only conclude that that book had vanished in the same direction as the other. I seem to remember that I had showed it to Needham once, and he had been very interested in what it contained.

"The reason I didn't mention this to you before is that you were new in these parts, and I didn't want you to get off on the wrong foot with your neighbours. But you've been here long enough now to form your own opinions of them, so I feel I can speak more freely. And quite honestly, I always thought of Needham as deceitful and dishonest. To myself I always called him 'Mr Sly Needham'. If I were you, I shouldn't trust him an inch, or believe a word that he says."

"I don't really know what to say to that, I am so surprised," returned Blake after a moment, sounding utterly taken aback. "But I thank you for your honesty."

We spoke a few minutes longer without Mr Stannard really adding anything to what he had already said, and, just as we were leaving, he asked Blake if he would be attending the inquest into the death of Brookfield.

"When is it?" asked Blake.

"Ten o'clock tomorrow morning, in the Royal Oak."

As we left Mr Stannard's cottage and made our way back down the lane to the high street, Blake shook his head in a gesture of perplexity.

"Well," said he, "I don't know how you see it, Watson, but I don't know what to make of anything we have heard this morning. I feel more confused than ever, and feel I know nothing of what is going on about me. The only thing I do know for certain is that I am very thankful that you are here."

"I am glad if my presence is of any help to you," I returned, "although – to speak frankly – I think I am probably as confused about everything as you are. I feel we ought to do something – act in some sort of positive way, rather than simply wait to see what happens next – but I cannot think what to suggest."

"I'll tell you what we will do," said Blake after a moment. "We'll go and see Needham, and see what he has to say for himself!"

9: A VISIT TO LOWER CROPLEY

LIKE A SCENE FROM a children's story-book, the village appeared to have sprung to life as if by magic while we were in Mr Stannard's cottage. The high street was now very busy, with all manner of folk passing this way and that with their shopping-baskets, small groups pausing to exchange their news, and even a queue outside the baker's shop.

"Well, *there* is a surprise," said Blake to me as we strolled along. "Over there," he continued, nodding his head in the direction of a youth of seventeen or eighteen and a girl a little younger, who were some distance away, on the other side of the street. "That is Ashton's son and daughter. We don't see them in the village high street very often. In any case, I thought they were still away at school."

"Perhaps the school terms have ended," I suggested.

"You are probably right, Watson. Let's go and say hello."

We crossed the street and approached the young couple. As we did so, I observed an unusual thing. I have often seen, in satirical cartoons and the like, the depiction of those who regard themselves as superior to the mass of mankind as passing among their fellow-citizens with their noses held high in the air. I think I had always assumed it was some sort of artists' convention, an exaggeration of reality, as I had certainly never seen such an expression in real life. But as we drew nearer to Ashton's children, I realized that that was precisely how they

132

were holding themselves, the girl especially. I realized, too, at the same moment, why they were doing so. It was not, as I think I had always assumed, that they were avoiding the smell of their social inferiors, but rather that they were endeavouring to avoid their eyes meeting those of another, which might have obliged them to engage in conversation.

As we drew nearer, I saw the youth say something to his sister, and they made as if to cross to the other side of the street. Blake evidently saw this, too, for he quickened his pace.

"Good morning, Giles!" he called in a loud, clear tone. "Good morning, Miss Ashton!"

"Good morning, Mr Blake," they returned.

"It is a very fine morning, is it not?" Blake observed.

"Yes, sir."

"School finished for the summer?"

"Yes, sir."

"This is Dr Watson, who is staying with me for a few days."

"Good morning, sir," said the youth to me.

"Well, well," Blake continued. "Give my regards to your father. He is well, I trust?"

"Yes, sir."

"Perhaps we shall see you at the village pageant," Blake remarked as we parted.

"Yes, sir."

"Trying to engage those youngsters in conversation is like trying to open a clam-shell," remarked Blake to me as we continued along the high street.

133

I laughed. "Don't be too hard on them," I responded. "I think I was not so very different myself at their age. You know a lot of facts that you have learned at school, but you do not have the experience to judge what is most important or relevant in any given situation; you therefore find the best rule is usually to keep your mouth tightly closed. At least Ashton's children are very polite!"

"That is true. I know, from remarks he has made, that Ashton has very strong views on politeness, propriety and that sort of thing. I wonder where they are going. They hardly ever deign to set foot in the village."

"The girl was carrying a small posy," I remarked. "Perhaps they are visiting their mother's grave, in the churchyard."

"Of course!" cried Blake. "That must be it. This is perhaps their first opportunity to do so since returning from school. It was observant of you to notice that, Watson, and I'm sure your inference is correct. I thought it was only Mr Holmes who observed such small details!"

"Perhaps his skill is beginning to rub off a little on me," I remarked. I laughed as I said it, but, all the same, I felt rather pleased that Blake had been impressed by my observation and deduction, which Holmes never seemed to be.

Upon our return to the Grange, Blake found that a telegram had been delivered. He tore it open and scanned the contents.

"This is a nuisance!" he said in a tone of annoyance. "It's from *The Popular Railway Magazine*. I was due to do an article for them next week on the rival braking-systems used on

134

modern trains, but they say they have been let down by another author and must have my article by Thursday at the latest."

"That is very short notice," I remarked.

Blake nodded his head with a sigh. "I have all the material to hand, but I haven't even looked at it yet. It means I shall have to devote myself to it today and tomorrow, and even then it will be touch and go whether I manage to get it finished or not. I will never catch the post tomorrow, so I shall have to take it up in person on Thursday. I'm sorry, Watson, but I'm afraid I shall have to postpone our visit to Needham."

"I understand perfectly," I returned. "If there is anything I can do to assist you, just let me know."

After lunch, with further apologies from Blake, and further protestations from me that no apology was necessary, my host disappeared into his study with his secretary and I was once more left to my own devices.

For a while, as I had done the day before, I sat in a shady corner of the garden and watched the birds flitting this way and that and the butterflies and other little insects fluttering about the flower-beds. It was warm, peaceful and quiet, and I felt drowsy after my lunch, so it was not surprising that I drifted off to sleep.

I awoke abruptly. What the immediate cause was, I did not know. It may have been the buzz of a large bumble-bee which I could see on the flowers to the side of where I was sitting, but it may also have been my own thoughts. For, even in the instant of awakening, I found myself pondering the mysterious events which seemed to surround Farringdon Blake and Foxwood Grange. Who had hurled that large stone at us the

135

night before? If Mrs Booth was right, and her husband had not visited Foxwood in the last eighteen months, then all our assumptions about the matter must be wrong. But if Booth was not responsible for sending the warning message which had been attached to the stone, then who was? And what conceivable purpose could this other person have?

I filled my pipe and put a match to it, and as I did so, I reconsidered the whole matter afresh. When Holmes had suggested that it might be Booth who had sent that warning, it had seemed to explain everything so satisfactorily. No other explanation made any sense, as far as I could see. I therefore considered if there were any way in which Holmes's theory might be reconciled with Mrs Booth's testimony. I was aware, of course, that by the canons of scientific research a single conflicting piece of evidence was sufficient to disprove a hypothesis. That was certainly the theory, anyway, the principle under which all scientific research was conducted. In practice, however, matters were not always so clear-cut, and it was always worthwhile examining the apparently conflicting evidence to see if it really did contradict the hypothesis. In laboratory experiments dealing simply with combinations of chemicals, there was generally little room for doubt. But in other spheres, the apparently conflicting evidence was often open to different interpretations, some of which might not be so fatal to the hypothesis. Could that be so in this case?

After several minutes' reflection, it occurred to me that the fact that Mrs Booth had not seen her husband for eighteen months did not conclusively prove that he had not been to Foxwood more recently than that, simply that she was not aware that he had. He might, for instance, have come in some sort of disguise, such as a false beard and tinted glasses, have stayed at the village inn, and made sure that he did not run across his wife. As he had only visited the village once before, and that eighteen months ago, it would be unlikely that anyone other than his wife would recognize him. He might even have visited the district several times in this way, and managed to spy on his estranged wife's comings and goings. In this way he could have learnt of her friendship with Farringdon Blake. This, it seemed to me, was a perfectly valid sub-hypothesis which might yet save the main hypothesis. It would, of course, itself need to be put to the test. Clearly, we should need to ask at the inn if anyone had stayed there recently whom we could possibly identify as Booth. Even if that enquiry proved fruitless, there might be other possibilities. For instance, there might, for all I knew, be an inn in the village of Thuxton at which a visitor could stay. According to Holmes, whoever had flung the stones at us had run off in the general direction of Thuxton, so that certainly could not be ruled out.

For several minutes I sat there feeling pleased with myself, and considered how we should phrase our enquiries to the inn-keeper at the Royal Oak. Had Blake not been so preoccupied with his article on railway braking systems, I should have gone straight away to tell him of my new theory, which, it seemed to me, might solve all our difficulties. And yet, all the time, there was something nagging at the back of my mind which I could not quite bring into focus. I was just on the point of abandoning my reflections altogether, and taking myself off for a walk, when I realized what it was that was troubling me. It was not that there was anything specifically wrong with my own new theory. What it was that bothered me was just as much a problem for the whole notion that Mrs Booth's husband was the root cause of the recent puzzling events. It concerned the telescope on the viewing-platform up the tree: if Booth was determined to discover what his wife did with herself in and around Foxwood, then it made sense that he should spy on her wherever she went, including her visits to the Grange. But why on earth should he spy on Blake in his study or in the cobbled yard behind the house? What could he possibly hope to learn from that? It seemed unlikely to me that Mrs Booth ever went into Blake's study or the back yard; more probable, I thought, was that he entertained her in the drawing-room, which was not visible from the viewing-platform, or, on fine days, in the garden. I wondered, as my mind went back and forth over this problem without reaching any conclusion, if this particular difficulty had occurred to Holmes, and I wished he were there, so I could put the point to him. However, he was not, so I should have to decide matters for myself, and act on my own initiative.

Having nothing else to do, and thinking that I was unlikely to see Blake and Whitemoor again that afternoon, I resolved at length to walk down to the village once more and put my enquiries to the landlord of the Royal Oak. Having walked that way with Blake in the morning, I had a feeling of familiarity with each bend in the lane, each tree and bush that I passed. It is always surprising how quickly such a feeling takes hold of one, and as I turned into the road to the village, I was recalling the way I walked to the very first school I ever attended, in which I quickly became familiar with almost every paving-stone and door-step along the way.

There were no customers in the Royal Oak, and the landlord was sitting on a stool behind the bar, reading one of the sporting newspapers. He greeted me cordially, and asked me what I would like, so I asked for a glass of beer.

"I was wondering," I said in a casual tone, as I paid him for the beer, "if a friend of mine has stayed here recently."

"What's his name?"

I had prepared a detailed story to explain my query, but for some reason I had not anticipated this most elementary of questions, and I hesitated over my reply. "Henderson," I responded at length, that being the first name that entered my head.

"No, he ain't."

"He may not have been using that name," I remarked after a moment. "He sometimes uses a different one."

"Oh? Man of mystery, is he?"

"No, not exactly. But he sometimes uses his mother's maiden surname for some reason, and I can't remember what that is."

"You don't seem to know much about him, considering that he's a friend of yours."

"Not so much a friend as an acquaintance," I returned. "Our connection is really just a business one. The fact is," I continued, seeing an opportunity to get my prepared story into the conversation, "that I've just heard from him. He says that he thought he would look me up while he was in these parts, but he couldn't remember the address I was staying at, so he put up at an inn."

"You've just heard from him?"

"Yes, he sent me a letter."

"How could he send you a letter if he didn't know your address?"

I paused. I could have kicked myself for my stupidity in including such an obvious inconsistency in my story. I decided to meet the difficulty head on. "Yes, that puzzled me, too," I said. "It's a bit of a mystery. I suppose he must have asked someone when he got back to London."

"A Londoner, is he?"

"No, not really," I replied, thinking that from what I had heard of Booth, he might well have a Midlands accent. "He's actually from near Birmingham."

"That's another mystery, then, isn't it, why he went back to London?" observed the landlord.

"His business obliges him to divide his time between the two cities," I responded. "I believe he stays with his sister."

"What, a sister in London, or a sister in Birmingham?"

"I don't know," I replied, feeling I was getting into deeper water than I had intended. "I don't really know him very well at all."

"No, well, the only man who's stayed here in the last month was a commercial traveller from Bristol, and that was nearly two weeks ago."

"I don't think that can have been my acquaintance," I said. "Was he a short to medium man, perhaps with a beard or spectacles?"

"No, he wasn't. He was a good six foot tall, with a bald head and a ginger moustache."

"That's not him," I said, and, with a great sense of relief, took my glass of beer off to a table in the corner of the room. I hope my readers will appreciate my honesty in including this unfortunate and somewhat chastening episode in this narrative. I am sure that many authors would have suppressed the episode altogether to save embarrassment and preserve their dignity, but I thought I would include it to illustrate how difficult it can be for one who has no training or experience to make real progress with enquiries in the sort of mystery in which we were involved. It also shines a light indirectly on the skill with which Sherlock Holmes conducted his enquiries. I am sure that he would have adroitly avoided all the pitfalls into which I seemed to stumble, and would certainly never have found himself answering more questions than he was asking, as I did.

At least, I thought, as I walked back to the Grange, I had established that Booth had not stayed at the Royal Oak recently. I should have to ask Farringdon Blake if it was possible to stay at Thuxton or anywhere else in the district. If it were not, then we were back at the point at which Holmes's hypothesis concerning Booth might have to be rejected altogether. In that case, we should have no idea at all who had sent the warning and thrown the stones at us.

When I reached the Grange, I decided not to linger there, but passed straight through the garden and by the side gate into the field beyond. There was no-one about, and, save the ever-present bird-song, it was very quiet. I had no particular aim in mind, but thought I would stroll up to the ash spinney, look about, and see if any fresh thoughts struck me. I knew from odd remarks Holmes had made to me in the years we had lodged together that this was his method on those occasions when he was at a loss in a case and was unsure what to do next. As I ambled up the hill and through the ash spinney, however, I found that absolutely nothing whatever occurred to me. Eventually, for want of anything better to do, I climbed up the rungs in the ash tree and stood surveying the countryside round about from the old wooden platform.

Not a breath of wind disturbed the leaves on the trees, and, as far as I could see through the thick foliage which surrounded me, not a soul was about in any of the neighbouring fields. I glanced down at Farringdon Blake's study window in the Grange, but I could not make anything out. I sat down on the platform, leaning my back on the trunk of the tree behind me. It seemed very strange to me that I was now in the very place in which Farringdon Blake's mysterious enemy had stood just a week or two ago, and yet I had no idea who he was or what he wanted. I placed the palms of my hands on the wooden boards of the platform with an utterly illogical but overwhelming feeling that, by getting as closely in touch with this spot as I could, and concentrating all my thoughts upon it, I might yet learn who had been here, and for what purpose.

And then, an odd thing occurred. I had closed my eyes, to help concentrate my thoughts, but a brief moment later they were wide open again. For my ear had caught a sound that broke the silence of the wood. It sounded like footsteps, and someone brushing against the low undergrowth from the far end of the wood. I sat perfectly still and listened. Yes, it was definitely someone approaching, drawing ever closer. Then, abruptly, these light sounds ceased. As far as I could tell, whoever it was had stopped right beside the tree up which I was sitting. A moment later, I thought I heard the scrape of a boot on one of the iron rungs attached to the trunk of the tree, and then another. I held my breath. Whoever it was, he was evidently climbing up to the platform upon which I was sitting. Every muscle in my body tensed, as I waited to see who it would be. My mind raced. Would I discover who Farringdon Blake's mysterious enemy was? Did he know I had climbed the tree? Had he been watching me? If not, he was likely to be as startled as I was when he saw me there, which might give me an advantage.

All at once, the sound of his boots ascending the iron rungs stopped. For a moment, all was silent. I did not move a muscle, as I waited to see what would happen next. As far as I could judge, he was about half-way between the ground and the platform. Then I heard the sound of a boot on one of the rungs again, but there was something different about it. He was climbing down! As I heard him reach the ground and begin to walk away, I scrambled forward as silently as I could and peered over the edge of the platform. He was already a little distance away, making his way towards the far end of the ash spinney, evidently returning the way he had come. He appeared to be a small man, and was clad in a brown suit and had a soft-brimmed brown hat on his head. It was certainly no-one I had ever seen before. Who was he, and why, at the last moment, had he changed his mind about climbing to the platform?

As he disappeared from my sight, I determined to follow him at a distance, and try to see where he went to. I began to climb down the iron rungs, making as little noise as possible. I was only half-way down, however, when I heard another noise, but this time from the opposite direction, from the path towards the Grange. It sounded to me like an animal of some kind, padding through the wood, and brushing past the undergrowth.

I had just reached the ground and turned, when the approaching sounds grew louder. Along the path, a very large, rough-haired dog came bounding. As he saw me, he let out a fierce growl and sprang at me. I put my arm up to protect myself, and he sank his teeth into my jacket-sleeve, the force of his attack knocking me clean off my feet and to the ground. At the same moment, a large man appeared in the clearing by the tree.

"Duke!" he shouted in an angry voice. "Get down! Leave him!"

Reluctantly, the dog released his grip on my arm, but remained close to me, growling menacingly. I stood up and knocked some of the dust and dirt off my clothes.

"Your dog is a somewhat aggressive beast," I said, none too pleased.

"What do you expect?" the man retorted. "If you go skulking around on other people's property, it's hardly a surprise if one of the dogs goes for you. That's what they're supposed to do. Who are you, anyway, and what are you doing on my land?"

I did not feel much like discussing the matter with him, but I explained that I was a guest of Farringdon Blake's at the Grange, and had been under the impression that no-one would mind if I took a walk in the woods. His manner towards me changed then, although he seemed reluctant to admit that he or his dog were at all at fault in their aggressive behaviour.

"A friend of Blake's, eh? Well, why didn't you say so?"

"I didn't have much opportunity," I said. "Anyway, I'm telling you now."

"Well, I'm sorry, I'm sure, if Duke's upset you," said he in a gruff tone, as if it cost him an enormous effort to apologize, even though it was only on behalf of his dog. "No lasting harm done, I hope?"

"I don't think so."

"Pearson," he said in a loud voice, stepping forward and thrusting out his hand. He was one of those people who seem to have been constructed on an altogether larger scale than most of their fellow-men, with large, prominent ears and a large nose and chin, and the hand that he offered me was suitably enormous. I took it and shook it simply out of politeness, but with little enthusiasm. "Watson," I said.

"Well, Mr Watson," said he. "Any friend of Mr Blake's is a friend of mine. I'm sorry we got off on the wrong foot. Can I offer you tea? I'm sure my wife would be pleased to meet you. She doesn't get out much these days and is always glad when somebody calls by, whether they've got anything interesting to say or not."

I was about to decline this somewhat graceless invitation, but it occurred to me that if I saw something of Pearson's household at Lower Cropley farmhouse it would give me something else to put in my report to Holmes. I therefore accepted the invitation, and we set off together, the dog generally running backwards and forwards ahead of us, save when it barged past us on the narrow path and nearly sent me flying.

As we walked along, Pearson explained to me that he had been doing a grand circuit of the boundary of his property, as he occasionally did, so he said, to ensure that all was as it should be.

"It is always good to keep an eye on things," I observed. To myself, though, I reflected that his statement did not tally with his previous remark to Blake that he had only set foot in the ash spinney a couple of times in the last twenty years. Whether there was any significance to this discrepancy, however, I had no idea.

Our way took us by the disused quarry where old Brookfield's lifeless body had been found. As we passed it, I asked Pearson if he had known Brookfield.

"Everybody knew Jacob Brookfield," he returned. "He'd been a fixture in this parish since before anyone can remember. It's not everybody as liked him, though. He drank a lot and didn't always pay his way, if you know what I mean; a bit of a trouble-causer."

As we passed over the brow of the hill by the quarry, the chimneys of Lower Cropley came into view, thrusting up through a clump of trees. A few moments later, we arrived at the gate. Set behind a small, scrubby garden was a broad, spreading old house, half covered in ivy, which appeared to be several centuries old, built of the local brownish-grey stone, no doubt excavated from the nearby quarry.

Inside, the house was dark and cool, and had a faint musty, damp smell, even on that warm summer's day. Pearson conducted me down a dark passage and into a large cluttered room which I took to be some kind of parlour, where a middle-aged woman with faded brown hair sat reading a magazine in an armchair. This, Pearson informed me, was his wife.

"Mother," he said, addressing her, "this is Mr Watson, who is staying with Mr Blake at the Grange. We ran across each other in the old ash spinney. At least, he and Duke ran across each other first, before we'd been properly introduced."

The woman laughed, so much so that her whole body shook. "Yes," she said, "he can be a bit forward in his greetings, can Duke, but he's very friendly." I murmured some non-committal response to this observation, privately reflecting that if Duke were their idea of a friendly dog, I should certainly not want to meet one that they considered unfriendly.

Mrs Pearson rang a bell, and, when the maid appeared a moment later, ordered a pot of tea. While we waited for the tea to arrive, Mrs Pearson asked me how I came to know Farringdon Blake. I told her we both contributed articles to magazines, implying without specifically stating it that that is how we had met.

"What name shall I kook out for, then?" she asked, holding up the magazine she had been reading. "Is it 'Mr Watson', or do you use a *nom-de-plume*?"

"I use my own name, but it's *Doctor* Watson, rather than *Mister*."

"You're a doctor?"

"Yes, but I'm not in practice at the moment. I used to be an Army surgeon."

"Ever been overseas?" asked Pearson.

"Yes, I was in Afghanistan a few years ago."

"Seen any action?"

"More than I could have imagined – or wished for."

"Then that's what you should write about!" cried Pearson thumping his right fist into his left palm. "That's what people want to read about: military exploits, leading through adversity to triumph!"

"It's not as straightforward as that," I returned. "For a start, I was wounded twice, nearly died twice, and then spent weeks and weeks in a hospital bed. I didn't have much triumph!"

"But we won through in the end!"

"No thanks to me, I'm afraid. Besides, people have written about the Afghan campaign already; publishers aren't interested in any more accounts at the moment, so I have been told."

"More fool them, then," said Pearson in an indignant tone and seemed about to give me the benefit of his opinions on the book trade, when there came a loud and rowdy interruption from just outside the room.

"It sounds as if someone has fallen downstairs," I remarked.

"That'll just be James or Anthony larking about," responded Mrs Pearson dismissively. "I've told them they'll break their necks one day, but do they listen?"

She was interrupted by a terrific crash, as the door burst open and two very large young men, who were apparently having a wrestling match, came tumbling into the room and continued their grappling on the carpet beside my chair.

"Damn and blast!" cried Pearson in a loud voice. "You'll break that damned door one of these days!"

I glanced round. In fact, they had succeeded already, for the wood was splintered and the lock was hanging out at an odd angle. The young men had stopped their wrestling, but began talking very loudly, both at the same time.

"Boys! Boys!" said Mrs Pearson, in a tone of mild remonstrance. "Where are your manners? Have you not noticed we have a visitor?"

"In other words," shouted Pearson in a fierce tone, "shut your infernal racket, and say hello to Mr Watson here."

The young men rose to their feet and bade me a "good afternoon", almost in unison.

"He's staying at the Grange. We met at the top of the hill, in the old ash spinney."

"Do you mean," said the older of the two young men, "near where there are those rungs going up a tree like a ladder?"

"I don't know anything about that," said Pearson.

"Yes you do, Pa," said the other young man. "I remember you said it would be a good place to spy on old Stannard from. Then you could see if he ever found that ancient treasure that's hidden at the Grange."

"I never said any such thing!" cried Pearson fiercely, "and don't you tell such damned lying stories!"

"Well, someone did," the young man persisted.

"It must have been James, then," said his father, "and I told him not to be so stupid."

"It wasn't me," said the other young man. "I've never had any interest in the Grange. Not like Anthony, who, as we all know, is *very* interested."

At this, Anthony took the magazine from his mother, rolled it up and hit his brother on the head with it. "No I am not!" he said, emphasizing each word with a blow.

"Oh, yes you are," said James, snatching the magazine from his brother's hand with a laugh, and returning the blows. "Do you remember, Ma," he said after a moment, "how we used to play up there in the ash spinney when we were little?"

His mother shook her head. "I never knew where you used to get to," she replied. "You'd go off somewhere and not come back for hours, and I'd have no idea where you'd been or what you'd been up to – and it's just the same now!"

At that moment, the maid brought in a tray of tea-things, and set it down on a little round table.

"Where's my cup?" asked one of the young men.

"If you want a cup, you'll have to go and get one yourself," said Mrs Pearson, and the two young men left the room almost as noisily as they had entered it. "They can be a bit rowdy," she said to me, as she poured out the tea, "but they're good boys, really."

"I'm sure they are," I said, as I accepted the cup she passed me. It was certainly a relief to the ears that the young men had left the room, but I had gone off the idea of engaging the older Pearsons in conversation; I could not see that I was likely to learn anything of interest there. I therefore finished my tea as quickly as I could, and said I had best be getting back to the Grange. Shortly afterwards, with a great sense of relief at having escaped that noisy and chaotic household, and revelling in my peaceful solitude, I made my way in the warm afternoon sunshine over the hills towards the Grange.

It took me some time to clear my head of the idiotic racket which had filled it at Lower Cropley, but gradually my brain began to function normally once more and I found myself reflecting on the afternoon's events. When I was about half-way back to the Grange, I happened to pass an old tree-stump at the side of the road so I decided to sit down for a while, smoke my pipe and concentrate my thoughts on what had happened.

Concerning the Pearsons, I did not really know what to think. On the one hand their thought-processes appeared too shallow and unimaginative for them to have had anything to do with Farringdon Blake's mystery, but on the other hand it was odd that Mr Pearson had claimed to have hardly ever been in the ash spinney in the last twenty years when that was precisely where he and I had met. It was also odd that he should claim to know nothing about the rungs in the tree when even his own family disagreed with him on that point. I shook my head in puzzlement. Perhaps, after all, Pearson simply had a bad memory, or was one of those people who tend to disagree with what anyone else says as a matter of course.

But if I was inclined to dismiss the Pearsons from consideration, what of the other man I had seen in the wood? Presumably what had happened was that, as he was ascending the rungs, he had seen Pearson approaching, and that was why he had changed his mind and hurried away. But who was he? Why was he climbing the tree? And what would he have done if Pearson had not turned up when he did?

10: THE INQUEST

THAT EVENING, at supper, I recounted to Blake and Whitemoor my experiences of the afternoon. They were interested in my enquiries at the village inn, which seemed to establish that Mrs Booth's husband had not stayed in Foxwood recently.

"I'm afraid I have no idea if it is possible to stay at the inn in Thuxton," said Blake in answer to my query. "We'll have to find out. If it isn't, then we'll just have to rule out Booth as a possibility for the stone-thrower, and try to think who else it could have been."

"I don't think it's likely to be Pearson or any of his family," I said. "In the first place, I can't conceive of any motive they might have. In the second place, they don't strike me as the sort of people to go creeping about in the dark, throwing stones at people. I think it more likely that if Pearson had any grievance against you, he would simply come round here in broad daylight – with or without his vicious dog – and have a violent quarrel with you."

"I quite agree," returned Blake. "That is my experience of them, too. There's not much subtlety at Lower Cropley. If Pearson wanted to attack me, he'd be more likely to confront me with a bludgeon in his hand than creep up behind me with a rapier. I think we'll be on safe enough ground if we dismiss the Pearsons from our calculations, then. The other man you saw in the woods interests me, though, Watson. It's a pity you didn't get a better look at him."

I nodded my head. "I can't really tell you anything about him, I'm afraid, except that he did not appear to be a very big man and he was wearing a brown suit and hat. It was certainly not anyone I've seen before, anyway."

"I wonder if it could have been Booth," suggested Whitemoor. "A brown suit and hat does not sound so much like a countryman's outfit as that of a town-dweller, such as Booth."

"That's a fair point," agreed Blake. "Also," he continued in a thoughtful voice, "from your account of it, Watson, the fact that he made himself scarce when he saw Pearson approaching suggests that he did not wish to be seen there."

"Yes," I said. "That seemed pretty clear. I feel certain now that he did not know that I was up the tree, because when I first heard him approaching he was still some distance off, too far away for him to have seen me climbing the tree."

"I wonder what he intended to do up the tree?" said Blake.

"Could you see if he was carrying a telescope or field-glasses?" Whitemoor asked me.

"No, I don't think he was carrying anything."

"Then it is a mystery, unless, of course, he had been up there earlier and left something behind, and was, when you saw him, returning to retrieve it – whatever it was."

I shook my head. "It's an ingenious thought," I said, "but I was up there some time and saw nothing. There was certainly nothing on the platform, and I'm fairly certain there was nothing hanging on a branch, either. It is, as you say, a mystery."

Later that evening, in the quiet of my bedroom, I made a record of all that had happened that day and all that I had learnt, so that I should be able to give Sherlock Holmes a full account when he returned. As well as the afternoon's events, I made detailed notes of our visits to Mrs Booth and Mr Stannard, and even included a mention of our encounter with Ashton's children in the high street. There were two reasons why I was determined to be as thorough as I could possibly be: in the first place I did not want to give Holmes any reason to find fault with my reports, and in the second place, as the mystery surrounding Farringdon Blake was such a puzzling one, it seemed to me that it was impossible to say which of the many details I was noting down might be important and which might not, and thus the safest way of proceeding was to include everything I could recall, however trivial.

By the time I had finished, the house was in complete silence, and had been for some time. As I blew out the lamp on my writing-table, yawned and climbed into bed, I wondered what the next day of this singular week might bring.

I awoke to the light pitter-patter of raindrops against my bedroom window. It had evidently rained quite heavily in the night, for as I drew back the bedroom curtains I could see that the trees and shrubs in the garden were all wet and bedraggled, and there were little pools of rain-water on the paths.

"This rain will freshen up the gardens a little," said Blake as we sat down to breakfast together.

"It must have been quite a heavy downpour," said Whitemoor, "for it seems to have knocked the heads off some of the flowers, which is a great shame."

Blake nodded. "But no doubt they'll soon burst forth with renewed vigour. Speaking of renewed vigour, incidentally, Watson, I feel a bit like that myself this morning. I got on so well with railway braking systems yesterday that I don't feel under so much pressure about it today, and I think I might go to the inquest this morning, at the Royal Oak. It's something of a melancholy business, but I feel I perhaps ought to be there."

"I'll go with you," I said. "I imagine it will be a fairly routine proceeding, but I should like to hear it nevertheless."

"What about you, Whitemoor?" asked Blake. "Would you like to see how an English coroner's court proceeds?"

The young man shook his head. "I don't think I will," he replied. "As Dr Watson says, it will probably be a routine matter, and I have a number of references to dig out for you from the back numbers of the *Journal of Mechanical Engineering*."

It had stopped raining by the time Blake and I left the house, and we reached the Royal Oak in good time. This was fortunate, for the tap room was already almost full. I had expected a large number of people to attend, Jacob Brookfield being a very well known local character, but the size of the crowd exceeded my expectations. Blake and I managed to find a seat near the back of the room, but those who came after us were obliged to stand. I wondered, as I waited for the proceedings to begin, if anyone would raise any of the objections to Brookfield's death having been an accident which

Sherlock Holmes had mentioned to me. In accordance with his wishes, I had not mentioned Holmes's views on the matter to anyone, but those views were uppermost in my mind when the coroner took his seat, rapped his knuckles on his desk and opened the proceedings.

After taking preliminary testimony from the local police constable and Brookfield's daughter as to the identity of the deceased, the coroner called the surgeon who had examined the body. I made brief notes of all the evidence presented, from which I can reconstruct the following exchanges:

Coroner: "Were you able to determine the cause of death?"

Surgeon: "Yes. There was a severe wound at the back of the head which would undoubtedly have caused death, probably instantaneously."

Coroner: "Were there any other wounds or injuries?"

Surgeon: "Yes. Several bones were broken, both in the limbs and in the chest."

Coroner: "What did this suggest to you?"

Surgeon: "That the deceased had fallen from a considerable height. I have seen such injuries on other occasions, and the circumstances were always thus."

Coroner: "Is it possible, in your experience, that death could have been caused in any other way?"

Surgeon: (after a moment's consideration) "Yes, there is one other possibility: that the deceased was struck on the head with a blunt object – say, a large stone – which killed him, and that his lifeless body was then flung from a great height into the quarry."

Coroner: "Is there anything in the state of the body to distinguish between these two possibilities?"

Surgeon: "No. All the injuries occurred either at the same time or within a very few moments of each other. This would have been the case whether the death was an accident or the result of foul play."

Foreman of the jury: "There was nothing specifically in your findings which would suggest foul play?"

Surgeon: "No."

The constable was then recalled and asked if there had been any evidence in the quarry to indicate which stone, of all those there, might have been the one upon which Brookfield struck his head.

Constable: "No. There were several stones in the vicinity of the deceased which, from their shape and size might have been responsible."

Coroner: "There was no stone on which there were traces of blood, for instance?"

Constable: "No. It had rained quite heavily between the probable time of death and the time the body was discovered, and I think that some of the blood-stains had been washed away. For example, although there was some blood around the head where the deceased lay, as you would expect, even that was not of uniform appearance, but was blotchy and partly washed away.

Evidence was then taken from Brookfield's friends and acquaintances, and others who had been in the Royal Oak on the evening of his death. The coroner asked each of them first if they knew of anyone who might have wished Brookfield ill, to which all answered "no". He then asked each of them if Brookfield's manner had seemed in any way different on the evening of his death, and all agreed that he had been more morose than usual. There appeared to have been two reasons for this: first that he had had little money, and, second that he had earlier had a quarrel with his daughter, which he regretted. The general opinion, also, was that he was somewhat more inebriated than usual. The coroner asked how this could be so if Brookfield had had little money, to which several of those who had been present in the Royal Oak stated that Brookfield had "borrowed" a drink from them with the promise to return the favour at some future date – although no-one entirely believed this promise.

The coroner also asked each of the witnesses in turn if they thought it possible that Brookfield might have considered taking his own life. Each declared that such a thought was inconceivable.

Coroner: "I am asking this question in an attempt to shed light on the reason why the deceased should have approached the edge of the quarry on the night in question, which matter seems to me to be in need of explanation."

At this, one of the witnesses, Thomas Hopkins, asked to be recalled, and gave the following additional testimony:

Hopkins: "Mr Brookfield said to me, on the evening of his death, that he did not wish to go home until he could be sure that his daughter and son-in-law were in bed and asleep, as he did not wish to face them after the row they had had earlier in the evening."

Coroner: "Are you suggesting, then, that the deceased went to sit by the edge of the quarry on that occasion simply in order to pass a little time before going home?"

Hopkins: "Yes, sir."

Coroner: "Would the edge of the quarry be a suitable place for anyone to sit down to pass the time? Is there nowhere safer or more comfortable?"

Hopkins: "There is nowhere much on that road to sit down, sir, which is comfortable, except for that stretch of grass by the quarry. I have sat there myself occasionally in years past on sunny days. But I would not go there at night, and nor would I go near the edge of the quarry, for it's a mighty drop."

The coroner made a note of all this, and then called Brookfield's daughter, Mrs Elizabeth Naylor. He apologized for doing so, and said he had hoped it would not be necessary, but said that the court needed to know about the quarrel that was said to have occurred on the evening of Brookfield's death, as that was thought to have played a part, if only indirectly, in what had later taken place.

Mrs Naylor: "My father lived with us. He did odd jobs about the house, for which I gave him a small allowance. On the day in question, he asked for some money, but I had already given him some the day before and I told him I could not afford to give him any more, which was true. He then said that I did not appreciate the work he did – which wasn't true – and that he would go where he was more appreciated, mentioning his sister at Banbury. I told him that he was welcome to go there as far as I was concerned, but that she wouldn't put up with him as I did, and we had a quarrel about it all."

Coroner: "Had he ever threatened to move to his sister's house before?"

Mrs Naylor: "Yes, once or twice, but he had never done so. He visited her occasionally, but never as a result of a quarrel with me."

Coroner: "Were you surprised when your father had not returned by the time you retired for the night?"

Mrs Naylor: "No. He was often late home if he stayed to chat to a crony of his in the village after he had left the pub."

Coroner: "And when he did not return at all that night, or, indeed, for the next two weeks, were you not then surprised?"

Mrs Naylor: "A little, but I assumed he had gone to his sister's, as he had threatened, and that he would turn up again eventually."

The coroner then asked all those present if any of them had stood talking with Brookfield after leaving the inn on the night in question. One man, Arthur Streedbank, stood up and stated that he had done so.

Coroner: "Did the deceased mention to you the quarrel he had had with his daughter?"

Streedbank: "No, your honour."

Coroner: "What did you talk about, then?"

Streedbank: "Country matters, your honour: rabbits and suchlike."

Coroner: "For how long were you in conversation?"

Streedbank: "I don't rightly know. At least half an hour, I should say."

Coroner: "So there was probably not really much need for the deceased to pass any further time by sitting by the quarry, but, of course, he might have wished to make absolutely certain that his daughter had retired for the night before he returned."

The coroner wrote for some time, then, looking up from his papers, summarized the evidence we had heard. He then asked the jury if they had understood it all. A short discussion ensued among the members of the jury, then the foreman, a tall, distinguished-looking man with white hair and a long, thin nose, stood up and said that they had understood it all perfectly. The coroner then asked them to consider their verdict on all that they had heard. Another discussion, somewhat more prolonged, ensued, during which there seemed to be some disagreement between the foreman and a large man sitting directly behind him, but eventually the foreman stood up once more and gave their verdict as follows:

"It is our belief that the death of Jacob Brookfield was an accident, and that no-one else was involved in any capacity whatever. We believe that he had gone to sit by the quarry to pass a little time, and that, his judgement, and perhaps, also, his physical capability being impaired by the amount of alcoholic liquor he had consumed, he came too close to the edge of the quarry, stumbled, and so fell to his death."

"Is that the verdict of you all?"

"It is. May we make a further observation?"

"By all means."

"We feel that the owner of the land on which the quarry stands, whom we believe to be Mr Pearson of Lower Cropley

Farm, should be obliged to erect a wire fence at the place where the quarry comes close to the road, to prevent any repetition of this tragic accident."

"I will make a note of your recommendation," said the coroner. He then thanked the jury for their efforts, formally closed the proceedings, and we made our way out into the street.

"The foreman of the jury was a well-spoken man," I observed to Farringdon Blake, as we stood amid a large throng of people, milling about outside the inn. "I don't know what Pearson will think of the suggestion that he should be obliged to erect a fence," I added. "It tends to imply that Pearson himself was partly culpable for the death."

"Yes, I had the same thought," returned Blake with a dry chuckle. "Pearson won't like that at all. The foreman of the jury was Ashton, by the way."

"What, your rival for Mrs Booth's interest? Why, he looks old enough to be her father! Surely, he can't be much of a rival?"

"Oh, I don't know about that, Watson," returned Blake. "You know what widowers are like – or, perhaps you don't: they mourn their wives for some time, but eventually come to the point of fancying a little more company about the house. And when they do, they nearly always set their sights on someone a lot younger than wife number one."

"If that is really what he has in mind," I returned, "he is a little premature. Mrs Booth is still married to someone else."

"Yes, of course. But I suspect that, like a careful and methodical architect, he may be laying the groundwork now, in a general sort of way, groundwork upon which he can later erect an attractive edifice of wealth and position, with which to lure Mrs Booth in his direction."

I nudged Blake in the ribs as surreptitiously as I could. "He's approaching now," I said.

A moment later, we were greeted by the tall, white-haired man I had seen acting as foreman of the coroner's jury.

"Good morning, Blake!" he cried in a pleasant tone. "Well, that's that business out of the way. I don't know why the coroner prolonged the proceedings by raising the possibility of foul play in the way he did. It was obvious from start to finish that it was just a ghastly accident!"

Blake returned his greeting and introduced me.

"A doctor, eh?" said Ashton. "Pleased to meet you! It's something of a coincidence, actually: I've just been reading about the part played by the doctor who sailed with Christopher Columbus. It's fascinating, I can tell you!"

"I'm sure it is," I responded, hoping that he would not launch into an account of it there and then.

"With regard to the coroner and the question of foul play," said Blake: "I suppose he was duty-bound to consider all possibilities. After all, he did also raise the possibility of suicide."

"Yes," returned Ashton, "but that was ridiculous, too. Men like Brookfield don't kill themselves – too old, too set in their ways! And as for foul play: who'd want to kill him? He might as well have raised the possibility of the man in the moon coming down and pushing Brookfield over the edge of the quarry! Anyway, enough of that! Must be off! Looks like it might rain again! Nice to have met you, doctor! You must come over and have supper with us one evening!"

As we made our way back to the Grange under heavy skies, Blake asked me what I thought of the inquest and the verdict which had been reached.

"Of course," he said, "it is apparent that Ashton, and no doubt others, were already convinced that Brookfield's death was an accident before the inquest even began, and I suppose that, all things considered, that is the most likely explanation. And yet, I can't help harbouring a few doubts. What do you think, Watson?"

I shook my head. "On the evidence presented," I replied cautiously, having in mind Holmes's instruction not to divulge his own view of the matter, "I would have to agree that 'accidental death' was the most reasonable verdict. I did notice, however, that, to begin with, at least, there appeared to be some disagreement between the jurors on the point. That large man who was sitting behind Ashton seemed to be arguing about something."

Blake nodded his head. "I noticed that, too. The large man was Perkins, an old crony of Brookfield's. He evidently thought that there was something not quite right about the whole business."

"And yet, Ashton's view prevailed in the end," I remarked. "I could not help but wonder if the fact that Ashton was more eloquent and probably more highly educated than the other jurymen had more to do with that than the actual facts of the case. Perhaps without Ashton they would have reached a different verdict."

Again Blake nodded his head. "That is always the trouble in these rural parts: the large landowner states his opinion and other men tend to defer to him and go along with what he has said, as much because of his social position as his arguments. I don't know, Watson. Perhaps my own recent experiences have made me suspicious of everything that happens, and have inclined me to see plots and conspiracies where none exist, but it seems something of a coincidence that Brookfield should have met his death in this untimely fashion at just the same time as I am being spied upon at the Grange and having stones thrown at me in the dark. You must remember that this is a parish in which nothing out of the ordinary occurs from one year's end to the next, and now, all at once, odd things are happening all the time, one after the other. There was no connection between Brookfield and me – I had probably only spoken to him four or five times in three years – but, still, the coincidence of his death strikes me as odd. Did Mr Holmes express any opinion about it?"

"He was certainly interested in it," I responded. "As you will imagine, with a mind like Holmes has, he is always trying to fit things into some overall pattern. He dislikes treating anything as simply a coincidence unless it is absolutely impossible to connect it up to other things; but sometimes, of course, coincidences do occur."

"So he has no particular opinion on the matter?"

"I should not say that, exactly," I returned. "But, as far as I am aware, he has no definite evidence which would prove the matter one way or the other. if he did have, he would certainly have communicated it to the authorities."

With that somewhat evasive answer from me, our discussion of the matter drew to a close. Upon our return to the Grange, Blake at once retired to his study to continue his essay on railway braking systems. He was evidently able to get back into it again very quickly, for over lunch he explained to me in great detail some of the intricacies of the subject, including the latest developments in the United States of a brake which would be applied automatically, very quickly and with permanent effect should the vehicles of the train part for any reason. I have always found this sort of technical discussion fascinating, I must say, and I was glad that Blake had something to occupy his mind other than the mysterious and unpleasant events which had beset him recently.

After lunch, Blake returned to the study with Whitemoor. "It shouldn't take us above an hour or two at most," he said to me. "Whitemoor is helping me with a couple of diagrams to accompany the text. They don't have to be works of art, as the journal's own artist will almost certainly re-draw them for publication, anyway, but they must be clear. I'll let you have a look at them later on, Watson. You can act as our 'Mr Everyman', if you wouldn't mind, and let us know if you can understand them!"

"By all means," I returned. "I shall look forward to it."

After they had left me, I sat for some time, reflecting on all that had happened recently, but could make little sense of it. As it had begun to rain again, I decided to take the opportunity to write an account of the morning's inquest for Holmes's benefit, so took myself off to my bedroom and laid out my foolscap once more. I glanced at what I had already written. It seemed quite a pile. Holmes had been gone for little over twenty-four hours and yet I had covered sheet after sheet with my reports of the people I had met and the conversations that had taken place. Holmes might find my reports inadequate in some respects, but I was sure he could not fault my thoroughness.

It took me some considerable time to complete my account of the inquest and of our brief meeting with Ashton afterwards, and by the time I had finished I felt so exhausted that I lay on my bed, closed my eyes and, within a few moments, had fallen fast asleep.

11: MR NEEDHAM OF ABBEYFIELD HOUSE

I AWOKE to the sound of someone tapping on my bedroom door. As I opened my eyes, the door opened and Farringdon Blake put his head in.

"Sorry to disturb you, Watson," said he.

"That's perfectly all right. I should probably be up, anyway. Do you know what the time is?"

"Just after four o'clock. I came to tell you that my account of railway brakes is all finished. It's stopped raining now, too, so we could walk over to Needham's place if you felt up to it."

"Certainly," I said. "I'll be with you in a few moments."

"I've asked Ann to make us a pot of tea," Blake added, "so we can fortify ourselves before we set off."

Five minutes later, we were sitting in the drawing-room and Blake was showing me his latest article and the illustrations that were to accompany it.

"What you have labelled a 'triple valve' looks an ingenious device," I remarked.

"It is," said Blake. "It's extremely simple in conception, but very effective in practice. It was invented by George Westinghouse, in America. He seems to be a very prolific inventor of such things. I imagine it must be very satisfying to see a problem and come up with a solution to it. Most of us don't even see the problems, let alone find solutions to them."

"That's true. This Westinghouse fellow sounds like a modern-day genius!"

"Of a sort, certainly. But however you regard him, his approach to life has a lesson for all of us: meet problems head on, solve them and then move on to the next one. In that way you are always advancing, always looking to the future, rather than the past. That's the exact opposite of how some people live their lives, dwelling on the past all the time, and also, in some ways, the exact opposite of Samuel Harley, one-time owner of this old pile. Harley seems to have been a very clever young man, but when he came into all that wealth, it seems to have knocked all the drive out of him. Instead of looking to the future, meeting problems and solving them, he spent most of his time finding ways to waste all the money that had been accumulated by previous generations. He was thus, essentially, backward-looking and never advanced at all. I remember reading somewhere that he had a habit of referring to his own unhappy childhood, and people said of him that even when not specifically speaking of it, it never seemed to be very far from his thoughts."

"An unhappy childhood can sometimes stay with a man throughout his life," I remarked.

"Yes, of course, but one should strive not to dwell upon it unnecessarily. After all, what's past is past, and there's nothing anyone can do about that."

"That's true. Some people certainly expend a lot of energy in raking over the past, as if hoping to change that which cannot be changed. Most people, I suppose, just drift along through life, and a few – like this Westinghouse man you mentioned – change things as they go along, generally to the benefit not only of themselves but of everyone else, too. Holmes is of this latter type. He spends his entire life solving puzzles and problems for other people. He hardly ever refers to what one might call his own personal life – apart from declaring how bored he is when he has no problem to challenge him – and has almost never, in all the time I have known him, referred to his own early life or childhood. It is almost as if, however good, bad or indifferent his past was, he has quite closed the door on it, and now looks only to the future. It is a cast of mind I have sometimes wished I could emulate, but so far without complete success!"

Blake laughed. "I know what you mean, Watson. It is an odd thing," he added in a reflective tone, "how many different and very diverse characters the human race can display. Take my neighbours here, for instance: I can scarcely imagine there could be half a dozen such different people, and all in this one small parish!"

"They certainly seem a varied collection," I agreed with a chuckle.

"Yes, and you haven't yet met Needham, whom we'll go and see as soon as you have finished your tea. He is perhaps the oddest of the lot. I was reflecting last night on Mr Stannard's suspicions that Needham had stolen a book from him. Although I had been surprised and shocked at that, I realized last night that I was somewhat less surprised than I would have been if he had levelled the accusation at any other of my neighbours. It was as if – without ever putting the thought into words, even in my own head – I had already instinctively marked Needham down as sly, or dishonest."

"I can scarcely wait to meet him!" I cried, laughing as I put my tea-cup down.

A few minutes later we had left the house, and were making our way up the field towards the ash spinney. The rain had quite stopped now and a weak sunlight was struggling to penetrate the clouds, but the countryside was very wet and the trees dripped upon us as we passed beneath them. When we reached the place at which I had encountered Pearson the previous day, I asked Blake if he had ever had the misfortune to run across one of Pearson's dogs, at which he shook his head.

"From your description, I'm glad I haven't," he replied. "I did once hear a couple of them fighting with each other, though, when I was over at Lower Cropley, taking tea with the Pearsons. They were in the yard behind the house, and the fighting sounded so loud and violent that I thought one of them must surely kill the other. In the end, Pearson had to go out and lay into them with a large stick, all the while bellowing just as loudly and violently as the dogs. Anyway, it did the trick. They shut up their racket and Pearson returned to the parlour to finish his tea as if nothing had happened!"

As we passed out of the further end of the ash spinney, we followed the path across the top of the field until we came to the farm track, where we turned right. A little further on, we came to the garden of Abbeyfield House, which was surrounded by a tall, thickly-growing evergreen hedge. The house itself was a substantial, square brick structure, built in the last forty-odd years, I judged, and more solid than attractive.

171

Our knock at the front door was answered after a moment by a gaunt, grim-looking middle-aged woman in the uniform of a housekeeper. Upon Blake's enquiring if Mr Needham was at home, she showed us into a reception room on the right of the hall, closing the door firmly but noiselessly upon us. As we sat there in silence, I looked about the room. A large table in the centre was covered with a thick, heavy cloth. The other items of furniture – the chairs around the table, a sideboard and a tallboy – were all of some dark wood and highly polished. In the centre of the table was a large glass fruit-bowl which was empty, and in the alcoves either side of the fireplace hung a couple of old dark prints of some kind. Other than that, the room was perfectly devoid of any decoration, and presented an austere, cold appearance. It did not appear that the room was ever used, and I found myself wondering if the rest of the house was as sombre and unwelcoming in appearance as this room.

My thoughts were interrupted by the silent opening of the door. A small, dark-haired and sallow-faced man entered the room, closing the door behind him.

"Good afternoon, Mr Needham," said Blake, rising to his feet.

"Good afternoon, Mr Blake," returned the other. His oddly hooded eyes flickered momentarily in my direction.

"This is Dr Watson, a fellow-journalist, who is staying with me for a few days," said Blake by way of explanation. I stood up, leaned across the table and offered Needham my hand, which he shook in a very brief and perfunctory manner, almost as if the touch of another's hand was distasteful to him. I had the impression that this mild distaste was not a consequence of any manifest shortcomings on my part, but was his customary manner towards anyone he did not know.

"Please be seated," he said, although he himself remained standing, as if to indicate that we should not stay long. "To what do I owe the pleasure of this visit?"

"A couple of things," returned Blake. "First, as we were out for a walk – I was showing Dr Watson round the local countryside – I thought we might just call by and I could introduce the two of you."

A wan smile appeared briefly on Needham's face, but was gone almost as soon as it had appeared. He nodded his head slightly. "And the second thing?" he asked after a moment.

"I happened to be talking to Mr Stannard recently," replied Blake. "When I mentioned to him that there was a book I believed to be in the library at the Grange, but which I could not find there, he remembered that he had lent it to you some time ago, and he thought that you might still have it."

"What was the book?" asked Needham.

"A volume of local history, which included a lot of information about previous owners of the Grange and so on."

"Ah, yes," murmured Needham. "I did borrow that book from your cousin several years ago, but I also returned it to him. I had no need to borrow it again, as I subsequently acquired a copy of my own. One moment," he added, then he turned and left the room without further remark.

I had turned to my companion and was about to express surprise at Needham's odd manner, when my thoughts were abruptly interrupted by a sudden flash of recognition. For as I had, in a state of bemusement, watched Needham turn his back on us and leave the room, I had realized all at once that this was the same person as I had seen walking quickly away in the ash spinney, the man who had begun to climb up the rungs in the tree before being disturbed by the imminent arrival of Pearson and his dog. The surprise I felt at this realization must have shown on my face, for Blake raised his eyebrow, an expression of curiosity on his features.

"What is it, Watson?" he asked in a low tone.

"Never mind," I replied. "I'll tell you later."

A few moments later, Needham returned with a slim book in his hand, which he passed to Blake.

"I imagine this is the volume your cousin was thinking of," he remarked, "but, as you can see, this copy is mine."

Blake showed me the front of the book, then opened it at the first page. On the right-hand side was a book-plate, printed with an elaborate border of curving, twining lines and little flowers, and the words *"Ex Libris"*, under which, written in a neat and precise hand, was the name 'Matthias Needham'.

"I have tried to get hold of a copy of this little volume for myself," said Blake, addressing Needham, "but no-one seems to have one. Can you remember where you got this one from?"

"I forget the name of the dealer," replied Needham. "It is some years ago, now. It was one of those who advertise occasionally in *The Times*, offering to search for any book you name."

"Would you mind if I borrowed it for a few days?" asked Blake.

There was a look of hesitation on Needham's face. "Not at all," he replied, "under normal circumstances. However, I am, as it happens, using the book at the moment in connection with some historical research I am engaged in, so I would rather hang on to it just for the moment, if you don't mind."

"I understand perfectly," said Blake. "Perhaps another time, then,"

"Certainly."

"That reminds me," continued Blake: "you don't know anything about Mr Stannard's grandfather's note-book, do you? That's something else I can't find, and Mr Stannard thought you might have borrowed that, too, but he can't quite remember."

Needham shook his head. "I don't know anything about that," he said. "Perhaps Mr Stannard has simply forgotten where he put it. I believe he is a little absent-minded sometimes. What is in this note-book, anyway?"

"Some ideas about Samuel Harley's puzzles, I believe, among other things. Never mind. It's probably in the Grange somewhere. I only asked you on the off-chance that you might know where it was."

"I'm sorry I can't help you," said Needham with another shake of the head.

"We'll leave you to your historical research, then," said Blake in an amiable tone, rising to his feet.

A minute later, Blake and I had left Abbeyfield House and were crossing the top of the large sloping field towards the ash spinney.

"You appeared surprised about something when we were in the house," said Blake as we walked along. "What was that?"

I glanced back to make sure that we could not be observed from Needham's house, and that there was no-one behind us. "You remember I told you I saw a man in the spinney yesterday – not Pearson, the other one?"

"What, the man who started to climb the tree, but then hurried off when he saw Pearson approaching?"

"Precisely. I now know who that man was. It was Needham."

Blake stopped. "What!" he cried. "Are you sure?"

"I'm certain of it. It was when Needham turned away from us to go and fetch that book. I realized as I saw his back that it was he: the figure and the gait were precisely the same as those of the man I had seen walking away in the spinney."

"So," said Blake, "he obviously knows all about the platform up the tree. I don't suppose he was carrying a telescope by any chance?"

"I don't think so. he didn't appear to be carrying anything, as far as I could see. He might have had a pair of field-glasses slung round his neck, I suppose – I couldn't tell, as he was walking away from me when I saw him."

"Where does that leave us, I wonder," said Blake, stroking his chin.

"I don't know," I said, "but I'll tell you something else."

"What is that?"

"That local history-book he showed us: I'm convinced that he was lying, and it really was your cousin's copy."

"What makes you think so?"

"The book-plate. Didn't you notice anything odd about it?"

"Not that I can recall."

"It was not placed centrally on the page. In fact, it was not symmetrical at all. It was rather high up the page, and offset to the right. To judge from that room in which we were sitting as we waited for him, I surmise that Needham is a man who has a strong, almost fussy inclination with regard to neatness, order and symmetry. I cannot imagine he would have gummed in the book-plate in such an unsatisfactorily asymmetrical manner unless he had a good reason for doing so."

"Such as?"

"I suspect he placed it where he did in order to cover up something that was already written on the page – the owner's name, for instance."

"That certainly sounds plausible," said Blake. "How very observant of you!"

"Of course," I continued, "even if I'm right as to his motive in placing the book-plate where he did, the inscription he has deliberately covered up might not necessarily be that of Mr Stannard's father or grandfather. Needham claims to have acquired the book from a second-hand book-dealer. If that were true, the name beneath the book-plate might be that of a total stranger. But he did seem oddly reluctant to let you borrow the book – almost as if he feared we might take the opportunity to steam his book-plate off and find the name of Stannard beneath it."

Blake nodded. "Yes, I agree. He certainly seemed strangely mean about it. What the significance of that might be, though, I don't know." He shook his head in a gesture of puzzlement. "Anyway, Watson, now I'll tell *you* something."

"What do you mean?"

"Needham told us a bare-faced lie when he pretended to know nothing about Mr Stannard's grandfather's note-book. He asked what was in it, as if he had no idea of its content, but – if you recall – Mr Stannard specifically mentioned that he had shown the note-book to Needham, and said he had been very interested in it. They cannot both be right; one of them is not speaking the truth, and I know which of the two I am more inclined to believe."

"I quite agree, I shall have to make a note of all this to tell Holmes when he returns."

"I wonder what he will make of it," said Blake, as we resumed our progress through the ash spinney.

"I can't imagine," I said. "I just hope he returns soon, to perhaps impose a little light and order on things that I confess seem only dark and chaotic to me at present."

On our return to the Grange, we found that a telegram had been delivered for me while we were out. I opened it eagerly, and scanned the brief message, which ran as follows:

INQUEST ADJOURNED AS EXPECTED.
RETURN DELAYED.
WILL WRITE AGAIN SOON – S. H.

"That is disappointing," said Blake. "I had hoped he might get back this evening. I wonder what has delayed him, and whether it is anything to do with my case, or something completely different."

"We can only guess," I returned, "and, having had some experience of Holmes's mysterious ways, I can tell you that our guesses are unlikely to be anywhere near the truth!"

That evening, the Caxtons had left us a meal of cold meats and salads, as they had been given the evening off. A challenge match had been arranged between the skittles team of the Royal Oak and a team from another village. I could see from Caxton's manner as they set off that he was still affected by the death of his old crony, Brookfield, but Blake informed me that nothing short of a foreign invasion would have prevented Caxton from turning out for the team.

"Does he always take his wife with him?" I asked.

Blake shook his head with a chuckle. "Not usually," he replied; "but these occasional challenge matches between the villages are a different matter. The men generally do all the playing, but it's a great social occasion for the ladies, too, who spend their time exchanging local gossip and cheering on their menfolk!"

As we ate our supper, I heard the rain begin to fall heavily again outside. Afterwards, Blake, Whitemoor and I repaired to the drawing-room, where the maid brought us a pot of coffee, and we sat smoking our pipes and discussing and debating the most significant scientific inventions of the previous two centuries. Later, we had several hands of cards. This was entertaining enough, but I found it difficult to keep my mind on the game. Time after time, when it was my turn to play, I would find that my thoughts had wandered off from this trivial pastime to the more substantial question of the vague and nebulous mysteries that seemed to surround us there at Foxwood Grange.

Some time after nine, when the light had quite gone, we all felt that we could do with a little refreshment, but could not at first think what to have.

"I certainly don't want any more coffee," I said. "That last lot was rather strong. If I have any more, I'll never get to sleep tonight."

Blake nodded. "It scarcely seems worth opening a fresh bottle of wine," he remarked. "I know," he cried, with a sudden rush of enthusiasm: "I'll make us all a hot toddy!"

"That sounds a somewhat wintry suggestion!" said Whitemoor.

"Perhaps so," said Blake, "but I think it's justified by this very heavy rain!" He glanced at the clock. "Ann will be in bed by now – I told her to take herself off when she'd put the plates away – and, if past experience is anything to go by, Mr and Mrs Caxton will not be back for another forty or fifty minutes. Fortunately, however, I know a good recipe, involving Scotch Whisky, hot water, half a lemon and a spoonful of honey."

"It sounds like what I generally prescribe for a sore throat!" I said, laughing.

"No doubt; but it's a tasty recipe, as you will see, Watson. If either of you finds it a bit on the strong side, you can let it down with a little more hot water. Come along, gentlemen! Let's re-kindle the kitchen fire and get the kettle on the hob, and then you'll see what a good nightcap it is!"

We had left the drawing-room and were making our way to the kitchen, at the back of the house, when Blake abruptly stopped. "What was that?" he said.

"It sounded a bit like a footstep," I said, "but it was probably just the rain dripping onto something. The rain sounds very loud here in the hall."

"No, no," said Blake with a frown and a shake of the head. "That wasn't just the rain, Watson. I'm sure it was a footstep."

"It certainly sounded like one," said Whitemoor, "outside, in the yard."

We hurried forward, and into "the long gallery" at the back of the house. It was very dark, but I could see at once that one of the casement windows was wide open and swinging in the wind, which explained why the noise of the rain had seemed so loud in the hall.

Blake struck a match and lit a sconce on the wall, and it was evident that the rain had been coming in through the open window for some time, for the rush matting immediately below the window was sodden.

"It's very odd that this window should have been left open," said Blake.

"This rain seems to have come with quite a wind," I said. "Perhaps the window wasn't properly fastened, or just slightly ajar, and the wind blew it wide open."

"We'll get it shut now, anyhow," said Blake, then he stopped again. "What was that?" he said sharply.

"It sounded like someone moving about upstairs," I said.

"I agree," said Blake. "Let us take a look." With a bound, he set off up the narrow back stairs, Whitemoor and I following closely behind him.

We reached the first landing in a few seconds, where Blake struck another match and lit a lamp on the wall. There was no-one there. For a moment we stood perfectly still, our ears straining to catch any sound, but the whole house was in utter silence.

"Let's have a quick look in all the rooms," said Blake, lifting the lamp from its hook. This we did, but found no-one there.

"I think the sound of the footstep – if that is what it was – may have come from higher up," I said.

Blake nodded his agreement, and we set off up the next flight of stairs. The upper landing, which was much smaller, was as silent and deserted as the lower landing had been, and though we prowled around for a few minutes, looked in the rooms and followed a long corridor along to a box-room at the other end, we found nothing.

"That is Ann's bedroom straight ahead," said Blake, as we returned to the landing. "She can't be long in bed. Let's see if she's still awake. If she is, she may have heard something."

"And if she's asleep," I said, "someone might have slipped into the room without her knowing."

Blake tapped on the door and pushed it open. It was a small room, right under the roof of the house, with a steeply sloping ceiling. Immediately ahead of us, illuminated by the lamp Blake was carrying, was a bed, whose occupant sat up abruptly as we entered, the sheets pulled up to her chin and a startled expression on her face. I had a quick glance round the room, as Blake addressed her.

"I'm sorry to disturb you, Ann," said he. "We thought we heard a noise up here. Were you asleep?"

"Not quite, sir."

"Did you hear anything?"

"No, sir. Only the creaking of the floor."

"How long have you been in bed?"

"About ten minutes, sir."

Blake glanced to the side. The little bedroom window that overlooked the back of the house was open, and rattling in the wind. "This rain has made the night a chilly one," he remarked. "Would you like me to close your window?"

"Yes, sir," said the girl. "It seems to be rattling more now than when I got into bed. Perhaps it's because the door's open."

"Here, I'll do it," I said, stepping to the window. It was certainly a dark and tempestuous night outside, and for a second, as I had my hand on the window-latch, I gazed out into the darkness. As I did so, I had the impression, just for an instant, that there was some movement, down in the yard behind the house. I pulled the window shut without saying anything about this. I didn't want to frighten the girl unnecessarily, and, besides, I could not be certain that I had really seen anything.

As the three of us descended the stair, Blake shook his head. "I don't know what to make of it," said he. "Perhaps, after all, the noises we heard were just the old floorboards creaking. It's been so hot and dry lately that the wood will have shrunk, I suppose, and this heavy rain and the cold air it's brought with it might have been just enough to cause the wood to expand again slightly. It certainly doesn't take much to get these old timbers creaking and groaning, as I know from past experience. Perhaps, if we're being strictly scientific in our approach, we should move this incident out of the column containing the stone-throwing and other things, and into the column headed 'natural occurrences'."

"And yet," I said, "we cannot be sure." I told Blake and Whitemoor then that I thought I had seen something, or somebody, moving about in the yard, as I was shutting the maid's bedroom window. "Of course," I said, "I cannot say for certain that I saw anything at all. When one is in a state of heightened awareness, it is well known that one's own imagination can make something out of nothing."

"That is true," said Blake. "But if there really was an intruder in the house, he could have hidden in a dark corner somewhere downstairs, and then when we went up the staircase, made his escape into the back yard. I don't think we examined the door in the long gallery, to see if it was locked."

"I'll soon remedy that omission," I said as we reached the ground floor. "It's locked," I continued as I tried the door-handle.

"It's bolted on the inside, too," observed Whitemoor. "So no-one has left that way."

"But look," I said. "This window that was wide open is still not fully closed. You set off at such a lick up the stairs, Blake, that you put it on the peg, but never finished closing it properly. It's certainly big enough for anybody to climb out of it easily."

Blake nodded and appeared to be about to make some remark about the window, when he abruptly stopped. "What's that by your foot, Watson?" said he. "I didn't notice that before."

I followed his gaze and saw that just by my boot, near the edge of the rush matting, where there were a few old leaves and other small bits of clutter that had probably blown in at some time when the door was open, there was a tiny slip of paper, about two inches long by an inch wide. I picked it up and examined it.

"It might just be something of ours," said Whitemoor to Blake. "I sometimes use slips of paper like that to keep my place in a book, or to remind me of something I need to look up. Is there anything written on it, Dr Watson?"

I nodded. "All it says is 'shrub'," I said, as I showed it to the others.

"That doesn't mean anything to me," Blake remarked after a moment. "And it's not my writing, nor yours, Whitemoor, is it?"

The young man shook his head. "Perhaps it's something Mr Caxton wrote to remind himself to do something in the garden," he suggested.

Blake nodded. "I suppose that seems most likely," he said, but his features expressed doubt. "The trouble is," he continued, "that it's not Caxton's handwriting, either. In any case, I can't really see Caxton bothering to write 'shrub' on a piece of paper – it's not the way he does things! What do you think, Watson?"

"I have no idea," I said. "It could have blown in here from anywhere and is probably of no importance whatsoever; but I'll hang on to it for the moment, anyway."

I slipped the scrap of paper between the pages of my note-book, as we followed Blake into the kitchen. There, he threw a few sticks onto the glowing embers of the fire, put the kettle on the hob and began to mix up the ingredients for the hot toddy. When all was ready, we carried our drinks back to the drawing-room, filled our pipes, played a few more hands of cards and scarcely mentioned again the strange interlude that had disturbed our evening.

Later, however, as I lay in bed, listening to the rain pattering against the window, I went over the matter again in my mind. Had we really heard footsteps, either downstairs or upstairs? If we had not, and the sounds we had heard were simply the rain and the creaking timbers of the old house, why, then, had the window in the "long gallery" been unfastened and standing wide open? What, if anything, was the significance of that little slip of paper with the word "shrub" written upon it? There had been something about that paper which had been nagging away at the back of my mind ever since we had found it. Now, all at once, an idea came to me.

I struck a match and lit the candle on my bedside table, then leaned over to where my jacket hung on a nearby chair and extracted my note-book from the inside pocket. I took out the little slip of paper and examined it again, by the light of the candle. Yes, I was surely right! I still had no idea what it might mean, but I was convinced I now at least knew who had written it. The style of writing was identical to the style in which

Matthias Needham had written his name on the book-plate in the book of local history he had showed us earlier that day. Why he had written "shrub", I could not imagine; how the paper had ended up at Foxwood Grange, I could not imagine; but that Needham had written it, I now had no doubt.

12: ENCOUNTER IN THE WOODS

WHEN I DESCENDED TO BREAKFAST the following morning, it was to find a scene of hustle and bustle. Blake had already finished his own breakfast and was preparing to leave for the railway station.

"Caxton is bringing the trap round now," said he to me. "I have to leave in the next few minutes if I'm to catch the train. I'm sorry to leave you at a loose end, Watson, but it can't be helped. I'll conclude my business in London as quickly as I can, and if I can get an early afternoon train I should be back by tea-time. Perhaps Mr Holmes will have returned by then. Who knows?" he added with a smile.

"Indeed," I responded. "Who knows?"

I had heard the rattle of the trap outside the front door as Blake was speaking, and a moment later he was gone. I finished my breakfast in the company of young Whitemoor, and we discussed the subjects that Blake would be tackling next.

"We're staying on the subject of railways for the moment," said Whitemoor. "The next thing Mr Blake wishes to do is a survey of the history and development of railway signalling, for *The Popular Railway Magazine*. Originally, it wasn't going to be needed for another couple of months, but as he has had to write the article on braking systems earlier than expected, he thought he had best get on with the signalling article as well, in case that, too, is required earlier than planned. It's not particularly technical or scientific, simply a broad survey, but it means I've got to look up every reference to signalling that I can find in books and journals. As you may know, Mr Blake is very thorough, and would not wish to omit any interesting thread in the complicated tangle of the subject, however slight its contribution to the general development of signalling may have been."

"Best of luck with that, then," I remarked with a chuckle, thinking of the mountainous piles of technical journals on the floor in Blake's study.

After breakfast, I took a stroll in the garden. The rain had passed on, but had left the garden looking drenched and sodden. The sky was still a cloudy one, but there was a brisk breeze in the air which seemed likely to blow the clouds away in an hour or two, and the day was already beginning to warm up. For no particular reason, I ambled through the side-gate into the large field belonging to Ashton which lay next to the garden, and from which someone had hurled stones at us on Monday evening. As I stood there, surveying the view, I saw that there was someone standing at the very bottom end of the field. As far as I could make out at that distance, it did not appear to be Ashton himself, but I thought it might be his son, Giles, so I gave a little wave. He did not appear to have seen me, however, as at the very moment I raised my arm he turned away, passed through a gate into a little wood and vanished from my sight.

I returned to my bedroom to look again through my note-book and the sheaves of papers lying upon the writing-table, to try to bring my reports for Sherlock Holmes up to date. So much seemed to have happened in the two days since that sunny morning I had watched my friend walk off briskly down the drive to the railway station. Much of what had happened may have been trivial and unimportant, but as I did not understand the nature of the mystery which surrounded Farringdon Blake, I could not judge with any confidence what was important and what was not. All I could do was ensure that my records were as thorough and detailed as possible, and hope that Holmes would find something in them to assist him in forming his view of the matter.

As I opened my note-book, the little slip of paper bearing the single word "shrub" fell out onto the floor. I bent down and picked it up, thinking as I did so that I had had no opportunity before Blake left that morning to give him my opinion, that the hand that wrote it was that of Matthias Needham. For some time I sat, pondering the matter. Before I had formed the conviction that Needham had written it, I had been inclined to dismiss the paper as probably of no consequence; now I felt rather differently about it. Now I was sure it must have some significance, although what, I could not begin to imagine. Still, I would make a record of where we had found it, and the circumstances which had surrounded our finding it, and see if Holmes could make anything of it.

My mind ran on from the slip of paper to the footsteps we thought we had heard the previous evening. It is always difficult to be certain what it is you are hearing when rain is falling heavily and is at the same time dripping from the gutters, but, as I tried to recreate the sounds in my mind, I remained convinced that I had indeed heard footsteps in the yard behind the house. As to the other footsteps – the ones I thought I had heard within the house itself – I was not so sure. Perhaps, after all, they were simply the old house's timbers creaking with the sudden change in the weather. Perhaps after I had heard footsteps outside – or, thought I had, at any rate – I had been predisposed to interpret subsequent sounds in the same way.

There was a lot for me to record, and it took me until lunchtime to get it all down in a way that satisfied me. As Whitemoor and I took lunch together in the dining-room, there came a ring at the front-door bell. A moment later, the maid entered with a telegram for me. I tore it open and read the following message:

RETURNING TOMORROW.
BELIEVE MAY HAVE
SOLVED HARLEY PUZZLE.   S. H.

"Can it really be true?" said Whitemoor, an expression of astonishment on his features. "Can Mr Holmes really have solved the puzzle that has baffled generations?"

"He only says he 'may' have solved it," I pointed out, "although knowing Holmes as I do, I don't think he would have made even so cautious a claim as that unless he were pretty confident about the matter. His caution may be simply because he has a theory about the puzzle which he wishes to put to the test when he returns. He is every bit as scientific in his outlook as Mr Blake, and would not wish to claim success before he had subjected his theory to the most stringent of practical tests. I must say I am looking forward to hearing his thoughts on the matter!"

"Yes," said Whitemoor. "It is an exciting prospect! I am rather sorry I shall be away when Mr Holmes returns."

"You are going to visit your mother?"

"Yes. I shall have to leave tomorrow morning – I always go on a Friday – but I should be back on Sunday, all being well. I, too, am certainly very keen to hear Mr Holmes's conclusions."

"Then I shall make sure that he repeats his explanation for your benefit when you return," I said with a chuckle. "Whether his theory turns out to be right or wrong, his reasoning is bound to be instructive!"

After lunch, I decided to take another walk over the nearby fields and woods. The sky had almost cleared, the wind had dropped and the sun was shining, and as I set off I was struck anew by the beauty of the countryside, refreshed as it was by the recent rains. What I had in mind was to explore the woods over by Black Bank House, the residence of Professor Crook. The last time I had been over that way, earlier in the week, I had run across the professor's secretary, Dr Taylor, near the house, and, to avoid seeming to intrude upon their privacy, I had abandoned my explorations and left the wood. What I now hoped to do was to follow the path right through the wood and take a look at the countryside beyond. That, at least, would have been my stated aim had anyone asked me, but, if I am honest, I must admit I also hoped to get a good look at Black Bank House itself, something which had been denied to me on the previous occasion.

As had become my habit, I made my way up Ashton's field, through the end of the ash spinney and down through

Pearson's field on the other side of the hill. There was no-one about, and it seemed, as on the previous occasion I had come this way, that I had the whole of the countryside to myself. At the foot of Pearson's field I crossed the Thuxton road and entered the woods beyond. The trees were very tall and growing closely together, and their foliage was so dense, that even on what was now a sunny day the wood was a very shady one. As I made my way deeper into the wood, however, I found that there were some places where the sun managed to penetrate the canopy of the trees, and in these brighter spots the undergrowth was luxuriant, although it seemed to consist largely of stinging nettles and brambles. I followed a winding, slightly rising track between the trees, making a random choice each time I came to a fork in the path. There did not seem to be much bird-life in these woods, I noted, and, save only my own footsteps on the soft woodland floor, a deathly blanket of silence and stillness seemed to hang over everything.

At length, the way ahead grew a little lighter, the trees thinned, and I emerged from the wood into bright sunlight. In the field ahead of me, a healthy-looking cereal crop was growing and beginning to change its colour from the fresh green of the spring to the mature yellowish-brown of the summer. A little way along the edge of the field was a fallen tree which made a convenient seat, and there I sat, filled my pipe and let my mind wander over all that had happened recently.

Sherlock Holmes had considered it a distinct possibility, at the outset of the case, that one of Farringdon Blake's neighbours was involved in the mysterious events that had surrounded him, chiefly because only someone who had lived in the district for some time could know of the rungs up the ash-tree and the opportunity the viewing-platform presented for spying on the Grange. But I had now met, if only briefly, all of Blake's immediate neighbours, and most of them, whatever their other good and bad points might be, seemed unlikely to have had anything to do with the mystery. The one possible exception, of course, was Mr Needham of Abbeyfield House. I was convinced that it was Needham I had seen in the ash spinney when I had been sitting on the platform up the tree, and who had made himself scarce very quickly as Pearson and his dog approached. I also suspected that Needham had indeed stolen the book of local history from the Grange, as Mr Stannard had suspected. But what did any of this mean? After all, having met him, I could not really believe that it was Needham who had been trying to climb into the Grange through a window in the "long gallery" the previous evening. Nor could I believe that it was he who had thrown a large stone at us as we sat out in the garden on Monday evening, for what possible reason could he have had? Of course, Holmes had speculated that the stone-thrower had been Mrs Booth's husband, but he seemed to me scarcely more likely to be the culprit than Needham. After all, there was no evidence that he had even been in the area on the night in question. I sighed. There must, I thought, be a solution to all these mysteries – after all, in scientific terms, there was an explanation of some sort for everything that ever occurred – but what it might be, I really could not imagine.

After perhaps fifteen minutes, I put my pipe away, rose to my feet and re-entered the wood. I did not follow the same path back, however, but at every fork in the way, took the opportunity to make my way leftwards, to the eastern end of the wood, which is where Black Bank House was situated. At one point, the path I was on came to a dead end, or, at least, was effectively blocked by enormous banks of stinging nettles, about four feet tall, on either side, which had leaned over the path so much as to unite in one impenetrable mass. I was just retracing my steps, to try to find a way round this obstruction, when I heard voices, as of a number of people approaching.

I stopped and listened, as the voices grew louder. Then, off to the right, through the trees, I saw two men and a woman coming my way, whom I recognized at once as Professor Crook and his two companions. They had evidently been for one of their customary walks and were making their way back home.

"Yes, of course it is!" I heard Professor Crook cry in a loud, irritable tone of voice. "It is perfectly obvious; I have explained it all already!" Dr Taylor made some reply, but in a lower tone, which I could not catch.

As they spoke, they reached a point on a path parallel to my own which was close to where I was standing. It was clear they had not seen me, and I felt a little uncomfortable to be standing there in silence, as if I were eavesdropping upon their conversation. I therefore made a move to return the way I had come. At once, Professor Crook turned my way and stared at me. Then he turned back to Dr Taylor and cried out.

"See!" he cried, in a loud, belligerent tone. "It is as I say! There is your proof! This is what I have to put up with!" Then, without further warning, he left the path and at a great rate plunged through the shallow undergrowth towards me. So startled was I by this sudden rapid approach that, for a moment,

I could neither move nor speak. "Hargreaves!" he cried out. "You devil!" Next moment, with tremendous force, he ran into me so violently that he knocked me to the ground. An instant later, his hands were around my neck with a grip like a vice and his thumbs were pressing into my throat.

Quite what happened then remains something of a blur in my memory. In vain I struggled to pull his hands from my throat. In vain I aimed a blow at his face which he easily avoided. As we struggled on the ground, I saw the figure of Dr Taylor loom up behind my assailant, then the woman I took to be Crook's wife pushed her way past him. As she did so, she produced some kind of wooden baton from a pocket in her skirts. A second later she had brought it down with great force on the back of Crook's head. The grip upon my throat abruptly slackened as his hands went limp, and he collapsed, insensible, on the path beside me.

For a moment I lay there, breathing heavily and scarcely understanding what was happening. Then Dr Taylor was bending over me and asking me if I was all right, in a voice full of contrition and sympathy. I murmured something, then he held out his hand to help me to my feet.

"I am terribly sorry about this," he said. "Are you sure you are all right?"

"I will be in a moment," I replied, dusting myself down. "What on earth got into Professor Crook? Why should he attack me? I have never even met him before."

Dr Taylor glanced down at the senseless figure stretched out upon the path. "I hesitate to ask," he began after a moment, "but I wonder if you would do me a favour? If you would help us get the professor back to the house," he continued, as I looked at him in surprise, "I will explain everything to you, and you will realize that what has happened does not reflect on you personally in any way."

"Very well," I said, somewhat reluctantly.

Between the three of us we lifted Professor Crook and carried him by winding pathways back to Black Bank House. As we passed through the gateway between the high hedges which surrounded the garden, I saw that the house was similar to Needham's, solid-looking and square but not especially attractive.

We deposited Professor Crook on a sofa in one of the downstairs rooms, and Dr Taylor bent over and examined him closely, removing the professor's jacket and rolling up his shirt sleeve. Then, taking a slim box from his pocket, and extracting from it a hypodermic syringe, he injected half the contents into the professor's arm.

"He will sleep now for about two hours," Taylor remarked, turning to me. "When he awakes he will remember nothing of what happened in the wood."

"You are a medical man?" I asked in surprise. "I had rather assumed you had a doctorate in astronomy or some related subject."

Dr Taylor nodded his head. "I am aware that people in these parts have taken me to be a scientific colleague of Professor Crook's. I have made no effort to correct that impression for reasons that I will explain in a moment."

"I am a little concerned for the professor even if he did attack me," I remarked. "The blow he sustained appeared quite a severe one."

"I think he will be all right," returned Taylor. "It may have appeared to you to be very violent treatment, but Miss Dawes really had little choice. He would not have stopped until he had throttled the life out of you. Come, let us go to the other room, and I will tell you all about it."

We left Professor Crook in the care of the woman, and Dr Taylor led the way to a room across the hall.

"Do you know anything of Professor Crook's academic career?" he asked me as he closed the door. "No?" he continued as I shook my head. "I will tell you then that it was a brilliant one. In his field, his name is known and honoured throughout the world. His publications are practically countless, and almost every one of them is regarded as the last word on the topic it addresses.

"In his latter years at Cambridge, however, and quite unknown to the wider world, his character underwent an odd transformation and he became secretive in his manner and suspicious of others. At first, this alteration in his previously open and generous manner was slight, and passed unnoticed. As time went by, however, these tendencies became more marked and he became convinced that others were spying upon him, trying to steal his ideas and take for themselves the recognition that he considered should be his. Eventually, the situation deteriorated so much that his relatives became seriously concerned, not least because a tinge of violence had now entered the behaviour of this previously mild-mannered man. He had taken to carrying a sharp knife about with him in his jacket pocket. This he showed to some of his academic colleagues, and to his relatives – who were all, of course, horrified – declaring that he was 'more than ready' to deal with his enemies should they attack him or attempt to steal his research."

"He appeared to address me as 'Hargreaves', when we were in the wood," I interjected. "Is that the name of some academic rival of his whom he distrusted?"

"Such a mistake would be bad enough," replied Taylor with a shake of the head, "but in fact it is even worse than that. The truth is, there is no such person as 'Hargreaves'. He does not exist except in Professor Crook's own head. Where he plucked the name from, I have no idea. Perhaps he chanced to see it on a shop-front one day and it stuck in his memory for some reason. Who can say? Whatever the origin of the name, this non-existent 'Hargreaves' soon became the focus of all the professor's suspicion and hatred. By this time, it was clear that he was suffering from what might be termed a persecution mania, as was now recognized by his relatives and by his doctor in Cambridge.

"At length it was decided that both for his own good and for that of others, the best thing would be to remove him from the hustle and bustle of the university to somewhere peaceful and quiet, where he could perhaps continue his scientific work without interruption, and under the watchful eye of an experienced medical man. As someone who has had great experience of such mental diseases, I was honoured to be appointed by Professor Crook's family to that position. Miss

Dawes – the woman you saw with us in the woods – is a nurse who has also had great experience in such cases."

"Did the professor's sequestration have the desired effect?" I asked.

"At first, certainly. He adapted to his new surroundings very quickly and spent long hours at his desk, preparing a great work which would sum up all his opinions and all his theories in one large volume. At the same time, I encouraged him to take frequent walks in the countryside, as I have found physical exercise and fresh air to be beneficial in such cases. After a time, however, the occasions when the suspicious and sometimes violent side of the professor's character were manifest began to occur more frequently. I had learnt to predict such episodes from a certain increased agitation in his manner, but occasionally they took me quite by surprise. One day, for instance, without warning, and for no apparent reason, he attacked me with a carving-knife he had taken from the kitchen. As it turned out, I was not badly hurt, but I easily could have been. This is my souvenir of the occasion," he continued, showing me the back of his right hand, across which ran an ugly scar. "As a result of that, we have had to hide all the knives, and watch carefully to see that the professor does not take any cutlery from the dining-table.

"Now," Dr Taylor continued after a moment with a shake of the head, "I am really not sure how much longer we can continue in this fashion. The professor's attacks of mania are becoming more frequent with each week that passes. Several times I have found him standing on a stool, looking in some high cupboard, in the kitchen or elsewhere, and have suspected he was looking for a knife or something else he could use as a weapon. On top of these problems, he isn't really managing to write very much any more, even in his most calm and lucid periods."

"What is it you discuss when you are out on your walks together?" I asked. "I have heard that the conversations always appear very intense ones, and Mr Blake has assumed you were discussing the professor's theories on astronomical matters."

Dr Taylor shook his head. "If only it were so," said he. "What we discuss most of the time these days are the professor's theories about 'Hargreaves' or his supposed agents: what, according to his theories, they are plotting to do next, and so on. Sometimes it is utter gibberish. I used to try to dismiss his anxieties and tell him he was worrying about nothing, but now I generally tend to go along with them, for I have found that if I disagree with him too bluntly he becomes very angry and is likely to launch a physical attack upon me."

"I understand," I said. "Does the professor ever go out alone?"

"He used to, occasionally. I would sometimes leave him working in his study, only to find later that he had climbed out of the window and gone off somewhere. He always came back eventually, but, of course, I never knew where he had been or what he had been doing in the meantime. Eventually, I felt obliged to secure the window, which I did by banging a large nail through the bottom of it, into the frame. But when Professor Crook discovered this, he showed it to me as evidence that Hargreaves's agents were getting closer and plotting to trap him in the study while they robbed the house. He claimed he had heard them running past the house in the night-time and had wondered what they were up to, but now, he said, he knew. The other day, when you and I met in the woods, the professor had tricked me, and while I was looking for a pencil he said he had lost, he ran off, out of the front door. I found him a few minutes later, wandering aimlessly in the woods. He told me he had got lost, and accompanied me peacefully back to the house."

I nodded, and expressed sympathy for the difficulty in which Dr Taylor found himself. "Incidentally," I said, as if I had just remembered something, "does Professor Crook have a telescope?"

"What an odd question!" returned Taylor in surprise. "As a matter of fact, he does, although I don't know what he has done with it, as I haven't seen it for a while. Why do you ask?"

"It was just something that crossed my mind," I replied, not very honestly. "Mr Blake was wishing the other day that he had one, to look at something in the night sky. It might have been the moons of Jupiter, although I can't quite remember. Anyway, it doesn't matter; it's not important."

I thanked Dr Taylor for sharing his confidences with me and wished him well in his thankless task of watching over Professor Crook. He in turn apologized profusely for what had happened.

"If I could beg a favour," he said, as we shook hands on the doorstep.

"Certainly," I returned. "What is it?"

"You will of course wish to inform your friends at the Grange of what has happened. But I should be very obliged if you did not pass on the information to anyone else in the district, at least for the present."

"You have my word," I said.

As I walked back to the Grange, I reflected on the afternoon's events. My visit to north Oxfordshire was certainly proving a surprising one, but whether Professor Crook's mental illness had any bearing on Farringdon Blake's mystery, I had no idea. I had established that Crook had sometimes left the house by himself and stayed out for some time. I had also established that he had a telescope. Were these facts of any significance or not? I had no way of telling.

By the time I reached the Grange, I realized that I was quite exhausted. My brow was wet with sweat, and it was clear that my body had succumbed to that physical weakness which had afflicted me intermittently ever since my return from the war in Afghanistan. I therefore retired to my bedroom, where I lay on the bed, closed my eyes, and slipped swiftly into the deepest of sleeps.

When I awoke, much refreshed, Farringdon Blake had returned. I told him of the telegram I had received from Holmes, and asked him how he had fared in London. Then he, Whitemoor and I sat for some time in general light-hearted conversation. I had wondered whether I should perhaps hold back until Holmes returned the news of my encounter with Professor Crook in the woods and what I had subsequently learnt about him, but in the end, when supper was concluded, I decided I would tell them. Both Blake and Whitemoor were shocked at what had happened, although I stressed that I was none the worse for it. They were also shocked, of course, to hear of the terrible mental deterioration with which Professor Crook was afflicted.

"Poor fellow!" cried Blake. "I am very sorry to hear that, but it at least explains why Dr Taylor won't let anyone see him, which is something that had always troubled me."

I nodded. "I hope Holmes is not too late back tomorrow," I said. "I can scarcely wait to tell him all that has happened since he left. We seem to have had several weeks-worth of events packed into just a couple of days!"

"It will be interesting to see what Mr Holmes makes of any of it," said Whitemoor.

Blake nodded his head in agreement. "Yes," said he, "and I am also very much looking forward to hearing Holmes's thoughts on Samuel Harley's riddle."

13: SHERLOCK HOLMES DISCOURSES

AT THE BREAKFAST-TABLE the following morning, after Whitemoor had left us to make his way to the railway station, Farringdon Blake declared himself to be in "a lazy frame of mind".

"I don't think I shall do any work today," said he with a yawn. "Yesterday I delivered a lengthy article on railway braking systems to one journal, an article on Pythagoras's theorem to another, and a third, on the general pattern of winds around the world, which I prepared last week, to another, so there is nothing immediately pressing that I have to attend to. I get very few such free days from one month's end to the next, so I think I shall make the most of this one. I have a few small tidying-up jobs to do in the study, but after that there is nothing I would rather do than give you a guided tour of the garden. What would you say to that, Watson? There are, I believe, some parts of it that you have not yet seen."

"There is nothing I should like better," I replied. "Now we know that Holmes is returning some time today, I feel at something of a loose end. There is nothing in particular that I wish to do, either, so a leisurely tour of the gardens would be ideal."

An hour later, therefore, the two of us made our way, with many a detour to terraces and quaint corners I had not seen before, by winding paths and stone steps towards the bottom of the garden. There, Blake showed me a little spring, which trickled down a low rock face and fed a small, reed-girt pool. On the other side of the pool was an old, lichen-covered stone wall, about six feet high, beyond which, as far as I could see, was a wood.

"That wall marks the boundary with Ashton's land," said Blake as we sat down on a wooden bench beside the pool and filled our pipes. "The wood is his, and his house is just the other side of it."

It was a pleasant, shady spot in which to sit on such a balmy summer's day, and for some time we remained in companionable silence, watching the little birds flitting in and out of the trees, and listening to the trickle of the spring into the pool.

"You certainly have some curious neighbours," I remarked at length, breaking the silence.

"That can scarcely be denied," returned Blake. "Did you have anyone in particular in mind?"

"I was just reflecting again on my encounter yesterday with Professor Crook and his household."

Blake nodded. "It sounds, to judge from what Dr Taylor told you yesterday, as if they have just about reached the end of their tether, and it won't be possible for Crook to stay there much longer."

"So I should say," I agreed. "It is certainly a sad state of affairs, but his family must face the reality. A potentially violent man cannot be allowed to go wandering off round the countryside by himself, however eminent he may be. In any case, it doesn't sound as if he is able to do much work or write anything much these days."

We discussed Crook further, and Blake told me of some of the professor's contributions to astronomical theory and practice over the years. Eventually, when we had exhausted the subject, Blake suggested we return to the house for a little late-morning refreshment.

"In the light of the latest information you gleaned from Dr Taylor yesterday," remarked Blake, as we made our way up the narrow, twisting paths of the garden, "I have been wondering if it was in fact Professor Crook who was spying on me through a telescope. He may have conceived the notion that I was in league with his imaginary enemy, Hargreaves, or even that I myself was Hargreaves."

"Indeed," I said, "although I doubt whether he could have been responsible for hiring that private detective to follow you about London."

"That is certainly a problem," agreed Blake, "unless, of course, someone else agreed to do it, to humour his delusions. I suppose we must accept that what Dr Taylor told you was all true – we have no reason to think otherwise – but it seems a little odd and unlikely to me that he should claim not to know where the professor's telescope is at the moment."

As he was speaking, we ascended a shallow flight of stone steps and came onto a grassy terrace, when Blake abruptly stopped. I followed his gaze. Off to the right, in a secluded bower, half-hidden by climbing roses, was a wooden bench which faced away from us, and upon that bench a man was sitting. I could make out very little of him other than a rural-looking soft cap of some sort and the left sleeve of a tweed jacket.

"Hello!" cried Blake, taking a step towards the bench. "Are you waiting for me?"

For a second there was no response, then the man sprang to his feet and turned to face us, and I saw that it was none other than Sherlock Holmes himself.

"Holmes!" I cried. "What are you doing here?"

"As a matter of fact, I was just examining the behaviour of some honey-bees on the flowers," returned Holmes. "I heard your approach, but it was so fascinating I found it difficult to tear myself away!"

"But we were not expecting you until some time this afternoon," said Blake in a tone of puzzlement. "How on earth did you manage to get back so early?"

"I came a different way," replied Holmes.

"Not to Rushfield station?"

"The station is irrelevant to my time of arrival, although, as it happens, I did not alight at Rushfield, but at the next stop on the line, Little Broadstone Halt."

"That would seem an odd choice," said Blake. "It is the other side of Thuxton, and quite a bit further to walk from there."

"Perhaps it is," responded Holmes, "but I had a particular reason to come *via* Little Broadstone. As a matter of fact, that is also the station I used when I left here the other day. Anyhow, I am here now, so, if we could postpone this discussion of trains and stations to a later time, I should very much like to get on with the matter in hand."

"I saw in the telegram you sent Dr Watson that you think you may have solved Samuel Harley's riddle," said Blake in a hesitant tone. "Of course, I was fascinated to hear that, but I was a little surprised that that was the main point of your telegram. I had understood from what you said when you were here before that you regarded the old puzzle as something of a recreation, which you might look at if you had any time to spare when not pursuing my own very current and pressing mystery. Might I ask if you have made any progress in the latter business?"

"I spoke lightly of Harley's riddle before for two reasons, Mr Blake. In the first place, I did not wish to raise hopes which I could not satisfy – some of these old riddles are the very devil to understand, let alone solve – and, in the second place, although I already suspected that Harley's puzzle might be connected to what you term the current mystery, I could not be certain. Now, however, it is clear to me that the two mysteries are indeed intimately connected, the threads of the one intertwined with the threads of the other. The reason I am so certain about this is because I have solved both mysteries, the current one and the hundred-year-old one. Before I explain it all to you, however, I wish to make sure I am in possession of all relevant information. Has anything of significance occurred in my absence?"

"You could say that," I replied with a chuckle. "I have been physically attacked twice, once by a dog and once by a man, and that is not all."

"Have you made a note of all these things, Watson?"

"I have made very detailed notes," I replied. "I have kept what amounts to a diary these last few days, and I am sure you will find it of interest."

"Where is this diary?"

"Such as it is – a note-book and a pile of loose foolscap sheets donated by Blake for the purpose – it is in my bedroom."

"Then let us waste no more time," said Holmes, turning and leading the way to the house. "If you will fetch your materials, Watson, I will seclude myself in the library for a little while and study it all."

Forty minutes later, Blake and I were sitting on the little terrace outside the French windows of the drawing-room, enjoying a cup of coffee, when Holmes joined us.

"Thank you, a cup of coffee would be most welcome," said he in answer to Blake's query. "Now, Watson," he continued, "I have read your diary with great care, and it is indeed most interesting! You have a decided gift for observation, which I don't think you fully recognize."

"It is kind of you to say so."

Holmes shook his head. "Not at all. It is not a mere empty compliment, but a statement of fact, and there is thus no kindness involved. I have remarked your powers of observation before when I have read other things you have written. Sometimes you compare yourself unfavourably to me and exaggerate my achievements in the field of deduction, but if I am indeed more accomplished than you are at deduction, it is often only because you are too timid in drawing conclusions from what you see before you. In the fundamental power of observation, you are arguably my equal, at least when circumstances – such as having to keep a diary for my benefit – push you into making an effort. Your reports in here," he continued, tapping the bundle of papers in his hand, "illustrate the matter perfectly."

"What do you mean?"

"I mean that you have recorded numerous interesting facts, with great clarity of expression, and yet you have failed to draw the inferences that the facts suggest."

"I have gone over and over those events in my mind," I responded, "but, save only the belief that Needham did indeed purloin Mr Stannard's book, have been unable to reach any conclusions."

"Very well. Let us look at one particular incident, then, the mystery of the footsteps you heard the night before last, which you describe so very vividly. As I understand it from your report, the three of you – you, Blake and Whitemoor – were making your way down the back hall towards the kitchen. The noise of the rain seemed unusually loud – a circumstance subsequently explained by your discovery of the open window – when all three of you thought you heard a footstep, outside in the cobbled yard. Am I correct so far?"

"Precisely so."

"Then, as you stood there a moment, pondering the open window, you thought you heard another footstep, this time inside the house, from somewhere upstairs. You quickly ascended the back staircase, but found no-one on the first landing or in the rooms there. You then ascended to the attic, and, after establishing that there could be no-one in any of the other rooms, knocked and entered the bedroom of the maid, Ann Wallingford."

"That is correct."

"The room was in darkness and she was in bed, but sat up in alarm as you entered – not surprisingly, under the circumstances. You had a look round the room?"

"Yes, because as I mentioned in my report, I thought it possible that if she had been asleep someone might have slipped in there quietly and hidden in a dark corner. However, there was no-one there."

"Did you look behind the door?"

"Yes, there was no-one there."

"Was anything hanging on the back of the door?"

I paused, closed my eyes and tried to recreate in my mind the scene as I saw it on Wednesday night. "Yes," I said at length, "there was a dressing-gown hanging there."

"Colour?"

"Dark red."

"Anything else?"

"No."

"What about the wall behind the door?"

"There was a wash-stand there, with a jug on it, a bar of soap in a saucer and so on. There was nothing else on that wall."

"And the rest of the room?"

"It is not a very big room, and there is not much furniture in it. While Blake was speaking to the girl, I had a good look round. Against the right-hand wall was a small chest of drawers, on top of which was a hair-brush, a comb and some small ornamental boxes such as might have contained trinkets."

"Was there a wardrobe in the room?"

"No, but in an alcove on the wall facing us, to the right of the chimney-breast, was a rail, with a shelf above it."

"Was anything hanging on the rail?"

"Yes," I said. Again I closed my eyes to concentrate. "There was an outdoor coat, and, next to that, another outdoor costume of some kind."

"Anything else?"

"No."

"And to the left of this alcove was a chimney-breast, you say?"

"Yes, with a small fireplace. Above the fireplace was a small mantelpiece with a candlestick and a few small ornaments on it. To the left of the chimney-breast was another alcove. That is where the bed was. To the right of the bed as we looked was a wooden chair."

"Anything hanging on the back of it?"

"No, but upon the seat was the maid's cap and some hair-pins, and, beside it, a pair of shoes. To the left of the bed, between the bed and the window, was a small, circular table. On that," I continued, pausing to concentrate my thoughts once more, "was a candle in a holder, and a book. The casement window, as I mentioned in my report, was wide open. There! I think I have mentioned everything that was to be seen in the room."

"Do you agree?" Holmes asked Blake.

"Yes," replied Blake, "although I'm not clear what the point of this exercise is. Watson is certainly very observant – I don't think I would have remembered all the details he has mentioned – but why are you asking? If you wish to see the room, I can take you up there now."

"It is not how the room is now, but how it was on Wednesday night which is the question at issue," returned Holmes. "I trust Watson's powers of observation, and, because of that, I feel justified in reaching a conclusion."

"Which is?" queried Blake.

Holmes leaned forward and lowered his voice slightly. "That Ann has not been entirely honest with you."

"But she scarcely said anything," returned Blake in surprise. "I apologized for intruding into her bedroom, and asked her if she had heard any footsteps. She said she hadn't, Watson closed the window for her, we withdrew after a brief glance round, and that was that."

"I am not saying that she lied directly to you," said Holmes. "Rather, she lied by omission."

"What do you mean?" queried Blake in a tone of bafflement.

"Watson's detailed description of the room and its contents can surely mean only one thing," said Holmes. "Something is missing. Can you not see it, and see what it must mean?"

"Although I have described to you everything I can remember," I said, as Blake shook his head, "I may have missed a few odd details. I think, for instance, that there may have been a box of matches on that small table by the bed."

Holmes shook his head. "It is a somewhat larger omission than that," said he. "Where, in your inventory, is the maid's dress? It was not hanging on the back of the door, it was not hanging on the rail in the alcove, it was not thrown over the back of the chair by the bed, so where was it?"

"I have no idea," I said.

"Surely," said Holmes, "the most likely explanation for its apparent absence is that the girl was still wearing it. You state in your report of the incident that when you entered the maid's bedroom she sat up in bed, a startled expression on her face and with the sheet pulled up to her chin. What I suggest is that this was not simply a matter of maidenly modesty, but was to prevent you from seeing that she was still wearing her maid's uniform. What this in turn suggests is that there was indeed an audible footstep on the stair, as you initially supposed, but that the footstep was that of Ann Wallingford herself, hurrying ahead of you up the staircase. I imagine she just had time to remove her shoes and cap before climbing into bed fully clothed, mere moments before you knocked on her door."

"There is something else I remember now," I interjected. "As we were speaking to her, I noticed a piece of white cloth sticking out from under her pillow. I gave it no thought – I think I took it to be a part of the pillow-case – but now I consider it again, I think the texture of the cloth was different from that of the pillow-case, and that it was more likely to be a corner of her nightdress which, if your theory is correct, she had not had time to put on."

"How observant of you," said Blake. "I didn't notice that at all."

"That illustrates admirably the point I was making before," said Holmes, "that your powers of observation are indeed excellent, but you do not make the inferences that your observations warrant. There is something else, too, which supports my view of the matter."

"What is that?" I asked.

"The open window in the maid's bedroom. It was a chilly and damp evening. Why, then, was her window open so wide? What I suggest is that just after she retired to her bedroom, someone, seeing the light in her room, called up to her from the yard below or perhaps threw a pebble up at her window to catch her attention. She opened the window wide, and leaned out to see who it was. Recognizing the caller, she descended to the downstairs hall to converse more conveniently through the open window there. Upon your sudden arrival in the hall, she dashed back upstairs, but had no time to close either of the windows."

"Are you suggesting," I asked, "that the maid is in league with Blake's mysterious enemy?"

"I can't believe it of her," said Blake. "I'll send for the girl straight away, so that we can get to the bottom of this business once and for all."

Holmes shook his head. "No," said he in a firm tone. "I would rather leave the matter there for the moment. I am confident that I know who it was she was speaking to, and there are other issues I wish to pursue first."

"As you have suggested that Samuel Harley's old puzzle is inextricably bound up with Blake's modern mystery, will you explain to us your thinking on that?" I asked.

"All in good time, Watson. First I wish to put some questions to one of your neighbours, Blake, and I should be obliged if you would introduce us."

"Certainly," responded Blake. "Who is it you wish to interview?"

"Mrs Booth."

"Mrs Booth?" cried Blake in surprise. "I'm sure she knows nothing of relevance to your investigation. Besides, Dr Watson and I have already spoken to her at some length."

"Perhaps so, but the questions I wish to ask her are different from the ones you asked, so the answers may be different, too."

"Very well," said Blake, somewhat reluctantly. "If you insist." He glanced at his watch. "She and the boy will probably be having their lunch now, so what I suggest is that we do likewise, and go to see her afterwards."

Holmes was agreeable to this, so after lunch we took the pony and trap, and, ten minutes later, the three of us arrived at Netherfield Lodge, where we were shown into the drawing-room. After a moment, we were joined by Mrs Booth.

"This is Mr Sherlock Holmes, Penelope," said Blake. "He wishes to ask you a few questions."

"By all means," said Mrs Booth, as she turned to Holmes, an expression of curiosity mingled with apprehension upon her face. "What is it you wish to know? Don't tell me you have had another stone-throwing incident!"

Holmes shook his head. "I simply wish to ask you how you came to be living here, in Foxwood."

"I do not understand. I imagined you would have heard from Mr Blake of my separation from my husband. Everyone else seems to know all my business."

"Indeed," said Holmes. "I do understand all that. My meaning is simply this: why Foxwood, rather than anywhere else?"

"The house just happened to be available," she replied, evidently surprised by the question.

"No doubt, but there must surely have been other houses available at the time, too. Where were you living before, when you were with your husband?"

"Solihull, near Birmingham."

"Is that where you spent your childhood?"

"No. I grew up in Aston, in Birmingham, where my family still live. My father owns an engineering business there."

"Did your father assist you in getting this house, either financially or in any other way?"

"Yes, he did."

"Why, then, did he look this way when there must have been properties available in Birmingham, or, at least, nearer to Birmingham than Foxwood? Did he, or you, have some previous connection with this part of the country?"

"Yes, he did, as a matter of fact. He had a number of friends who lived in these parts."

"Was your husband related to any of these friends?"

"Yes, he is the son of one of them. He and I first met when my family was paying a visit to his, some years ago."

"That connection must have created difficulties when you informed your family of your intention to separate from your husband."

"It did. My mother and father were very distressed and begged me to reconsider, but I remained resolute in my decision. At length, when they accepted that I could not be dissuaded, they were very helpful to me."

Holmes nodded. "And Mr Ashton? Is he, too, a friend of your father's?"

"Not especially. They have met once or twice at the house of a mutual acquaintance, but that is all."

"But he is, perhaps, a friend of your husband's family?"

"Yes."

"And when Mr Ashton calls round to see you, as I have heard he does, does he attempt to persuade you to return to your husband?"

Mrs Booth nodded her head. "His visits almost always begin simply as casual social calls, with chit-chat about the village and so on, but invariably end up with his trying to persuade me to heal the breach with my husband."

"I suspected it might be so. His visits are, then, perhaps, not especially welcome?"

"I have come to dread them."

Blake leaned forward, an expression of surprise upon his face. "You never told me anything of this, Penelope," said he.

"I did not wish you to become embroiled in my distressing family affairs," she returned.

Blake sat back in his chair, blew out his cheeks and ran his fingers through his hair. "Well, I never," said he.

"What?" said Mrs Booth with a little smile, reading the expression upon his face. "Surely you did not ever regard Mr Ashton as a rival? Your visits here are always welcome to me, John. His are not."

"When my friends here called upon you earlier in the week," continued Holmes after a moment, addressing Mrs Booth, "you informed them that although you had received a

219

series of letters from your husband, he had not been here to see you at any time in the last year."

"That is correct."

"But I fancy that that is no longer the case."

Mrs Booth hesitated. "How do you know?" she asked at length.

In answer, Holmes leaned forward. "May I?" he asked, then he gently pushed back the left cuff of Mrs Booth's dress. Upon her wrist was a dark bruise. "Is this your husband's work?" he enquired, at which she nodded her head, her gaze averted to the floor. "And the small cut I see on your eyebrow?" he continued, to which she again nodded her head.

"He appeared without warning on Wednesday evening," Mrs Booth said at length, "and would not be denied entry. Of course, we quarrelled, as you might expect, and he struck me."

Blake rose to his feet and put his arm around Mrs Booth's shoulders. "How dreadful!" said he. "You should have told me."

"I did not want you to become involved," she responded. "I just felt so ashamed of the whole business."

"Well, well," said Holmes, rising to his feet, after we had remained a few moments in silence, "Watson and I will be on our way now. I wish to speak to Mr Needham before I do anything else."

"Feel free to take the trap," returned Blake, who had seated himself beside Mrs Booth. "I shall walk back to the Grange a little later. But if you are going to see Needham, you may need to bang his door-knocker very energetically. His housekeeper is never there on a Friday, and he himself is a little deaf."

We took the pony and trap as Blake had suggested, and, a few minutes later, were rattling along the road in the sunshine.

"At least," said Holmes, "we are now justified in conjecturing with some confidence not only that it was indeed Booth who threw the stones at us, but also that he has been secretly staying at Oldstone House, Ashton's place."

"That certainly seems likely from what we have heard," I agreed. "In which case, it was probably Ashton who told Booth of the burgeoning friendship between his wife and Farringdon Blake."

Holmes nodded his agreement. "It is also possible," said he, "that Booth observed his wife driving herself round to the Grange on Sunday. If so, that was probably the incident which precipitated Booth's dramatic warning the following day, although, of course, Blake had not even been at home when Mrs Booth called." My friend fell silent then, and it was clear that his thoughts had moved on to some other matter. As for my own thoughts, they circled round and round the new information we had received concerning Booth and Ashton. What did it mean for the other mysteries in the case, which remained as yet unresolved? The only thing I felt certain about was that Sherlock Holmes would have an opinion on the matter, but what that opinion might be, I could not imagine.

It took us a little more than ten minutes to reach Needham's house. I had asked Holmes as we jogged along what it was he wished to speak to Needham about, but he was unforthcoming, saying only that he wished to ask him a couple of questions. As it turned out, however, my friend was destined to be disappointed. Our knock upon the door elicited no response, and though we repeated it several times, no-one came to the door, and the house remained in complete silence.

"It seems it is not only his housekeeper but Needham himself who is away," I remarked, as we made our way back to where we had tethered the pony.

"So it would seem," returned Holmes. "However, it makes little difference to my immediate plans."

"What, if I may ask, are they?"

"To return to the Grange, have a cup of tea and put my theory about Samuel Harley's puzzle to the test."

14: THE ERROR IN THE HEART

ONE OF THE MOST STRIKING FEATURES of Sherlock Holmes's singular character was his reluctance to share his thoughts on a case until he was certain that his theories had been proved beyond all possible doubt. As we sat together with a pot of tea, on the little terrace outside the French windows of the drawing-room, I endeavoured to draw him out on the mystery surrounding his client, but without success. To all my enquiries he simply replied that he would explain the matter later.

"Did you find my reports at all useful to you in refining your theories?" I asked, not because I was seeking to gain a compliment, but simply as another attempt to draw my friend out on the matter.

"They were very interesting and thorough," said he, as he put a match to his pipe.

"I feared they might better be described as rambling and incoherent," I remarked, "but, having no idea what might or might not be relevant, I felt obliged to include almost everything I saw and heard."

Holmes nodded. "That was not a weakness but a strength," said he. "If you had already had some strongly held theory about Blake's little mystery – whether right or wrong – it would have insensibly influenced your judgement as to what was important and what was not, and your reports would very likely not have been so comprehensive. I myself had formed a tentative hypothesis on the matter before I left here for London, and I am glad to say that there is nothing in your reports, even among the smallest details, which in any way contradicts my view of the matter. So, to that extent, they were certainly useful. Had there been some detail in your account which my theory could not accommodate, I should have been obliged to review it."

"Is that all?" I asked in some disappointment, "that my reports confirmed your views only in a negative sort of way, by not contradicting them?"

"Not at all," replied my companion with a chuckle. "The issues surrounding our client are manifold and complex. Some are linked and some are not. Your record of the week's events shed light on all of them in varying degrees."

"Did any one incident stand out?"

Holmes hesitated. "I am inclined to say that the most interesting thing you reported was the little slip of paper which you included among the leaves of your note-book."

"What!" I cried in surprise. "The scrap of paper which had the word 'shrub' written on it? You amaze me, Holmes! I considered that little scrap so utterly and completely irrelevant to anything else that I almost did not mention it at all! I only did so because of the circumstances in which it happened to come to light. Why, it could have blown into the house from anywhere, at any time!"

"Well, well, I am sure that the path it followed from its origin to the moment you found it was indeed a tortuous one. Yet it turned up when it did, and not at any other time, and I believe it to be of the very greatest significance. There!" he continued with a smile, "I have let you in to a part of my reasoning, Watson, and, now I have done so, I should be obliged if you did not mention it to anyone else."

"Not even your client?"

"No."

Blake himself returned shortly afterwards, while Holmes and I were still sitting in conversation, discussing the inquests we had attended.

"Mrs Booth should be all right now," he remarked, as he joined us on the terrace. "I think her husband's assault had shocked her deeply, but she had kept the matter to herself until you drew it out of her, Mr Holmes."

Holmes nodded. "Such affairs are always distressing for all concerned, but it is generally better to have these things out in the open. Will she now seek a divorce?"

"Yes, and, in the light of her husband's physical ill-treatment of her, I should think it will be granted."

"Very well," said Holmes, rising to his feet. "Let us now consider Samuel Harley's puzzle. If you will come with me to the library, I will explain to you my reflections on the matter."

Blake hesitated. "Forgive me for querying this point again, Mr Holmes," he began in a dubious tone, "but you are sure, are you, that this old riddle is relevant to the concerns for which I consulted you – that I was spied upon here, and followed in London?"

"I am certain of it."

"Then you have my full attention," said Blake in a brighter tone. "I could do with something to lift my spirits a little!"

In the library, Holmes took from his pocket several sheets of paper, which he unfolded and spread out on the table. One of them was the copy he had made of the puzzle-square in the orangery, except that he had now added a number to each column, one to thirteen, across the top, and to each row, one to thirteen, down the left-hand side.

"You will no doubt recall," he began, "that we discussed briefly a possible connection between the puzzle-square and the poem on the wall there. As I reflected further on this possibility, I discovered a curious fact. There are, as you are aware, precisely one hundred and sixty-nine letters in the array. Harley's moral poem, meanwhile, contains one hundred and eighty-eight letters. On the sheet I was working from" he continued, indicating another of his papers on the table, "I have noted the number of letters in each line, as you see."

I leaned over to study his sheet, which appeared as follows:

If error be in the heart,	19
Nor all thy diligence nor all thy talent	33
Nor all that learning can bestow	27
Shall bring forth fruit.	20
Like seed scatter'd unto rocks,	25
Or bulbs thrust into mud,	20
All that might have been	20
Is but a vain and empty vision.	<u>24</u>
	Total: 188

"You will observe," Holmes continued, "that the length of the first line is nineteen letters. If that line is discounted, the sum total of the remainder of the poem is therefore one hundred and sixty-nine letters, the same as the number of letters in the puzzle-square."

"What an odd coincidence!" I cried.

"Well, of course, it could simply be a coincidence," returned Holmes, "but if so it is certainly a singular one. As you know, Watson, I dislike simply accepting anything as a coincidence. In my line of work, anything which appears at first sight to be a coincidence is almost always open to some more constructive interpretation. So it is, I am sure, in this case. Fortunately, there is a simple way of verifying that we are on the right lines in our conjecture."

"I cannot imagine what that could be," I remarked.

"Nor I," agreed Blake.

"Really?" said Holmes in surprise. "It is a perfectly elementary matter. I am sure that if you reflected on what I have suggested for longer than five seconds, you could not fail to see it for yourselves. If we ignore the first line of the poem, and consider the rest, from 'Nor all thy diligence' to 'empty vision', and count the number of instances in it of every individual letter of the alphabet, we can compare that with a similar examination of the letters in the orangery puzzle. Here are the results," he continued, unfolding another piece of paper on the table, on which I read the following:

A 15	B 6	C 4	D 5
E 13	F 2	G 4	H 9

I 12	J 0	K 2	L 15
M 3	N 15	O 10	P 1
Q 0	R 11	S 9	T 20
U 6	V 3	W 1	X 0
Y 3	Z 0		

"You will note that there is only one list of letters on this sheet," said Holmes. "The reason for that is that the figures for the poem and the figures for the puzzle are in fact identical. You surely cannot still suppose that such an exact concordance is simply coincidence, Watson! Why, the odds against it must be almost beyond the wit of man to calculate!"

"I agree," I said. "You must be right!"

"Thank you. Now, when I first realized the facts I have just described to you, I conjectured that, as the rest of the poem matches the puzzle-square, letter for letter, the first line of the poem should perhaps be considered separately from the rest of it. Of course, in one sense – the obvious one – the first line is an intrinsic part of the poem. The whole piece is in the form of a conditional proposition – 'if this, then that' – in which the first line is, to use the traditional terminology of the schoolmen, the *protasis*. The next three lines form the *apodosis*, that is to say, the consequence if the first line is the case, and the four lines which follow are a sort of amplification of the *apodosis*, comparing it with other activities that the writer regards as equally futile. In that sense, then, the first line cannot be ignored without destroying the whole point of the conditional statement. However, I conjectured that it was possible that the first line had a double meaning: that is, some other meaning as well as the obvious one. But what other meaning could I attach to the phrase 'If error be in the heart'?

"For some time I pondered this mystery, convinced that I was on the right track, but unable to see what the next step forward should be. Then, as I read through all my material again, it struck me that the poem itself contains an error."

"What do you mean?" asked Blake, turning to study the framed poem on the wall once more. "It appears straightforward enough to me."

"Yes, the general meaning is clear enough," returned Holmes, "and the poem is composed in a thoughtful and convincing way. There is nothing wrong with it in that sense. But one of the individual letters is arguably incorrect."

"I cannot see anything which is obviously wrong," I remarked as I ran my eye over the poem.

"No doubt," said Holmes, "but that is the point of it. It is a subtle matter. Yet consider for a moment the fifth line, Watson: 'Like seed scatter'd unto rocks'. What I suggest is that the word 'unto' is incorrect. It is acceptable, but 'onto' would surely make better sense in the context. Arguably, then, the 'u' is an error and should be an 'o'."

I closed my eyes to concentrate. "Yes," I said at length, "I am sure you are right."

"I agree," said Blake. "The more I think about it, the more amazed I am that it has never struck me before!"

"Very well," said Holmes. "We are agreed, then, that what I am suggesting is possible, at the very least."

"I think it more than simply possible," I said. "I think it is a brilliant conjecture. I don't think it would have occurred to me if I had studied the poem for the next ten years. But where does it leave us?"

"It leaves us looking for a heart into which to put the error," replied Holmes.

"That seems somewhat cryptic," remarked Blake. "Surely the error is in the heart of a man."

"Yes, in the context of the poem," returned Holmes. "But don't forget that we are now considering that the poem's opening line has a double meaning which we have now related to a single letter, the letter 'u'. Where is a heart into which we could place the letter 'u'?"

"Of course!" I cried. "The puzzle-square!"

"Precisely, Watson. The puzzle-square consists of one hundred and sixty-nine tiles, and, that being an odd number, it follows that there is one tile – number eighty-five – which is inarguably the central one, or 'heart' of the whole array. We must therefore place the letter 'u' – the error – into the position of the eighty-fifth tile and fill in the remainder of the poem, minus the first line, accordingly."

"That certainly makes sense," said Blake after a moment, "but I can't see that that will get us anywhere. What will it achieve?"

"We cannot say." replied Holmes. "But as we have no idea what the purpose of the puzzle is, that is not so surprising. At least we shall have arranged the wooden blocks in a way which has never been done in over a hundred years. The sensible course of action, it seems to me, therefore, is to re-arrange the blocks as I suggest and consider how we might proceed once we have done that."

"It is possible," I said as a fresh thought struck me, "that when we have arranged the blocks as you propose, they may perhaps, reading down the columns, spell out a message of some kind."

"That would certainly be a plausible idea," said Holmes. "A similar possibility occurred to me. Unfortunately, however, it is not the case. I know because I have already drawn up a revised version of the puzzle-square with the 'u' of 'unto' in the central position. I filled in the rest of the poem in order from that point until I came to the bottom right-hand corner. I then went up to the top left-hand corner and continued from there, until I put in the last letter, immediately before the central 'u'. Here," he continued, "take a look."

I	G	E	N	C	E	N	O	R	A	L	L	T
H	Y	T	A	L	E	N	T	N	O	R	A	L
L	T	H	A	T	L	E	A	R	N	I	N	G
C	A	N	B	E	S	T	O	W	S	H	A	L
L	B	R	I	N	G	F	O	R	T	H	F	R
U	I	T	L	I	K	E	S	E	E	D	S	C
A	T	T	E	R	D	U	N	T	O	R	O	C
K	S	O	R	B	U	L	B	S	T	H	R	U
S	T	I	N	T	O	M	U	D	A	L	L	T
H	A	T	M	I	G	H	T	H	A	V	E	B
E	E	N	I	S	B	U	T	A	V	A	I	N
A	N	D	E	M	P	T	Y	V	I	S	I	O
N	N	O	R	A	L	L	T	H	Y	D	I	L

231

He had unfolded another large sheet of paper on the table as he had been speaking. Now, Blake and I bent over to study it.

"As you can see," Holmes continued, "there are, unfortunately, no hidden messages revealed when one reads up or down the columns or diagonals. I have tried numerous other approaches, but none of them makes any sense. That is a pity, but, still, I am sure we are on the right track. As I have worked out the position of every letter, it will not be necessary for us to shuffle the wooden blocks about individually and risk confusing ourselves. What I suggest instead, is that we remove all the blocks before we attempt to begin positioning any of them correctly, and arrange them into separate piles on the floor, one for each letter of the alphabet."

"There is a little number in the corner of each block," said Blake. "What do you think is the meaning of those?"

"I imagine that the numbers simply indicate the order in which each of the blocks of a particular letter should be placed in the array," said Holmes. He glanced at the sheet on which he had listed the number of instances of each letter in the puzzle. "If I have counted them all correctly, there should, for instance, be fifteen blocks with the letter 'A' on, numbered one to fifteen, six blocks with the letter 'U' on, numbered one to six, and so on. It matters which instance of each letter we use in a particular position because of the differing number of wooden prongs on the backs of the blocks."

My friend gathered up his papers as he spoke and folded them into a neat bundle. "One thing we do not know yet," he said, "is if we should begin counting off the numbers from the

232

'U' in the centre square or from the top left-hand corner, but no doubt we shall discover which is the correct procedure once we start trying to fit the blocks in position. What I propose is that we make a start on the task at once. I am keen to get on with it as quickly as possible."

Both Blake and I expressed our enthusiasm for this proposal, and we followed Holmes as he led the way from the library to the back door, across the yard and into the orangery. There he spread out his papers again on one of the old wooden tables, and we set about removing the wooden blocks from the large array on the rear wall. It was a fine, warm evening, and the low rays of the sinking sun sent bright shafts of light between the trees to the west of the house and bathed the orangery in their golden glow.

We set about our work with an energy born of enthusiasm, but removing the wooden blocks of the puzzle proved to be a little more difficult than I think any of us had expected. Some of them felt as if they had never been moved since they were first placed there, and were jammed in very tightly. Blake fetched some more tools to help us from one of the other outhouses, but it was still surprisingly slow and warm work, and after ten minutes' effort all three of us had taken off our jackets.

We had managed to pull out almost three-quarters of the blocks when we heard the sound of a gong from the house.

"Supper will be served in ten minutes," said Blake. "If you can tear yourself away from this work, Mr Holmes, we can continue afterwards. I'm sure a little nourishment will not go amiss."

A faint trace of annoyance crossed my friend's face. "You are probably right," said he, "but it is a pity. I had hoped to have finished removing the blocks by now. The light will have almost gone by the time we get back to it. We shall need several lamps in here."

Our meal was a hasty one. It was not only Holmes who was impatient to return to the task in the orangery. Neither Blake nor I had any inclination to prolong our supper for longer than was absolutely necessary and were keen to get on with Samuel Harley's puzzle. The excitement we felt at the possibility of solving this hundred-year-old riddle was almost palpable. For myself, I confess I had no idea what we would do when we had re-fitted all the wooden blocks according to Holmes's scheme. I just hoped that something, some fresh idea, would then occur to us.

In no time at all, therefore, we were back in the orangery, where the maid brought us a large pot of coffee and a tray of cups. As she set it down on one of the old tables there, I observed that there was an expression of the most intense curiosity upon her face. A few moments later, Caxton brought in an armful of oil-lamps which he proceeded to light. This was timely, for the sun had now sunk below the trees and the twilight was turning the orangery into a grey, shadowed place.

In a few minutes, we had removed the remaining blocks, and added these to the twenty-odd piles which I had arranged on the floor. Blake poured out some coffee for us, and we stood a moment, surveying the black expanse of the empty puzzle-square.

"Now," said Holmes, as he put down his cup, "let us see what will go where. If you will pass me the 'U' which has a '1' on it, Watson, I will see if that will fit in the heart of the array. No," he continued after a moment, "It won't. This block has five prongs on the back, and there are only two proper holes available in that position. This suggests that the numbering on the blocks begins at the top left-hand corner. Starting from that position, Blake, can you tell me where the first 'U' occurs?"

"The first square on the sixth row down," replied Blake after a moment, as he studied Holmes's chart.

"Hum! It certainly fits there," said Holmes, "but it is a little difficult to get in. The wood has probably swollen a little. Can you supply a hammer, Blake, and a piece of cloth, to protect the face of the block when I hit it?"

Blake brought a hammer and a yellow duster from one of the nearby outhouses, and, after a couple of smart taps, the wooden block went into position to Holmes's satisfaction.

"Now," said he: "the 'U' which is in the central position, the heart of the puzzle: what number will that be?"

"That is the second 'U'," returned Blake.

I passed Holmes the block inscribed with a 'U' and a '2', and he pushed it into position.

"I think that establishes clearly enough that the numbering is indeed from the top left-hand corner," said Holmes, "so let us now begin from there. What is the very first letter?"

"An 'I'," said Blake.

I passed Holmes the block inscribed with an 'I' and a '1', and he fitted it into position, although it needed a sharp blow from the hammer to drive it fully home.

"So far, so good," said Holmes. "What I suggest, Blake, is that you read out all the letters in order, row by row, Watson passes me the relevant block and I fit it into position."

So we proceeded. Most of the blocks fitted fairly easily, a few were more difficult and needed attention from the hammer, and about seven or eight would not seem to go in properly at all, although the number of prongs appeared correct for the holes available. These few Holmes decided to leave until the end to finish off.

It was just over an hour later that Holmes fitted an 'L' into the bottom right-hand corner and the array was complete.

"What now?" said Blake, sitting himself down on the bench beside the table, as the maid brought in another tray of coffee. "The puzzle is complete, the 'error' is in the heart, but where does that leave us?"

"It is not quite finished yet," replied Holmes. "I shall have to apply a little more force to the refractory blocks." He sat down, filled his pipe and put a match to it, as the maid poured out the coffee, then he sat for a time in silence, gazing at the array of letters. "You have no doubt observed," he remarked at length, "that most of the blocks which have so far resisted my efforts to force them home form a rough pattern."

"Why, so they do," said I. "there is a line of them, passing diagonally from the top right corner to the bottom left, and another line passing horizontally from somewhere near the middle to the right-hand edge."

"That is suggestive, is it not?" said Holmes with a chuckle.

"I suppose so," I replied, "but of what, I don't know."

"We shall soon find out," said Holmes. "When I have finished this coffee and this pipe, I shall try to hammer home the remaining blocks."

As he spoke, I thought I heard something, a footstep, perhaps, in the yard outside the orangery. I turned, but the night was now pitch black, and I could see nothing.

"Was that a spot of rain?" asked Blake.

"I don't think so," I replied. "Perhaps it was the wind, or a moth against the window."

Presently, Holmes drained his coffee-cup and put down his pipe. Then he took up the hammer and duster, and proceeded to tap on the blocks that still stood out a little from the rest. Each one in turn resisted being driven fully home, but gradually, as he moved back and forth across the whole expanse, giving each a sharp tap in turn, by tiny degrees they moved further in.

"There seems to be at least one cross-piece – perhaps more – behind the back-board of this array," Holmes remarked, "which is getting in the way of the prongs on the back of the blocks. I noted, however, that the some of the dowels which form the prongs are bevelled at the end, as if designed to get beneath something and lift it out of the way as they are driven home. Whatever it is, I believe I am now slowly forcing it out of the way. Whether its presence is intentional or a flaw in the design, it is impossible to say, although I think the former is more likely. Whichever it is, I think I am getting the better of it. There!" he cried as he gave one of the blocks a sharp blow with the hammer and forced it fully home, so that its surface was level with the blocks around it. At the same moment, there came a dull, clattering noise from behind the array.

"What was that?" asked Blake.

"I don't know for certain," replied Holmes, "but, whatever it was, I think I've got rid of it." As he continued banging the projecting blocks into place, there came another clatter. "There goes another impediment," he cried, a note of excitement in his voice. "I'll just finish this last two off!"

Then a very strange and surprising thing occurred. As Holmes banged the last two blocks firmly into place, the whole array moved slightly, and a narrow dark gap was revealed at the right-hand edge.

"The right-hand side has moved inwards!" I cried, excited by this surprising new development.

"Yes," said Holmes. "The array appears to be hinged on the left side. Put your shoulders to it, gentlemen, and let us see if we cannot force it open a little more!"

The three of us pushed as hard as we could against that strange wooden puzzle-square, and slowly, with much creaking and groaning, it swung inwards, until the gap was wide enough for us to pass through. Holmes took up a lamp from the table and passed into the darkness behind the back wall of the orangery.

"Bring the other lamps!" he called. "There is a large chamber of some kind here."

We followed him in, both bearing a lamp, and an astonishing sight met our eyes. It was indeed a large chamber, like a cave, carved out of the hill behind the orangery. About ten feet back from the entrance was an old wooden table, covered with dust, on which stood a couple of glass bottles, a tumbler and some papers, the whole festooned with cobwebs. Beside the table was a wooden chair, and on the chair was the skeleton of a man, a few rags and tatters of leather and clothing hanging from the bones.

For a long minute we did not speak, but gazed dumbstruck at this strange and terrible sight. At length, Sherlock Holmes broke the silence.

"It is Samuel Harley," said he. "It must be. He never left Foxwood at all. The story of his travelling to Italy and living out his last days there is untrue. No doubt he got a friend to spread the rumour, to conceal his true intentions."

"And no doubt he got the same friend to post the letter in Italy which was later received by Harley's cousin," said Blake.

Holmes nodded. "And all the time his intention was to die here, where he had spent most of his life. Well, well. I think that suits rather better what we know of his character. Having prepared his riddle, he entered this chamber, sealed himself in, took poison of some kind, washed it down with a bottle of wine and then passed forever from this earthly realm."

"So the only 'treasure' hidden here," I remarked, "was Samuel Harley's own decaying corpse, an object lesson in morality for those who came after him."

"Not necessarily," returned Holmes. "There is something on the table there." He leaned forward and poked with his finger at a small, dust-covered bundle. As far as I could see, it was the rotten, decaying shreds of a small canvas bag, and as my companion disturbed the shredded remains, the contents of the bag were revealed as a dozen or more large pearls.

"There is a paper here," said Holmes, carefully picking up a grimy sheet from the table and blowing the dust off it. "It is still legible," he continued. "The absence of all light in this chamber has saved the writing from fading. If you will hold your lamp up to it, Watson, I will try to make out what it says."

I did as he asked, and for a moment my friend squinted at it in silence.

"The signature at the bottom is that of Samuel Harley," said Holmes at length, "which confirms all our suppositions. The message is as follows:

Here before me in this little pouch
lies all my worldly wealth. Do
with it as you will, but heed my warning.
These baubles may purchase for you some
fleeting pleasures but can never buy true happiness.
One pearl alone can purchase happiness.
It is a pearl which cannot be seen,
but only sensed with the soul.
That pearl I have never possessed.
It is called Love."

Holmes looked up from the paper and appeared about to pass some comment on what he had just read, when there came a sudden interruption from the doorway behind us.

"Hand those pearls to me now," came a sharp voice, as the three of us turned round in surprise.

15: RESOLUTION

"PRAY, COME IN," SAID SHERLOCK HOLMES. "I have been expecting you."

"Whitemoor!" cried Blake. "What on earth are you doing here?"

"Never mind that!" returned Whitemoor dismissively. "Just hand me the pearls!" As he spoke he made a gesture with his hand, and I saw that he was holding a pistol.

"What are you talking about?" demanded Blake. "Why should I hand them to you?"

"Because they're mine by right, and you know it!"

"I don't know what you mean. Samuel Harley left these pearls here."

"Yes, for his heir. I am that heir. I have more right to them than anyone else. This house should be mine, too. Harley was swindled out of it. Everyone knows that."

"No," said Blake. "It may have been a disaster for Harley, but there's no evidence he was cheated in any way."

"Yes," persisted Whitemoor. "George Darcy was a swindler who took advantage of the fact that Harley was drunk to cheat him. He was a swine if ever there was one. I have studied the matter. You have, too, so you know I am right. You wouldn't show me your research, but I knew you were secretly working on it all the time. I have been watching you."

"Would you like me to read you the message Harley left with these pearls?" Holmes interrupted.

"No. I heard it. It's not surprising he was melancholic, having been cheated out of all he possessed. Just give me the pearls!"

"I thought you were visiting your mother," said Blake.

"He can't visit his mother," said Holmes, in a calm, unhurried tone, "not unless he calls at the cemetery. She is dead. She passed away nearly three months ago. He has used his supposed visits to his mother to secretly hide in the woods here and spy on you."

"How do you claim to know anything about my mother?" demanded Whitemoor, his voice raised in anger.

"I have been to Towcester and made enquiries there."

"I suppose I should have expected that," said Whitemoor in a sneering tone. "I knew that you would be sticking your nose into other people's business when Blake hired you to solve Harley's puzzle."

"You're wrong, Whitemoor," said Blake. "I didn't consult Mr Holmes about Harley's puzzle, but to find out who was spying on me, here and in London. I had no intention at all of even mentioning Harley's puzzle to him. It was Mr Holmes's own idea to look into that."

"I don't believe you," cried Whitemoor. "I knew you'd been working on the puzzle, but you hid all your workings from me and lied about it!"

"That is nonsense," retorted Blake. "My 'workings', as you call them, were all futile. I hid nothing from you, because there was nothing to hide. I had given up even thinking about Harley's puzzle until Mr Holmes came here and expressed an interest in it."

"Just give me the pearls or it will be the worse for you," said Whitemoor in a menacing tone, pointing the pistol at Blake.

Reluctantly, Blake turned towards the table and made to pick up the pearls. Just as he did so, I seemed to see some slight movement, some shadow in the orangery outside the door of Harley's secret chamber. Next moment, a dark figure appeared in the doorway, and as this figure advanced stealthily and in perfect silence, with a thrill of horror I recognized Professor Crook, a wild look upon his face, and a large evil-looking knife in his hand.

"Look out!" I cried to Whitemoor.

"Be quiet, you fool!" he shouted back at me.

Blake had turned and looked up as I called out. "No, no," he cried to Whitemoor. "It's true! Look out!"

This warning evidently had a ring of truth about it. Whitemoor hesitated just a fraction of a second longer, then turned to see what was behind him, but it was too late.

With a terrible cry, Crook launched himself upon the young man and plunged the knife into his chest. "So, Hargreaves!" he cried. "I have caught you at last, you devil!" At the same moment, the pistol was discharged with a deafening crash which echoed round and round the stone walls of that strange chamber.

Holmes sprang forward as Whitemoor and Crook tumbled to the floor in a heap and wrenched the pistol from the young man's hand, but it was to no avail. The weapon had done its evil work: Crook had been shot through the heart and was stone dead. I rolled his lifeless body to one side and examined Whitemoor's wound, but I was powerless to save him. Blood had poured from a terrible gash in his chest, and even as I struggled to find some way of stopping the bleeding, his heart gave out and it was clear that he, too, was dead.

A moment later, alarmed by the noise, Caxton hurried into the orangery. In a few sentences, Blake explained to him what had happened and sent him to notify Jenkins, the local constable.

I shall not weary the reader with a detailed account of all that occurred on that dreadful, tumultuous evening. A brief summary must suffice:

Constable Jenkins duly arrived and we endeavoured with some difficulty to explain to him all that had happened and what it meant. On receiving news of the deaths from Caxton, he had at once communicated with Banbury police station, who, he informed us, were sending a senior officer and some men. I was meanwhile concerned at what the state of affairs might be in Crook's household, so, while Holmes and Blake remained at the Grange, Constable Jenkins and I made our way over to Black Bank House. There, I was relieved to find that both Dr Taylor and Miss Dawes were still alive, although both were badly injured. Their cook had been locked in the cellar by Crook but was otherwise unharmed. Miss Dawes had been struck a vicious blow on the head with some heavy kitchen implement which had rendered her unconscious. Dr Taylor had received a serious knife-wound in the shoulder and had lost a lot of blood. I patched them up as best I could with Dr Taylor's medical materials and told them what had happened at the Grange, then Jenkins and I set off back.

We had only just reached the bottom of the track leading to the road from Black Bank House, however, when we saw someone stagger into the road from the track on the other side. We hurried over to see what was the matter and found it was Needham, who appeared battered and bruised. In answer to the policeman's questions he told us he had been bound and gagged for several hours in his own house, after a violent quarrel with Whitemoor, and had only just managed to free himself.

"I know he intends to go over to the Grange," he said. "He has taken my revolver, and I am very worried about what he might do there. I have become increasingly concerned in recent weeks at the violent course of action he proposes."

"You are too late," I interrupted. I told him briefly what had happened, and he covered his face with his hands in horror. Jenkins asked him if he wished to come with us, but he declined, and we left him there, standing in the road, shaking like a leaf.

By the time we got back to the Grange, a police inspector by the name of Philips had arrived from Banbury in the company of three constables, and we were obliged to explain the whole business all over again. Eventually, when midnight had long since passed, and we had all provided detailed statements for Inspector Philips, the bodies of the two dead men were removed. Then Holmes, Blake and I sat in a stunned, exhausted silence in the drawing-room of Foxwood Grange, a tumbler of whisky and soda in front of each of us.

"Whitemoor!" said Blake abruptly. "I simply cannot believe it! He always seemed such a placid, untroubled young man, a little youthful and naive in his thoughts sometimes, perhaps, but really no different from hundreds of other highly educated young men. And yet, all the time, he was secretly harbouring all these baseless grudges and grievances. It seems scarcely credible that he could be on the surface so cheery and helpful, while below the surface he was full of dark, poisonous thoughts. I really think, Mr Holmes, that you must tell us all you know about this business. I feel in a state of complete exhaustion, but I don't believe I shall be able to sleep until I understand all that has occurred here, and what lies behind it all. Don't you agree, Watson?"

"Absolutely," I said. "For instance, Holmes, you showed no surprise when Whitemoor turned up this evening, but spoke as if you had expected all along that he would do so. How could that be? Even if you already suspected that he was behind some of what has happened recently, you could not really have been so sure that he would be here this evening."

"But you are forgetting," said Holmes, "that I sent a telegram before I returned, in which I explicitly stated that I believed I had solved Samuel Harley's riddle. I did so deliberately because I knew you would tell Whitemoor, and I was certain by then that Harley's riddle was what interested him. I wished to ensure, you see, that he would reveal himself this evening – although I confess I did not expect he would come equipped with a pistol. But, really, if I am to explain to you my reasoning in this case, my glass will need recharging."

"Certainly," said Blake. He took our tumblers to the sideboard and busied himself with the whisky decanter and the gasogene. While he was so engaged, the door opened and the maid entered. She asked if Blake would be requiring her any more that evening, or if she could now go to bed.

"Oh, Ann, my dear," said Blake in a contrite tone. "I had no idea you were still up. I thought you had retired some time ago, when the Caxtons went. I am aware that you have been working like a Trojan all evening, supplying people with coffee and so on, for which I am very grateful indeed! Now, you run along!"

She turned and was about to leave the room when Holmes spoke. "May I ask Ann a question?" he said to Blake.

"By all means," returned Blake in a tone of surprise.

"Yes, sir?" asked the maid, turning to Holmes with a slight look of apprehension on her tired features.

"Are you friendly with Anthony Pearson?" he asked.

She appeared somewhat taken aback by the question, as if unsure of its purpose, and a slight blush tinged her cheek. "Well, I do know him, sir."

"Was it he you had been speaking to at the back window the other night, when you pretended you had been in bed?"

The maid hesitated. "Yes, sir," she replied at length, her eyes cast down to the floor.

"That is all right, Ann," said Holmes. "No-one is annoyed with you. You may see whoever you wish, I am sure. There is no need to be secretive about it," he continued, as Blake nodded his head agreeably, "but the other night, when Mr Blake heard a footstep in the house, your acting was so good that he was convinced that some dangerous intruder had got in."

"I am sorry, sir," said the maid to Blake. "I thought I might get into trouble."

247

"That is perfectly all right, Ann," returned he. "I am glad it *was* only you, and not an intruder. No harm is done, so we can forget all about it now."

When the maid had left us, I asked Holmes how he had known that it was Anthony Pearson that she had been talking to at the window in the "long gallery".

"I did not know for certain," replied Holmes, "but it seemed to me fairly likely. In your admirable reports of your recent activities, you mentioned your visit to the Pearsons at Lower Cropley Farmhouse. In the course of that, if you recall, you described an exchange between the two young men, James and Anthony Pearson, in which James said of his brother that he 'was the one who was *very* interested in Foxwood Grange', or words to that effect. This seemed to embarrass the younger brother, who proceeded to hit the other over the head with a rolled-up newspaper. It was apparent that James was teasing his brother, and what could be more likely to cause such embarrassment in a young man than an affair of the heart? As Ann Wallingford is the only possible focus here for young romance, the inference was not a difficult one to draw."

Blake laughed. "I suppose you are right," he said. "Such a possibility had not struck me before. When one is wrapped up in one's own work, it can be difficult to see things from another's perspective."

"In my line of work, by contrast," said Holmes, "it is often of the utmost importance that you can do so. There have been many cases which I should probably never have solved had I not been able to place myself, imaginatively speaking, in the position of the criminal. My recent travel arrangements, which you queried earlier, illustrate the point well. I reasoned, you see, that if I were Whitemoor – or anyone else – carrying a large telescope, whether in a case or not, and wished to leave the district by train but not be seen by anyone to do so, I should avoid the nearest station, where I might meet someone who knew me. The next stop on the line – Little Broadstone Halt – which is very little used, would be my choice.

"That is therefore the way I went, hoping to strike up a conversation with the guard, to see if he could remember anyone answering to Whitemoor's description boarding the train there. On the outward journey, I was out of luck. The guard had no recollection of such a person. But I learned from him that he and another guard roughly divide the duties between them, and on the return journey I was fortunate enough to coincide with the other man, who remembered Whitemoor and the case he was carrying very clearly. So you see, by putting myself in the place of the villain, I had managed to confirm my theory perfectly."

"That is an interesting illustration of your point," I remarked. "But what had led you to suspect that Whitemoor was behind all the mysteries in the first place? On the face of it, at least, he strikes me as perhaps the least likely candidate for any such villainy."

Holmes nodded. "When we first arrived here, I had no particular suspicions, but regarded everyone in the district as an equally likely – or equally unlikely – suspect. Last Monday lunchtime, however, after we had been up to the ash spinney to view the tree with rungs, Whitemoor came very close to giving himself away. I believe he realized his mistake at once, and quickly corrected it, but not before I had made a mental note of it."

"Whatever do you mean?" I asked.

"To explain, I must take you back to the murder in London of the enquiry agent, Wilson Baines. It did not, if you recall, appear to be premeditated. Baines had been struck on the head with a marble book-end from the shelf behind his desk. It seemed likely that he and his assailant had been having a quarrel and, in the heat of the moment, the other man had seized the first thing that came to hand – the book-end – and struck Baines with that. We speculated as to what they might have been quarrelling about, and one possibility was that Baines had demanded more money for what he was doing. I was reflecting on this possibility afterwards, and wondered if, in a sense, I might be to blame."

"You?" queried Blake. "How could you be to blame?"

"Only indirectly. The second time that Mr Coleford, the checker from Paddington station, called upon us, on Saturday morning, he described how he had been accosted in the street by a man pretending to be a police officer. Coleford said he had not come directly to my chambers after this encounter so that the bogus policeman – who I knew, of course, must be Baines – would not learn where he was going and thus perhaps guess where he had taken your letter the day before. But for all Coleford's efforts, I knew he was a novice in such matters, whereas Wilson Baines had a great deal of experience in following people about. It was possible, then, I thought, that, despite Coleford's caution, Baines might well have followed him and discovered that I was the recipient of your letter. Now,

Baines and I had never met, but I certainly knew of him and I have no doubt he knew of me. Could it be, I speculated, that it was because he had learned of my involvement in the matter, and believed that I might prove a somewhat more dangerous adversary than he had expected to face that he had demanded more money from his client, or had even refused to continue with the case at all? If so, this might have led to the quarrel between the two men, and so, indirectly, to Baines's death.

"Now, when Watson and I arrived here, we were described, as we had arranged, simply as friends of yours, Blake, and fellow-journalists. Yet, upon our return from our first visit to the ash spinney, it was noteworthy that Whitemoor initially directed his questions about it to me. Why me? Why not Watson, or you? It seemed to me to suggest that he knew more about me than simply what you had told him when you introduced us. Of course, his questioning of me could have been simply a matter of chance, but it did not seem that way to me. He appeared to recognize that he had made a little slip – perhaps he read something in my facial expression – and endeavoured to correct it by addressing questions to you and Watson, but the slip had already been made, and I had duly noted it.

"That afternoon, I returned alone to the ash spinney. My intention, although I did not announce it publicly, was to examine the ground there more thoroughly. I had already made a mental note of your footprints and Watson's, and also of Whitemoor's, which I had seen in the garden here, so that I could eliminate them from consideration when I came across them. In the ash spinney, however, I made an interesting discovery. Although the ground around the tree with rungs was too scuffed up to provide much useful information, further along the path through the wood the situation was quite different. There, the footprints were much fewer, and I was able to identify what I believed were Whitemoor's prints, all the way along the path to the other end.

"Even more interestingly, I found a place where the footprints left the path altogether and wandered off through the undergrowth until they came to a small clearing. There the ground was disturbed, and it looked to me as if someone had spent some time there, possibly even passed the night there. This suggested that the person who had been spying on the Grange, if these were his prints, was not a local, who would presumably have returned to his own house when he had finished his spying activities, but someone who did not live in the district or, at least, was believed to be elsewhere at the time. You will understand that this only strengthened my suspicions of Whitemoor.

"I might also mention that I was forced to the same conclusion by my consideration of the death of the unfortunate Mr Brookfield. whose body was found in the quarry. For various reasons, some of which I have explained to Watson, I did not believe this death was an accident. I conjectured that Brookfield had encountered someone on the Thuxton road late one evening as he was returning home, and this person, knowing that Brookfield was likely to mention the encounter to others, had decided to silence him permanently. But if the person Brookfield met had been a local man – say, Pearson or Needham – such violence would scarcely have been necessary. After all, there is nothing very unusual in a man taking an evening walk near his own home. This suggested that the man Brookfield met was not a local man, or, if he was, then he was someone who was not supposed to be there at that time. Again, then, I was led to speculate that the man in question was Whitemoor, the only man, to my knowledge, who was believed to be away from home on the evening in question.

"But if it was Whitemoor, as the footprints in the wood certainly suggested, why on earth, I wondered, was he spying on the Grange – presumably when he had pretended to go home to Towcester – when he already spent the greater part of every week here?

"For some time I wrestled with this conundrum. Then I considered again the small branches that had been cut off up the tree by the viewing platform, to provide a clear view for the telescope. I had already noted that the clipping of the foliage made it possible to see not only your study window, but also the yard and outbuildings behind the house. We had not really considered the latter, which seemed incidental and irrelevant, but now I wondered if we had not perhaps got the whole business back to front and it was the view of the orangery and the puzzle it contained that was important to the spy and the view of your study window largely irrelevant. The more I thought about it, the more convinced I became that this was so, and that the recent mysteries that had surrounded you were intimately connected with the century-old mystery concerning Samuel Harley and the puzzle he had left behind him. The valuables that Harley was supposed to have hidden somewhere here at Foxwood would certainly provide a strong motive for anyone who believed the story to pursue the matter relentlessly.

"Yet if it was Whitemoor who was intent on securing Samuel Harley's hidden wealth, as I now believed, I still faced the question of his bizarre behaviour. Why, I asked myself again, should he spy on you in this covert fashion, when he spent most of the week in your company? The only plausible answer that suggested itself was that he did not trust you and did not believe you when you said you had had no success in solving Harley's riddle. I speculated that he had, rather, convinced himself that you were secretly working on the problem when he was not there. If this were so, though, it suggested in turn that, despite his placid exterior, Whitemoor was of a very obsessed and unbalanced frame of mind, one of those odd people who get some fixed idea in their minds which no amount of evidence can ever remove. If he was of this type, that might also explain why he had hired the enquiry agent, Wilson Baines, to follow you about London. Of course, your activities there were perfectly innocent, and had no connection whatever with Harley's puzzle, but Whitemoor may have suspected that while there you were consulting some kind of specialist in connection with it, such as an historian or an expert in the solution of puzzles. The irony is, of course, that you did indeed consult such a specialist eventually, but only as a result of Whitemoor's perfectly fruitless spying upon you.

"But surely, I thought, Whitemoor could not have developed such an overpowering obsession in the relatively brief period of time he had been living here at the Grange. What seemed more likely was that he had already developed his obsession with Samuel Harley and his puzzle before ever he came here. In that case, his arrival here was very unlikely to have been the chance occurrence it appeared to be. In order to try to learn a little more about it, I wrote a letter before I left here on Tuesday to St Matthew's College at Oxford, which I posted at Banbury station. In the letter I mentioned that a friend of mine, Mr Farringdon Blake, had taken on a graduate student as a research assistant, to help him in his work. This, I said, appeared to be very successful for all concerned, and I wondered if there might be any other such student who would be interested in assisting me in a similar capacity. On Thursday morning, I received a reply. Unfortunately, they said, there was no such student available, and nor was there likely to be in the near future. The arrangement between Mr Whitemoor and Mr Farringdon Blake was probably unique and had only come about because Mr Whitemoor had expressed a keen interest in Mr Blake's work and, under the circumstances of his mother's illness, had requested that his tutor approach Mr Blake on his behalf. From this reply, it was clear to me that the moving spirit behind the arrangement was not anyone at St Matthew's College with whom you had had correspondence in the course of your work, and nor was it Whitemoor's tutor. Rather, it was Whitemoor himself. My suspicions were thus amply confirmed. Whitemoor had deliberately contrived to stay here at Foxwood Grange, which suggested that his obsession with Samuel Harley and his hidden treasure was of much longer duration than the few months he had spent here.

"It only remained, then, for me to try to find the ultimate source of Whitemoor's obsession. To this end, I spent most of Tuesday and all day on Wednesday, after the inquest, in the public records office in London. Yesterday I travelled down to

Towcester and continued my researches in the town records office there. I stayed the night in Towcester, incidentally, which is why I arrived back earlier today than you had expected. Anyhow, the result of all this weary work in the record offices was the discovery that Whitemoor was, on his father's side, a descendant of that cousin of Samuel Harley's who received the letter which Harley was supposed to have sent from Italy. I also discovered, to my surprise, that Whitemoor's mother had died some months ago."

"I suppose he kept that fact to himself so that he could use his visits to her as an excuse to go off at the end of each week," said Blake.

"No doubt," returned Holmes. "Another very interesting discovery was that the mother's maiden name had been Needham and that she was in fact a cousin of Matthias Needham of Abbeyfield House. As Needham seems to have had a long-standing interest in the history of Foxwood, and probably did steal that book as Mr Stannard suspected, I don't think we need to look any further to find out who it was that filled the impressionable young man's head with the grievance that he and his ancestors had been somehow cheated out of their inheritance."

"As Needham clearly knows of the rungs up the tree, and the viewing platform," I remarked, "it must have been he who told Whitemoor about it, and gave him the idea of using it to spy on the Grange."

"So I should imagine," said Holmes, nodding his head. "It seems, though, from what you reported to us earlier, Watson, that Needham had come to feel anxious about his young cousin's intentions, and tried to dissuade him from any violent course of action, which is why Whitemoor had imprisoned him in his own house. In law, I doubt there is anything Needham can be charged with; in morality, however, I think he bears considerable responsibility for Whitemoor's actions and thus for all the blood that has been spilt in this matter. Still, the knowledge of the monster he created, the trouble it has caused and the deaths that have resulted from it may be a harsher punishment than any court could impose."

"What on earth was the relevance of that little slip of paper with the word 'shrub' on it that I found near the back door?" I asked after a moment. "I have never been so astonished in all my life as when you said that that was of great significance."

Holmes had taken his pipe from his pocket and begun to fill it with tobacco, but now he paused, threw back his head and began to laugh, in that odd, silent way that was so characteristic of him. "You must excuse me," he said at length, "but I really could not have expected such a perfect confirmation of all my theories as that little slip of paper represented. The word 'shrub' has a number of different meanings, but one you may not be aware of, which was current in the middle of the last century but seems to have quite passed out of use now, is 'to reduce someone to poverty by winning his property at gaming'. You astutely recognized the hand that had written 'shrub' as that of Needham, Watson, and yet the paper was found here, in the Grange. How could that be? Surely only if Needham had written it and given it to Whitemoor, to stoke his sense of grievance. Thus, in a single word on that little slip of paper, there are connections to Needham, to Harley's loss of this house in a game of chance, and to Whitemoor – my entire theory of the case condensed into one word on a scrap of paper no bigger than a man's thumb."

"That is certainly striking," I said, "but how do you think it came to be by the back door?"

"There I can only speculate," replied Holmes, "but what seems most likely to me is that you put it there yourself, Watson."

"Whatever do you mean?" I cried in surprise.

"On the night you found it, you had stood for a few moments by the open window, where the matting was very wet. You then hurried upstairs and looked in the bedrooms for an intruder. I think that Whitemoor must have already accidentally dropped the slip of paper on the floor, either in his bedroom or on the landing, and that it stuck to the wet sole of your boot – you would not have noticed it in the dim light – and you brought it back downstairs with you, where it chanced to catch Blake's eye."

"Yes, that must be it," I agreed.

Blake nodded his head. "What a dreadful business it has been," said he. "Thank Heavens it is all over at last," he added in a tone of relief. "I think it will be a long time before this household feels normal again – if it ever does."

"Such upheavals can certainly have long-lasting repercussions," I remarked. "I hope you do manage to put it behind you, Blake, and that it does not affect your admirable work."

"I shall let you know how things go," responded Blake with a weary attempt at a smile. "And now, gentlemen, do not feel you must leave at once, now the mystery is solved and, from your point of view, at least, the case is over. You are welcome to stay here as long as you wish."

"That is very kind of you," said Holmes, putting a match to his pipe, "but, speaking for myself, at least, I really think I must get back to London tomorrow. Several letters arrived for me when I was at Baker Street, to which I was only able to give the most cursory attention, but what is clear is that my assistance is very urgently required in matters which are both fascinating and puzzling, and may have the most far-reaching consequences!"

ABOUT THE AUTHOR

Denis O Smith's first Sherlock Holmes story, *The Adventure of the Purple Hand*, was published in 1982, since which time he has revealed to the public many more previously unknown cases of the famous detective. Highly regarded, both for his great fidelity to the style and spirit of Conan Doyle's original stories, and for the freshness and ingenuity of his own new stories, Mr Smith remains committed to satisfying the curiosity of a public keen to learn the details of all those adventures which Dr Watson had previously neglected to chronicle.

His most recent collections of short stories are *The Lost Chronicles of Sherlock Holmes* and *The Lost Chronicles of Sherlock Holmes, volume two* (the latter published in the USA as *The New Chronicles of Sherlock Holmes*).

In addition to being a long-time student of the life and career of Mr Sherlock Holmes, Mr Smith's interests range very widely, from philosophical problems and historical mysteries of all kinds, to Victorian railways and society and the history of London.

Also from MX Publishing

MX Publishing is the world's largest specialist Sherlock Holmes publisher, with over two hundred titles and one hundred authors creating the latest in Sherlock Holmes fiction and non-fiction.

From traditional short stories and novels to travel guides and quiz books, MX Publishing cater for all Holmes fans.

The collection includes leading titles such as ⁣ ⁣ and ⁣ ⁣ which won the 2011 Howlett Award (Sherlock Holmes Book of the Year).

MX Publishing also has one of the largest communities of Holmes fans on ⁣ with regular contributions from dozens of authors.

Also from MX Publishing

The Missing Authors Series

Sherlock Holmes and The Adventure of The Grinning Cat
Sherlock Holmes and The Nautilus Adventure
Sherlock Holmes and The Round Table Adventure

"Joseph Svec, III is brilliant in entwining two endearing and enduring classics of literature, blending the factual with the fantastical; the playful with the pensive; and the mischievous with the mysterious. We shall, all of us young and old, benefit with a cup of tea, a tranquil afternoon, and a copy of Sherlock Holmes, The Adventure of the Grinning Cat."
Amador County Holmes Hounds Sherlockian Society

www.mxpublishing.com

Also from MX Publishing

The Detective and The Woman Series

The Detective and The Woman
The Detective, The Woman and The Winking Tree
The Detective, The Woman and The Silent Hive

"The book is entertaining, puzzling and a lot of fun. I believe the author has hit on the only type of long-term relationship possible for Sherlock Holmes and Irene Adler. The details of the narrative only add force to the romantic defects we expect in both of them and their growth and development are truly marvelous to watch. This is not a love story. Instead, it is a coming-of-age tale starring two of our favorite characters."
Philip K Jones

Printed in August 2021
by Rotomail Italia S.p.A., Vignate (MI) - Italy